Heath's and he plac _ _ _ _ _ _ _ .

"Truth is, you know another reason it bothers me? Another reason I don't want to meet my sister?"

"Why's that?" Nicolette asked, trying to ignore the warm spot where his lips had touched her skin.

"Because, it makes me wonder...makes me realize that I could be just like him."

"Like your father?"

She barely saw the nod.

"Disloyal. To Rudy."

"In what way?" she asked, but she thought she knew, and her heart seemed to beat loud enough for him to hear in the silence of the elevator. She waited breathlessly for his answer.

He sighed heavily. "In the way I want you. In the way I wanted you even while you were married to my best friend."

In spite of the guilt she heard in his voice, there was also longing. She turned her head just slightly. She wasn't sure exactly how it happened, but in the next moment, his lips found hers. He tangled his hand in her hair and pressed her more closely to him as his mouth moved urgently over hers. She moaned in the back of her throat, and he answered it with a growl.

Dear God. She was kissing Heath King. Those were *his* lips on hers. They felt as good as she'd always dreamed they would. Firm and skilled, his tongue warm and seeking. Her heart lurched, and for a moment, all the angst of the past year flew away. This was it. This was what it felt like to be kissed by Heath King.

Kudos for Alicia Dean and...

HEART OF THE WITCH:
"Alicia Dean has created magic with *HEART OF THE WITCH*. She's woven a riveting story of murder, witchcraft & the paranormal into a contemporary, heart-stopping romance and made me believe it. From the moment I sat down to read, to the very last page I was hooked!"
~Sharon Sala, best-selling author of The Warrior (Mira Books, April 2009)

NOTHING TO FEAR:
"Ms. Dean has written an explosive story filled with action and adventure. The action will have you sitting on the edge of your seat."
~Sherry, Coffee Time Romance

TRULY MADLY:
"The unpredictable storyline carries the reader through a whirlwind of emotions—not only from fear, to gratitude, but to downright hate. An amazing and powerful murder, romance, and more."
~Snapdragon, Long and Short Reviews

POETIC INJUSTICE:
"If you love a good police story filled with action, suspense, and some steamy romance on the side, you will like Poetic Injustice!"
~Steph B., The Romance Studio

A Knight Before Christmas

The Three Kings, Book II

by

Alicia Dean

Best Wishes,
Alicia Dean

A Knight Before Christmas: The Three Kings, Book II

Cover Art by Angela Anderson

The Wild Rose Press
PO Box 706
Adams Basin, NY 14410-0706
Visit us at www.thewildrosepress.com

Publishing History
First Champagne Rose Edition, 2010
Print ISBN 1-60154-855-9

Published in the United States of America

Dedication

To my fantastic editor, Cindy Davis and my
wonderful writing partners,
Claire Ashgrove and Dyann Love Barr.
I have so enjoyed working with you ladies.
And,
To my nephew, Jared. It's been a joy watching you
grow from a terrific little boy into an amazing young
man. I am so very proud of you. Love you much!

Chapter One

Given a choice between smearing honey all over his naked body and leaping into a bear cave, or returning to Kansas City for Christmas, Heath King would have stripped off his clothes, popped the top from a bottle of Cloverleaf, and asked for directions to the nearest den.

But no one had given him a choice, so here he was, driving along I-35, sixty miles north of Wichita, his dread ratcheting up with every click of the odometer.

He looked forward to seeing his mother and his brothers, Alex and Clint, but the memories he left behind were still too raw. The last two trips to Kansas City had been for funerals, his father's this past July, and his best friend's in January.

His friend, Burke, was looking out for Heath's security firm during his absence, so at least he didn't have to worry about that. No, it wasn't concern over his company that had Heath's stomach tied in a knot the size of Texas. It was the news he'd received nearly two weeks ago.

Heath, we have a sister.

Just like Alex to come right out with it, no softening the blow.

Dad conceived a child with another woman. When he was in Viet Nam.

Translated: the father Heath grew up believing could move mountains, could part the sea, would be the one person he could always trust, the one he learned his values from, was a cheating liar.

1

Loyalty schmoyalty.

What really pissed him off was that his mother seemed okay with it. Well, maybe not okay, but accepting, forgiving. She actually wanted to meet this woman, this mascot of betrayal.

He'd done a background check on his *sister*, Keeley Jacobs, and he didn't mind admitting he'd hoped to dig up some dirt. His quest had been unsuccessful. She was either on the up and up or good enough not to get caught.

He tilted a Pez dispenser to his lips and tapped a couple of candies into his mouth. Out the windshield ahead, a few snowflakes fell. It hadn't snowed at home in Oklahoma City yet, but it looked like there was a good chance they'd have a white Christmas in Kansas City, something he used to enjoy and hope for. Now he could care less. He just wanted it to be over.

The radio was dialed to a country station, the volume low, but Heath still heard the start of "Blue Christmas" and punched the power button to Off. He might have suffered through the song in spite of his uncharacteristic Grinch-ness had it been the version by Elvis. This one was by the Chipmunks, and their squeaky voices grated on his already frayed nerves.

His cell phone rang, and he checked the display, managing a smile as he answered. "Hey, Jesse, what's up?"

Jesse was a childhood friend who'd grown up with the King brothers. She was more of a sister than some stranger could ever be.

"Just checking on you," Jesse said. "How's the trip going?"

"The usual, long and uneventful, just enjoying the spectacular scenery."

She laughed. "Yeah, the plains of Kansas are breathtaking. What do you have planned for tomorrow night?"

Heath's only plan for the entire visit was to get through each excruciating moment as painlessly as possible. "Nothing yet."

"Great. Wasn't sure if you knew yet, but they're holding a dedication ceremony tomorrow night to honor Rudy Morgan. I knew you'd want to be there."

Did you now? Well, what would you think if I said it's the last place I wanted to be? The last place and the first, actually, which he had to admit, was pretty fucked up.

"Heath, you there?"

"Yeah. I'm here. Thanks for letting me know."

"So you'll go?"

"I'll try."

"I'm sure Nicolette would love to see you."

And there it was. Nicolette. The person he both dreaded and desired to see more than anyone else in the world. His best friend's widow. The woman Heath had been in love with since college.

He tried not to reveal his turmoil as he said, "Yeah. It'd be great to see her."

"I'll let you go so you can get your attention back to your driving. See you when you get here."

He flipped his phone closed and turned the radio back on. He felt marginally better after Jesse's call. Not because of the news she'd delivered, not by a long shot, but somehow, just hearing the voice of his childhood pal brought a small measure of peace.

Now that the call had ended, though, the peace filtered away like smoke in a wind gust. The only thing left was silence. Unwelcome silence. Too much temptation to let his thoughts roam...to Nicolette and to the new sister he hadn't known about and didn't want.

The DJ finally played an Elvis Christmas song, but it was "I'll be Home for Christmas" and again, Heath shut off the radio.

He'd be home for Christmas all right, but *home*

would never be the same again.

****

Nicolette Morgan peered out the window, scanning the street. She couldn't see the car now, but it had been behind her when she pulled into the neighborhood. The dark blue Crown Victoria had shadowed her, off and on, for nearly a year.

The car didn't belong to her blackmailer. For one, his calls hadn't started until August, four months ago. Besides, as long as she did as he asked, as long as she made the payments on time, he had no reason to follow her.

No. The occasional tail she'd glimpsed had to be the police. They wanted to monitor her activities and see if they could gather enough evidence to file charges. Even though they hadn't bothered her much since their initial questioning almost a year ago, she was still the prime suspect in her husband's murder.

The thought seemed like such an abomination, especially here, at Louisa's home where Rudy had grown up. Memories of Rudy were everywhere in this house. Rudy as a smiling infant; Rudy in a peewee football uniform; Rudy graduating from high school. Rudy and Nicolette on their wedding day, faces smiling with an assurance that their life together would be perfect, that nothing could touch them. Boy, what naïve fools they'd been.

Leaving her post at the window, Nicolette retrieved the watering can from the utility room. After filling the can, she made her way through the house, watering plant after plant until she worked her way into the living room where Louisa sat glued to the TV screen.

Nicolette's heart warmed at the sight of the sweet old lady. Louisa was still lovely, even though the ravages of severe osteoporosis had taken a toll. The disease had engraved deep wrinkles in her once flawless skin and caused her stately bearing to bow until she nearly doubled over. Most of Louisa's waking hours were spent in a wheelchair.

Louisa still had a sparkle in her eye, still had a zest for life, in spite of her condition and the fact that she'd lost her only child less than a year ago. Which brought up a question Nicolette hadn't really thought about before. Was Louisa still considered her mother-in-law, when the connection, the tie that bound them, the son, was no longer living?

All that mattered was what they felt in their hearts, and Louisa loved Nicolette as much as Nicolette loved her. They would always be family. However, being around Louisa was bittersweet, not only because of losing Rudy, but it reminded Nicolette of the other things she didn't have.

Her own mother died when she was a teen. She hadn't seen her father since she'd gone off to college. She had no idea if he even lived in the same town. At the time, she'd wanted to forget about everything that happened, forget about the hell her family went through. Now she would give anything to have her family again, even if her father was all that was left of it.

Nicolette smiled, infusing her voice with mock irritation. "If you had any more plants, your house could be declared a rainforest."

Louisa spoke without pulling her attention away from the episode of Dr. Lawrence, a talk show host/psychologist who Louisa watched religiously. "Since you kill a few of them a week, I thought I should keep back-ups on hand."

Nicolette laughed. Unfortunately, Louisa was right. A green thumb was not one of Nicolette's attributes.

"Be right back with your dinner," Nicolette said.

After returning the can to the utility room, she went into the kitchen where beef stew simmered in the crockpot. She dished up a bowl and a slice of the cornbread she'd made from a *Jiffy* mix. In the living room, Louisa still watched her television show.

"That Doctor Lawrence is one smart cookie," Louisa said proudly. "They can't pull the wool over his eyes, no siree."

"That's for sure," Nicolette agreed automatically.

Louisa's worshipful attitude toward Saint Doctor Lawrence was the same every time she watched him, although the clichés changed a bit from day to day. Sometimes it was, "you have to get up pretty early in the morning to fool Dr. Lawrence," or "that Dr. Lawrence is sharp as a tack," or "Dr. Lawrence cuts right to the chase, doesn't he?"

Nicolette placed Louisa's meal on the tray in front of her. Reaching an aged, spotted hand out, Louisa patted Nicolette's arm. "Thank you. It looks delicious, but you do too much. You're a godsend, my dear."

Nicolette bent and kissed Louisa's cheek, smelling Jean Naté on her cool, dry skin. "So are you."

As Nicolette headed back into the kitchen to clean up the mess, the phone rang.

"Would you get that, dear?" Louisa called.

The caller ID wasn't a familiar number; the name read 'private.' It sent a chill through her. The private calls she'd received lately had been less than pleasant. But, this was Louisa's phone, so therefore safe.

"Hello?" Nicolette bent to stick a bowl into the dishwasher as she spoke.

"Next payment's due Friday."

Nicolette's hand stilled. She swallowed back the fear that rose to her throat.

The voice was the same robotic, indistinguishable monotone, but in spite of its vapidity, her stomach lurched and her heart shot into overdrive. "How did you get this number?" she hissed into the receiver, casting a glance at Louisa, who was thankfully glued adoringly to her hero.

"You mean, how did I get the number for your mother-in-law, Louisa Jane Morgan, age sixty-three, address seven forty-two Willow Creek?"

Nicolette's insides quivered as the voice droned the stats on Louisa. She wouldn't have been surprised if he'd quoted her bra size. The fear that had her in its grip for the past three months magnified. Not only was she in danger, Louisa was, too. Poor, frail, loving Louisa. The bastard better not lay a finger on her, but what Nicolette would do about it she had no idea. Obviously, if she could have stopped his sick game, she'd have done so with that first phone call seven months after Rudy's death.

"You said ten thousand a month," Nicolette said quietly. "I gave you a payment two weeks ago. When is this going to end? I can't keep doing this. I'm not a millionaire."

"I'll let you know when you've paid enough. Until then, you'd be wise to do as I say. You don't want the people you love to suffer, do you?"

Nicolette gave a grim smile. Joke was on him. Since Rudy died, she had very few people in her life she loved. Right off hand, the only one who came to mind was Louisa.

"I'll have your money," she told the stranger.

"Yes. I'm sure you will."

"Nicolette, sweetie," Louisa called from the living room. "Who is it?"

"Just a telemarketer," Nicolette answered, hoping her voice didn't convey her fear.

"Tell them we're not interested and come back in here. Doctor Lawrence is about to give this cheating bastard the what-for."

"I have to go," she said into the phone.

"Tell her I said hello." A creepy chuckle issued

7

from the receiver. "Hope you don't force me to tell her myself."

Nicolette slammed the handset on the base and drew in deep breaths, trying to calm her nerves before Louisa saw her. The woman was shrewd. She'd know something was wrong.

Not for the first time, Nicolette wondered if she should go to the police about the blackmailer. There were a few problems with that, though. For one, the guy had told her—more than once—that if she went to the cops, he'd kill her, or someone close to her. For another, the charity Rudy founded, Renewed Hope, would suffer, probably fold altogether. The purpose of the charity was to help drug addicts get clean and give them a new start. If the contributors learned the founder himself was a drug user, donations would dry up. Once the police knew about Rudy's drug use, there was no way Nicolette could keep it from the public, and then her whole purpose for caving to the blackmail would be defeated.

There were also a few very good reasons to tell the police. One, maybe they could protect her and Louisa. Maybe they could find the guy and stop him. Two, if she told the cops her husband had been involved in drugs they might investigate that angle. They might think Rudy's suspicious death was drug related. They might stop suspecting Nicolette of murdering him. But then again, maybe not. If Rudy's murder had nothing to do with drugs, then all she would accomplish by revealing his drug use would be to destroy a lot of lives.

"You shouldn't waste your time on those people," Louisa said. "You're about to miss the best part."

Louisa loved it when Dr. Lawrence ripped cheaters a new one. Her own husband had been a cheater, and Louisa was extremely proud Rudy hadn't turned out like his father. She was proud of his faithfulness as a husband, his giving nature, his service to the community, and his devotion as a son.

Nicolette agreed her deceased husband had all those wonderful qualities, and she was proud to have been his wife, proud to have even known a man as good as Rudy Morgan. But she hadn't learned until after his death that there were things about Rudy that she nor his mother had known.

Now, those things were coming around to haunt her and she'd have to figure out a solution soon. She had to protect Rudy's memory, his reputation. For the sake of his loving mother, and all the people who benefited from the charity, she'd do her best to keep the truth from leaking to the public.

Even if it meant losing everything she owned to a greedy, sinister blackmailer.

****

Half a mile from his family home of Hollyfield, Heath saw his mother's Christmas lights. The closer he drew, the more details he could make out—bright red bulbs lining the roof, the wraparound porch, the stair railings. A glow hovered above the front yard, fallout from the display of Santa in his sleigh, complete with reindeer. Next to it, but no less spotlighted, was the life-sized nativity scene. He and his brothers had been raised to appreciate both the commercial and religious aspect of Christmas.

His mother must have heard his Tahoe because he'd no sooner pulled into the driveway than the front door flew open. Amidst the still-falling snow, he saw her standing anxiously in the doorway, the light from behind spilling over her.

He slammed the truck door and crunched up the porch steps into her waiting embrace, which was only slightly encumbered by a pair of crutches.

"Heath!" she cried. "I've missed you."

Whether it had been ten months or ten minutes since he'd seen or spoken to her, it was the same refrain, as if just the fact that he now lived 360 miles away would initiate her motherly longing to be near her middle child. But then, she acted the exact same way with his brothers.

"Hey, Mom. I've missed you, too." They finished the hug, and he looked down at her cast. "How's the ankle? You in much pain?"

"Nah." She waved a hand in dismissal. "Just feeling a little foolish."

"You tripped over cats in the garage. Those things happen. It's not like you tried sky-diving."

She laughed and playfully slapped his shoulder. "As if! At my age."

"Nothing you decided to try would surprise me."

She chuckled as she ushered him into the living room where Alex and Jesse were chatting in front of the fire. Jesse got up from her seat in the recliner and threw her arms around Heath's neck, hugging him long and tight.

When she released him, Alex shook his hand, then pulled him into a manly, shoulder pound, brother hug. "How's it going, bro?"

"Not bad. Glad to have the drive over with."

"Yeah. It's a bitch, and I live near the Plaza."

Alex stood a few inches taller than Heath's stocky, 5'11" frame. Where Heath was more of a blue jeans, country music, jock type, Alex was sophisticated and refined. Alex wouldn't be caught dead with his hair looking like Heath's shaggy mane. Alex's dark hair was styled and clipped short. Hell, his haircut had probably cost more than everything Heath wore.

"Hey Mom," Alex said, a devilish glint in his eye. "What do you say about cutting into that apple pie?"

Heath inwardly cringed. *Apple* pie?

"We'll wait until Clint gets here." She turned to Heath. "You're chilled to the bone. This ought to warm you up."

Without asking if he wanted it, she handed him

a large mug of steaming cider she'd plucked off a tray. He'd never had the heart to tell her he hated cider. Hated apples, for that matter. She'd been forcing the vile beverage and desserts on him during the holidays ever since he remembered. He'd suffered through it quietly.

Now that he thought about it, since she'd shared the earth-shattering news of his father's infidelity, maybe it would be acceptable for him to share his distaste for apples.

"Drink up, bro. Mom made it especially for you. I'm having plain old coffee," Alex said, making Heath want to hit him.

"Are you going to the ceremony for Rudy?" Jesse asked.

"I plan to."

"Expect quite a turn-out," Jesse said. "Around here, Rudy was second only to Jesus."

Heath smiled. "So, nothing's changed, huh?" He grimaced as he sipped the cider. "Has anyone talked to Clint?"

"I did a little while ago," Alex said. "He's about an hour out."

"The three Kings will be reunited once more." Jesse grinned, raising her coffee cup in a toast. Heath gazed enviously at the mug, wondering why his mother hadn't given him coffee, too.

Behind Jesse on the fireplace mantel were four stockings that had hung there every Christmas for as long as Heath could remember. One for each of the brothers, and one for Jesse, who'd been like a sister. Would a fifth stocking bearing the name Keeley be added?

They'd each put their own names on the stockings with glue and glitter when Heath was four or five. Clint's name was neat and spelled correctly, but then he'd been a few years older at the time. The 'E' in Heath was backwards. Alex had always been the smart one and the letters on his were correct, although they were out of alignment, with the 'L' sitting almost on top of the 'A.' Jesse's was only slightly neater. Part of the glitter on all four had fallen off over the years, but other than that, they were in pretty good shape.

Amelia lowered herself to the chair next to the hearth and leaned her crutches on the wall nearby.

Heath squatted down in front of her and searched her face. "You gave us quite a scare. Clint and I ripped Alex a new one when he called *after* the surgery."

"That was my doing. I didn't want to worry you."

"I'm allowed to worry about you, so get used to it." He kissed her cheek. "I'm just glad you're all right." He rose and settled into a chair near her and forced another drink of the cider down his throat. He looked at Alex. "I thought your fiancée would be here."

"She's out with friends." A scowl marred Alex's forehead, and he stared into space for a long moment.

Heath waited for Alex to elaborate, but there was nothing other than that blank stare. "Yo, Alex, where'd you go?"

Alex seemed to snap back. He kept the scowl as he said, "Nowhere, just thinking."

Whatever his brother was thinking, it didn't seem happy. "Wedding jitters?"

Alex shrugged. "You could say that. It's a big step. The last two times didn't work out so well."

Heath lifted his cup in a toast. "Well, here's hoping the third time's the charm. Hey, speaking of three, when do I get to meet my nieces? And Sydney," he added belatedly.

"Soon," Alex said, but the reply was short and clipped, like he wasn't quite thrilled about the meeting. Heath guessed it had more to do with his fiancée than his daughters.

Amelia clapped her hands together and pressed them to her heart. "Very soon, I hope. I can't wait for you to meet them." Pride beamed from her features, giving her a youthful glow in spite of her sixty years.

Heath shot a look at Alex and saw the same glow of pride coming from him. Alex only recently learned he'd fathered triplets five years ago. Unfortunately, he was engaged to a woman other than the mother.

Heath hadn't met the fiancée yet, but if the information he'd gotten from his mother about his future sister-in-law was accurate, he wasn't looking forward to it.

"They're adorable," his mother went on. "They look just like your brother. Zoe is bringing them by in a couple of days. She's doing the catering for the reception."

Heath had difficulty hiding his surprise. "Isn't that a little weird—the ex-wife catering the new wife's wedding reception?"

Alex shrugged. "Ask Mom, she's the one who hired Zoe."

"When I first hired Classic Kitchen, I didn't know Zoe owned the business. A friend recommended her."

Wow. As if there wasn't enough drama surrounding the holidays this year: a new sister, their first Christmas without their father, Alex learning *he* was a father, and now Alex's ex-wife catering his upcoming wedding.

Throw in a teenage pregnancy and an evil twin, and the King family would have their own daytime soap opera.

Heath's heart and mind were only half-involved in the discussion that followed as the group moved into the living room and turned on the television while they waited for Clint. He stood restlessly and

13

paced, pausing by the photos on the mantel. There were a ton of them, a photographic montage of the King brothers' childhood. Most of them featured their father.

Heath stopped in front of one that used to be his favorite. He and his dad at a Royals game. Clint and Alex weren't there. It was Heath's tenth birthday, and on each of the boys' birthdays, they got to pick a special thing to do with their father, just the birthday kid and his dad. Heath chose dinner at Gates Barbecue and a Royals game. They'd gotten George Brett's autograph. It had been the happiest day of Heath's young life. Boy, had Clint and Alex been pissed.

Heath smiled at the memory. His father's smiling face stared back, and Heath's smile faded. He wanted to ask his father why he'd done what he had, why he'd betrayed his mother and why he'd raised Heath to be upstanding and loyal, when he himself hadn't been.

But he would never be able to ask him any of that. Although his father's transgression—if that was his only one, and Heath wasn't positive about that—had happened before any of his sons were born, they hadn't learned of it until after his death, when Frank King's love child burst onto the scene. Amelia had known about it all these years but kept it from her sons. Just a little, Heath resented her for not giving him the opportunity to confront his father, to get an answer to the questions that plagued him.

A truck sounded outside, bringing Heath out of his reverie. After several moments, the front door opened, sending a blast of cold air into the room as the eldest King brother arrived. Clint's dark hair was dampened with snow. He towered over Heath, his broad shoulders filling the doorway.

"Hey, bro," Heath greeted.

A warm sense of homecoming swept through him. Now their little family circle would be complete, well, minus one member...Keeley Jacobs, the newest and, in Heath's opinion, unwelcome one.

Chapter Two

Immediately after breakfast the next morning, Heath headed out for a drive. He told his mother he had some people to see, but truth was, he needed to get away, clear his head. His mother's house, with its endless parade of guests and family, and memories of his childhood, was stifling.

He drove past leafless trees and lawns with patchy snow, heading into town under a graying sky. The forecast called for snow and more snow. Just his luck, he'd probably end up stranded in Kansas City.

The cemetery where both Rudy and his father were buried was only about five miles east of town, and he considered going to see their graves, but he couldn't bring himself to do that just yet. His resentment toward his dad made him reluctant to visit his grave, and if he visited Rudy's, his guilt over not visiting his dad's would eat at him. For now, he'd avoid them both.

When his aimless wandering and jumbled thoughts took him into town, Heath stopped at Juniper's Café. The door jangled with his entrance, and the head of every patron swiveled toward him as if directed by an invisible orchestra conductor. No familiar faces, but that was good. He wasn't in the mood for company.

He slid onto a stool at the counter, and a plump, middle-aged waitress wearing a white blouse and black slacks approached. "Coffee?" she asked, sliding a menu in front of him.

"Yeah, please. Nothing but coffee." He slid the

menu back. His mother had plied him with enough breakfast to feed a small country, and he wondered why he'd even stopped at the café.

When the waitress returned with his coffee, he took a swallow of the better than expected brew and glanced around. It was Monday morning and the place was nearly empty, mostly occupied with mothers and small children and a few retirees who looked as though, like Heath, they didn't have anywhere better to be.

"Heath? Heath King?"

He turned at the voice to find Jerome Badgett standing at his shoulder. They'd gone to high school together and made an attempt at being friends, but they each had a flaw that prevented it. Jerome was an irritating pain in the ass, and Heath wasn't saint enough to tolerate him.

Heath forced himself to dredge up at least a little congeniality. After all, it was almost Christmas. He stuck out his hand. "How you been?"

Jerome was thin, with greasy-looking hair and traces of acne that hadn't improved much since high school. "Good, man, good. When the hell did you get into town?" Jerome slapped Heath's back so hard the coffee he held nearly sloshed over the rim and onto his hand.

He set the cup down. "Last night."

"Here for the holidays?"

"Yeah."

"Hell, guess that was a no-brainer. Mind if I join you?"

"No, go ahead," Heath said, even though Jerome was already sliding onto the stool next to him.

"What the hell you been up to?"

Heath resisted the urge to ask why the hell he had to put *hell* into every question. "Private security in Oklahoma City. You?"

"Coffee and the lumberjack breakfast," he told

the waitress without looking at the menu, then to Heath, "I do maintenance for some duplexes. Matter of fact, they belonged to your buddy, Rudy. His wife's running them now. But then, you may know that."

Heath shook his head. "No. I didn't." He didn't know what Nic had decided to do about the property she and Rudy owned. Managing all those units was a lot for her to take on by herself, but then, that was Nic.

"By the way, sorry about Rudy, man. And your dad."

"Thanks."

"You seen Nicolette lately?"

Heath tried to ignore the tightening in his chest that came with every mention of her name. "No. Not since the funeral."

"She's something else, isn't she? Hate to sound like a vulture, but I think she's been alone long enough that I could make my move. What do you think?"

The tightening increased. "That might not be a good idea. She just lost her husband in January."

"Nearly a year, bub. She's young, and a woman has needs."

"You know, I'm not sure I'm okay talking to you about this. Nicolette's my friend, her husband was my best friend." *And I'm in love with her myself.*

"Oh, yeah, sorry, man. Wasn't thinking. Didn't mean to open any wounds." He brooded into the cup the waitress handed him before taking a swallow.

"No problem." Heath stood and picked up his ticket.

"You taking off already? Didn't offend you, did I?"

"No. I just gotta go. Mom's waiting on me."

"Okay, take care, man. Sorry if I said something wrong, but I gotta tell you, that's not gonna stop me from going after her. You let a woman like that be

18

alone too long, some other dog will be sniffing around, know what I mean?"

Heath knew exactly what he meant. He had to hurry away before he plowed his fist into Jerome's stupidly smiling face.

****

Nicolette's hand shook as she brought the mascara brush closer to her eye. She stopped, took a deep breath, and tried again. Not much better. She was still trembling.

You have to get through this night. It's for Rudy, but mostly, it's for the people who need your help.

Some of the proceeds from tonight's event would fund the Christmas party they held every year for the families of the men and women who'd gone through the program. There was a big dinner, a Santa with gifts for the kids, and groceries for the families to take home with them, along with gift cards to Wal-Mart for the parents to get things they needed to help them along in their new start on life.

In addition to raising money for the party, Rudy was being honored tonight with a posthumous Good Samaritan award, and Nicolette was to accept it for him. She'd never felt less deserving, more like a phony. Droves of people would be in attendance, paying homage to a fallen hero. What would those people think if they knew their hero had skeletons in his closet? That he was enslaved to the very demons his charity spoke out against?

She tried again and this time managed to get the mascara on her lashes, even eyeliner onto her lids. But the effect wasn't what she wanted. Pale skin, too-bright eyes and now, dark, vivid borders to bring attention to them. She wiped it off with makeup remover and settled for a light brushing of mascara. Blush on her cheekbones to give the illusion of a healthy glow, a pinkish gloss on her lips, and she was ready.

Her sea-green dress hung loosely in places where it once clung. She'd bought it before Rudy's death, before the blackmail and threats. Back then, she'd wanted to lose a few pounds, but even she was aware that now she'd lost more than a few. She was bordering on a sickly thin that was neither healthy nor attractive. But then, who cared? Who was around to see her anyway, to appreciate her attractiveness, or lack thereof? Rudy was gone. No other man had paid attention to her in a while. And, the man who she most wanted to appreciate her attractiveness wasn't around.

Well, that wasn't entirely true. Heath *was* around. She'd heard the news from her maintenance man, Jerome. She'd had to struggle to keep her reaction from showing on her face. She thought she'd been successful, that Jerome didn't guess how thrilled and excited she'd been at the thought of seeing Heath again. Although, that probably wouldn't happen. Now that Rudy was gone, Heath most likely wouldn't bother to contact her. She hadn't heard from him since Rudy's funeral, and while they'd been close friends, it appeared the death of his *best* friend had severed whatever ties they once shared.

Or, was he avoiding her because of what happened between them after Rudy's accident? Correction, what *almost* happened between them, while Rudy lay in a coma. No, surely that wasn't it. They hadn't actually done anything. They'd both been lonely, needing comfort, grieving.

Yeah. Great way to express grief over your dying husband. Try to get another man to jump your bones.

That was neither here nor there. It hadn't happened. She and Heath were no longer in touch with one another. He was in town, but as out of reach as if he were on another planet. She wouldn't contact him, and it was obvious he had no plans to contact her. Best to put him out of her mind.

Nicolette gathered her handbag and keys, turned off all the lights in the condo, and went into the garage and climbed into her LaSabre.

Put him out of your mind, indeed, she thought as she backed out of the garage. *Yeah, right.* She'd be better off attempting to fry bacon with a light bulb.

****

When Heath arrived at the dedication, he knew his concerns about what he would say to Nicolette were moot. He'd never find her in this crowd. The auditorium was filled to capacity. It appeared a small fortune had gone into decorations. Huge red ribbons hung from the stage and along the balcony railing. Glittering lights were strung from every available spot and a Christmas tree the size of Mount Everest stood at one end of the room. Soft strains of "Have Yourself a Merry Little Christmas" played from gargantuan speakers placed in each corner.

Heath realized right off he was underdressed for the occasion. Maybe it was a good thing he wouldn't run into Nicolette. He'd no doubt embarrass her. Most of the attendees had on evening wear, the colorful array of tuxes and gowns nearly outdoing the decorations on the tree. Heath wore dark jeans and a sports jacket with cowboy boots. No one had told him it was a formal affair. Maybe he should have assumed.

Milling through the crowd, drink in hand, Heath felt conspicuously out of place.

After some more wandering around, he'd talked himself into slipping out and had swallowed the last bit of scotch in his glass when her voice came over the microphone, "Welcome, everyone. Thank you so much for coming. It's a very special night for me and I'm thrilled to see all of you here."

Too late now. He couldn't leave. Not when he'd have a chance to hear Nicolette. To see her, even from a distance.

Still holding his glass, he made his way as close to the stage as he could, which wasn't close. But it was close enough to see her. As beautiful as ever, though a little too thin. She wore a light green, sparkly gown. Her hair was pinned on top of her head, revealing the smooth line of her neck...a neck Heath had wanted to run his lips across the moment he'd first seen her.

He shook off those thoughts and forced his attention back to Nicolette's speech.

"Rudy would have been so honored at the turnout tonight. I can't tell you what it means to me, but mostly to the charity, to have this kind of support."

The crowd cheered, and a man who'd been standing off to the side of the podium stepped forward to lean into the microphone. "We would like to present this posthumous award to Rudy Morgan for his tireless, selfless dedication to those in need. Mr. Morgan's cause, and his devotion to it, has changed the lives of countless people. With your generous donations, that momentum will continue. Not only has Renewed Hope done just that—given renewed hope to countless people who would otherwise have none—it has provided homes, jobs, schooling for families. The annual Christmas party will be held at the Historical Museum on Christmas day, and needy families will benefit from donations of food, money, and gifts. This will be the first year our dear friend, Rudy, will not be in attendance at the party that meant so much to him, but we all know he'll be there in spirit." He turned to Nicolette. "Nicolette, please accept this in honor of your husband." He handed a plaque to her and she took it, leaning forward to place a kiss on the man's cheek.

"Thank you," her tearful voice said into the mic. "Rudy had a dream of changing the world. He always said it could be done, one individual at a time. I believe that, too."

The crowd went wild with applause. Nicolette blew a kiss, then strode gracefully from the stage. Heath tried to keep her in sight, but the crowd swallowed her. He let out a breath, trying to loosen the tightness in his chest. Damn. It was the same reaction every time he saw her. Had been from the moment he'd laid eyes on her as she moved across the quad at MU in that same, graceful stride.

Rudy had spotted her then, too. Before Heath could lay claim, he'd whispered, "I'm going to marry that girl."

And that's exactly what he'd done. Lucky bastard. Heath shook his head. Envious of a dead man. Nice.

Suddenly, having another drink sounded better than leaving. He worked his way back to the bar and ordered another scotch.

The bartender traded the full glass for Heath's money, and Heath took a sip. When the liquor burned through his throat and settled warmly in the pit of his stomach, he decided he'd gotten the better end of the deal.

"Heath?"

He'd been in the process of taking a second drink; the liquor stayed at the base of his throat, refusing to go down. He forced a swallow and turned to find Nicolette at his elbow.

"Oh, my God, Heath! I can't believe it's you."

She stood on tiptoe to kiss his cheek, much the way she had the old guy who'd given her the plaque. Heath wondered if the man felt that same warm tingle in the spot where her lips had rested so briefly, if he also wanted to pull her softness into him and give her much more than that chaste peck on the cheek.

"Nicolette," he said. "Hello."

"How are you? I had no idea you'd be here."

"Yeah, well. Jesse told me about it, and I thought I'd show my support. Apparently about a million other people had the same idea. I didn't think I'd even get a chance to talk to you. I was just about to leave."

Her face fell in disappointment. "You were going to leave without seeing me?"

Heath took another drink, wondering why he felt so guilty, why the very idea of making Nicolette sad was unbearable. "I wanted to see you, but I just figured with so many people, that wouldn't be likely." He looked down at his attire. "Plus, I'm not exactly dressed for the occasion. I didn't know this was going to be such a classy event."

Her nose wrinkled, and she shook her head. "Nah. It's a whatever event. These people just love any opportunity to try to outdo one another. Come on."

She slipped her arm in Heath's and began walking him away from the bar. Leaning conspiratorially close, she said, "Don't think I'm complaining. It certainly doesn't hurt the donations."

She smiled, but her eyes didn't join in. For the first time, Heath noticed something not quite right about her. It was more than just the weight loss. In the places where her body touched his, he detected a slight tremble. Her voice was overly bright, and her eyes held a look of desperation, of fear. The signs were all subtle. Had he not known her for fifteen years, he might have missed them. She seemed on edge. Fragile. Like the wrong move, the wrong word, might cause her to shatter.

She maneuvered him into an alcove and once there, released him. He tried not to think about how much better it had felt with her warmth touching him.

"How long are you in town?" she asked.

"I'm here until Christmas day. I'll be heading out that afternoon."

"You have to leave on Christmas?"

He nodded. "I'm bidding a big job, and the client wants to meet on Christmas evening."

"Who would want to work on Christmas if they didn't have to?"

"Someone who doesn't celebrate Christmas. He's a Jehovah's witness."

"Ah. I see. To him, it's just another day."

"Right."

Nicolette seemed at a loss for what to say next. She glanced around the room, then back up at him, a worried frown tugging at her brow. He reached out and took her hands in his. They felt like she'd been ice fishing without a pole.

"Is everything okay?" he asked quietly.

She smiled, but it was small and forced. "Of course. I mean, I miss Rudy like crazy, but other than that, everything's fine. Why?"

Heath searched her eyes, noting a hint of fear before she let her lashes fall over them. "You seem upset, distracted, maybe a little scared."

"Scared?" Her laugh was as forced as her smile. "What do I have to be scared of in a room full of people?"

He moved his hands up her arms and felt a shudder run through her body. Something was definitely not right. He made his voice hard, authoritative, and tightened his grip. "I don't know, Nicolette, why don't you tell me?"

She flinched, and his guilt increased. Damn. He hadn't been around her for five minutes, and he was already making a mess of things. He tried again, "If there's something bothering you, if you have a problem, I want to help."

"I'm fine," she insisted.

"You don't seem fine. I think you're lying." He didn't know why he was so certain she was in some kind of trouble, but he was.

The right side of her mouth lifted in a humorless smile. "You always did say what was on your mind, didn't you?"

Not always, Heath thought, *I didn't tell you I loved you before it was too late.*

Aloud, he said, "Just remember—if you need me, I'm here."

She lifted a hand, running her fingertips down the side of his face and his heart sped up. "You always were, weren't you?" she whispered.

"Yeah. And don't forget that, okay?"

Before she could answer, a voice behind Heath said, "Nicolette. We've been looking for you."

The man was about Heath's age, well-groomed with sandy blond hair and a big, toothy smile. A small, curvy, red-haired woman stood next to him.

"Hello," Nicolette greeted them. "Donovan, Marla, I'd like you to meet an old friend, Heath King. Heath, these are dear friends of mine and Rudy's, Donovan and Marla Sussman."

Heath shook hands with the couple, but on the inside, he cursed their timing.

"I really should mingle," Nicolette said to Heath. "It was good seeing you. Maybe next time you're in town, we can get together for coffee or something."

Next time. Message received. He wouldn't be seeing any more of her during this trip. Trying not to let his disappointment show, he returned her smile as she gave his hand a parting squeeze and disappeared into the crowd.

Chapter Three

One more hour and you can get out of here. Be alone. Fall apart.

Keeping up the façade, the phony smiles, the pretend happiness, was wearing on Nicolette. All she wanted was for it to be over. Correction, that wasn't *all* she wanted. Damn it to hell, she also wanted Heath.

No use lying to herself. She'd had a thing for him all those years ago but had done her best to put it out of her mind when she married Rudy. Then, the almost kiss just before Rudy's death had brought it all back, and she knew. No way in hell was she over Heath King. Not even close.

But he was Rudy's best friend. *Her* friend. Nothing more could come of it. What would people say if she hooked up with Heath? She knew what they'd say, that they'd been having an affair all along. That she'd been screwing around on Rudy during their marriage. Even worse, the police would think she and Heath wanted to be together, and they would most likely consider it a motive. Might even think she and Heath planned and carried out Rudy's murder. She couldn't do anything to raise their suspicions.

Jesus. What a mess. As if the blackmail and the discovery of Rudy's drug use weren't enough. Nope. It would definitely not be wise to get involved with Heath. Even if he was interested, and in spite of his temporary moment of weakness, she had no reason to believe he was, nothing could ever happen between then.

No matter how good it had been to see him unexpectedly...to touch him, albeit briefly, nothing could ever come of it. *Yeah, and maybe if you tell yourself that enough times, you'll be okay with it.* But then again, maybe not.

As much as Nicolette was anxious to have the night over with, a sudden dread filled her chest at the thought of leaving alone, going home alone, maybe finding another message, a threat. Even worse than the memories at Louisa's, were the memories at home. Not a lot to look forward to there. Nothing but the cold spot in her bed where Rudy's warm body once laid, the quiet that somehow seemed gratingly loud.

Although their marriage hadn't been perfect, they'd loved each other. She missed him so much it was a physical ache. She would never hear his laugh again, never feel his strong arms holding her, never feel his warm body in bed as she instinctively scooted against him, seeking his warmth. His death had rocked her world, left a yawning void that was soon filled with loneliness, pain, and anger. Grief had settled over her like a smothering cloak. Then, just when she was really getting into the groove, really getting comfortable with her role as the pathetic, lonely widow, the calls had started. Now, she could add fear to the mix of emotions.

She'd been so lonely and so afraid for so long that she suddenly needed the comfort of someone she felt close to, someone she could confide in.

In spite of her denials about Heath, in spite of her good intentions, she found herself glancing around for him. When she didn't find him, she felt inexplicably deserted, abandoned. She had an uncontrollable urge to seek him out. She just needed to be with someone she could trust. Someone strong and safe.

A Knight Before Christmas

Wading through the sea of bodies, she made her way to the bar where she'd found him earlier. The journey took an agonizing long time between the jostling and the attendees who stopped her, some to offer congratulations on Rudy's award, some to offer condolences on his passing.

Finally arriving at the bar, her heart dropped when Heath was nowhere to be seen.

"Can I get you something?" The bartender, a twenty-something black man shot her a wide smile, but his eyes held sympathy. Good God, was she that transparent?

"Club soda with lime, please."

He poured the soda over ice, the white foam rising then settling gently just when it seemed it would spill over the rim. She was like that lately. Panic and despair bubbling to the surface until she thought she couldn't take anymore, then somehow finding a way to push it back down before it spilled over. How much longer, though? How much longer could she tamp down the erosion without exploding into a million pieces?

The bartender squeezed a lime wedge and dropped it into the clear liquid, then handed her the glass.

"Thank you." She sipped at the drink, thinking she should have ordered something with a little kick, but she'd had two glasses of wine earlier and she was driving tonight. All she needed was a DUI. Wouldn't the cops love that? Wouldn't the papers love it? She could see the headline now, *"Woman suspected of killing her husband, Philanthropist, Rudy Morgan, arrested for DUI."*

Well, maybe that was a little long for a headline, but the press would be all over it.

A few moments later, she was still standing at the bar, enjoying the brief moments of solitude when she spotted Heath. Her heart did a little stutter

29

skip, and pleasure swept through her. His dark head was bent toward a woman she didn't recognize as he listened intently to whatever she was saying. He'd always been like that, had a way of focusing all his attention on whoever he was with at the time, making that person feel special.

A shiver ran through her, and she wanted him to give her that same intent attention. Wanted to feel his arms around her, have him comfort her. She wanted to pour her heart out to him, tell him everything that had been going on since Rudy died.

Heath would be the one person she could trust, the one person who could help her. But she couldn't do it. She couldn't tell anyone.

Lifting the glass to her lips, she took another sip, trying to wash down the lump that had risen to her throat. If she could tell anyone, it would definitely be Heath. He would understand, and he would do whatever it took to make this all go away.

Heath wouldn't do or say anything to hurt Louisa, or to destroy the legacy Rudy had built, the charity he'd created. Heath wouldn't judge Rudy. He would want to protect him, even in death. She knew all this as well as she knew her own name. After all, Heath had loved Rudy as much as she did.

Leaning a hip against a bar stool, she sipped her drink, content to simply watch Heath, something she hadn't been able to do in a long time. His head rose, his eyes meeting hers. A slow smile spread across his face, and he winked. Her skin warmed, her heart thudding crazily in her chest.

She set her glass down on the bar and took a deep breath, gathering her courage to seek Heath out once more. She'd only gone a few steps, when she halted. What would she say? She couldn't tell him about the trouble she was in, and she couldn't tell him she wanted him. Other than that, what was really left? Before she could give in to temptation and do something she'd later regret, she reversed course and headed for the exit door.

****

As she rode the elevator to the parking garage, Nicolette relived those moments with Heath. It had been wonderful to see him, yet frustrating at the same time. Not being able to continue their friendship, or have something more, caused an intense sadness deep within.

Maybe it wasn't really about Heath. In spite of the unpleasant truths she'd learned about Rudy, she missed him terribly. He'd been a loving, attentive husband; they'd had ten great years together. She thought they'd have a lifetime, but a terrible accident, or something more sinister if the police's theory was correct, had ended that dream.

The elevator reached her floor, and she stepped out into the parking garage. There were security cameras and plenty of lighting, but apprehension worked its way down her spine as she headed to her car. The sound of her heels clacking against the concrete echoed and bounced back. If someone approached, she might not hear them with all the noise her shoes were making.

She shook off the thought. She would not let all that was happening make her paranoid. Pausing to fish out her keys, she heard the elevator ding, then open. Good. Company. Not that she thought anything would happen. The blackmailer hadn't approached her thus far, no need for him to do so now. Just the same, she was glad to no longer be alone in the eerie, cavernous space.

Unless...whoever was getting off the elevator posed a threat. After all, it could be him.

She made herself turn to look. Relief swept through her as a group of two men and three women stepped off the elevator. The relief dissipated when they headed the opposite direction of where she was parked. Still alone.

Glancing around, she realized that she was indeed alone, which meant no one was here to threaten her, cause her harm. Feeling foolish and melodramatic, she found her keys and continued her loud journey to the car. Only a few more feet to safety.

Just as she reached her car, she felt rather than heard a presence behind her, and she started to turn. A hand grabbed the back of her head, holding her in place so she couldn't see behind her.

"Oh, God," she whimpered. Her legs shook so hard she thought they'd give out on her, that she'd crumple at the assailant's feet, be at his mercy. *Yeah, like she was any less at his mercy standing upright.*

"Shut up," a harsh voice hissed in her ear.

"What do you want? What are you going to do?" She clutched at her evening bag, wishing it concealed a weapon. That's what she should do. Buy a gun. To hell with being scared out of her mind and continually threatened.

But would you use a gun if you had it?

"I said shut the fuck up." The man's fist clenched in her hair and pulled so hard it stung her scalp and brought tears to her eyes.

Hell yes, she'd use a gun if she had one.

"What do you want?" She tried to make her voice sound strong, tried to note details about the man in case she ever had the opportunity to identify him. He seemed to be about her height and smelled of some cheap cologne.

"I thought maybe I should pay you a visit to let you know I'm not playing."

"Please let me go," she whispered. "I know you're not playing."

"Yeah? You sounded a little reluctant on the phone today. Can't have you getting cold feet."

"I won't. You'll have your money."

"I'd better have it. Or you won't like the way I show my displeasure. You have five days, *capice*?"

She realized he wasn't going to hurt her. He wouldn't want his funds to dry up. The knowledge made her braver than she would have been otherwise. "Yes. I *capice*, dammit. Now, please. Let me go. Leave me alone!"

He jerked her head back, pulling at the tendons of her neck, and she rethought her assumption. Maybe he wouldn't kill her, but there was nothing to keep him from hurting her. Injured or not, she could still fork over his cash.

She waited, barely able to breathe, for whatever pain he would dole out, but it didn't come.

Instead, he loosened his hold enough that she could once more breathe freely and said, "Don't fucking turn around until I'm gone. You do, I make you bleed, got it?"

She nodded, not trusting herself to speak. He released her and she felt him move away but didn't hear footsteps. He must be wearing soft-soled shoes, because not only did she not hear him now, she damned sure hadn't heard him when she'd been clomping through the garage like a horse.

She gave him plenty of time, then with shaking hands, unlocked her car and slid inside. She locked the door, laid her head down on the steering wheel and sobbed. Her earlier pleasure at seeing Heath had been shattered. All that was left was fear and dread.

Would she ever be free of the hold this asshole had on her? Or would she keep giving until she had no more to give? And then what? He'd kill her? Kill Louisa?

No. She couldn't let that happen. Something had to be done before the money ran out. She just wished she knew what the hell that something was.

****

When Heath entered the kitchen the next morning, his mother was limping around, making breakfast. "Mom! What are you doing?"

She swiveled on her crutches as naturally as if she'd been wearing them since birth. "Oh. You're up. Your brother's still in bed. I'll have your breakfast ready in a jiff."

"No way. Sit down." He took the carton of eggs from her hand. Bacon was already sizzling in the skillet. "I'll make breakfast. You're hobbled."

She slapped him lightly on the shoulder. "Now, watch it, buster. A little broken ankle's not gonna hobble me." She took the eggs back from him. "Sit. Let me cook. I'm perfectly capable of taking care of my boys."

Heath had learned long ago not to argue with her, so he poured a cup of coffee and let her have her way. "You in pain?"

"No, hon. No pain. Just a pain in my butt because it takes longer to do all the things I want to do."

"So the injury didn't stop you, just slowed you down."

She turned and flashed him a smile. "*Barely* slowed me down."

Heath didn't understand how she could be so jolly, so happy, under the circumstances. Her husband of forty years had cheated on her. Had a *child* with another woman. Heath hadn't spoken directly with his mother about it, and he didn't particularly want to know details, but he needed to get it out in the open.

"Mom, I need to talk to you."

Something about his tone must have conveyed the gravity of the situation. She turned, her expression one of wariness. "Yes?"

"How can you be okay with this?"

"With what?"

"Dad. The affair." Heath rose and went to stand beside her. "How did it not tear your marriage apart?"

She was silent for a moment, then she picked up an egg and cracked it on the edge of the skillet before dropping the contents onto the melted butter. She picked up a second egg and did the same. "I am *not* okay with it." Her voice was low but steady. "I could never be okay with that kind of betrayal, but I tried to understand as best I could. I loved your father more than anything else in the world. He was lonely, had faced death, saw his friends die in front of his eyes." She shrugged. "I could understand how something like that could happen. Don't you?"

Heath shook his head. "No. He made a commitment to you. You were a good wife to him."

"Yes. And he was a good husband. Everything's not black and white, Heath darling. You have no idea what your father was dealing with over there. He was so very young. People aren't perfect. They make mistakes."

"Yeah, and nearly forty years later, his mistake is coming into our lives. And he's not around to face the music."

"Heath!" She looked at him, eyes wide. "Don't speak ill of your father."

"I'm sorry, Mom. You've had years to get used to it. I haven't."

"Yes, but I'm the one he cheated on. If I can handle it, I'd think you can."

"It goes against everything we were brought up to believe. All those years, him shoving loyalty down my throat. For what?"

She flipped the eggs over, her movements jerky, as if using the spatula as a fencing sword. When she turned to Heath, he could see she'd lost her patience. "I'll tell you *for what*. Because it's what he believed.

35

And, for the fact that he raised three beautiful, kind sons, and if you ended up getting an extra dose of loyalty because your father wasn't using all his, then I reckon that's something you should be thanking the good Lord for."

Heath stared back at her for a moment, then turned and headed for the kitchen door, but halted before he reached it. He wouldn't walk out on his mother, wouldn't be that disrespectful. After all, she wasn't the one he was really angry with. And since the guilty party wasn't here to explain himself, it was best to just drop it.

He walked over and put his arms around his mother. At first, she stiffened against his hug, then her body relaxed, and she hugged him back.

"I'm so sorry, son. I'm sorry your father couldn't be perfect. But mostly I'm sorry you had to find out that he wasn't. Please don't think it didn't hurt me. It did. And trust me, I'm proud as can be that you're not like that. Proud of you for being a man of principles. Just remember, your father loved you, and he'd want you to forgive him."

"I know," Heath said, but he didn't promise he would. Maybe it would happen someday, but that day wasn't here yet.

"We're having Christmas dinner early," his mother said. "So you can eat with us before you head back."

"Good. I would have hated to miss out."

"I still don't get why you have to meet that man on Christmas day. Doesn't he realize it's a holiday?"

"He does, but he doesn't celebrate it."

"Yes, but you do."

"I'm sorry, Mom. It's business. Very important business for the company. I have to be there."

Besides, he was certain by then, he'd be ready to flee.

Amelia dished up his breakfast and handed him

the plate. She sat across from him at the kitchen table and watched while he put away eggs, hash browns, bacon and toast.

In a not so subtle attempt to steer the conversation away from sensitive matters, she said, "So, tell me, son. How are things going for you? Your company doing well? I know you had a hard time deciding to give up being a police officer."

She was right. It had been a difficult decision, but after years of seeing his fellow officers risk their lives—and some lose them, only to see the same assholes back out on the streets—he'd had to call it quits. He was no longer able to sleep at night, knowing everything he'd done that day had been for naught.

In truth, the picture wasn't quite that bleak, but he drove himself crazy thinking it was. After a particularly disturbing incident, he'd finally turned in his badge.

He and his partner, Joe, went out on a domestic disturbance call and found a coked-out thug pounding on his wife. Before they could cuff him, he pulled a gun and shot Joe. Heath wrestled the suspect to the ground and disarmed him, then called for an ambulance.

Once Heath cuffed the guy and was performing CPR on Joe, trying to keep him alive until help arrived, the wife went into a rage, kicking at Joe, screaming at the two of them, telling them not to take her husband to jail. It was all Heath could do not to finish what her old man had started. His partner lay bleeding on the ground after she'd called them for help, and now she was furious at him, the man who'd saved her ass.

Joe survived, but Heath's love for the job hadn't. The thug was back on the streets the next day. Not long after, he beat his wife to death. That had been enough for Heath. He'd left the force and never looked back.

Heath finished chewing, then swallowed the food with a drink of coffee. "It's going well. I like what I do. Business is good."

"Is it dangerous, this security work?"

"Nah. Concerts, frightened women in divorce proceedings, the occasional celebrity in town, stuff like that. Nothing to worry about."

"Well, you do know how I like to worry."

Heath grinned. "That, I do. A mother's curse, right?"

"Right." She grinned back. "Maybe someday, you'll have a child of your own to worry about. You have a girlfriend? Any women in your life I should know about?"

An image of Nicolette flashed through his mind, but he quickly banished it. "No. No one serious. I date once in a while."

"You must be lonely. I wish you lived closer. Wish you and Clint both did. Especially when—" She gave him a stern look. "*If* you give me grandchildren. I don't want to see them only on the holidays, you know."

"I tell you what, Mom. When I have kids, I'll make sure you see them once a month, how's that?" Heath felt confident making that claim. He didn't believe he'd ever have children. Unlike his baby brother, who'd been married twice and was currently engaged, he'd never met anyone he wanted to dedicate the rest of his life to, much less procreate with. Well, other than Nicolette. And that had been a foolish college dream born of youth and misplaced optimism.

"Don't lie to me, young man. I won't forget your promise."

Before Heath could respond, footsteps sounded at the doorway. Alex and a stunning blonde walked in. She wore dark blue jeans and a form-fitting blue

T-shirt. To Heath's untrained eye, her outfit appeared expensive and probably had been designed by someone with a name Heath couldn't spell or pronounce.

Alex made the introductions. Heath's suspicions were confirmed; this was Sydney, his future sister-in-law. Heath instantly disliked her, and he couldn't help but wonder if Alex's third foray into marriage would end as disastrously as the first two.

He sighed and inwardly chastised himself. Maybe he was just projecting his own dismal outlook of happily-ever-after onto his brother. It wasn't Sydney and Alex's fault that Heath's Mrs. Right married his best friend.

Alex and Sydney joined him at the table while his mother rose to make eggs for Alex.

"I'll just have dry toast and a fruit cup," Sydney said, her tone insinuating that eating anything else would be preposterous.

Heath tried to make small talk, but he liked Sydney less and pitied Alex more with every second that passed. His appetite waned, but he forced down as much of the breakfast as he could. He knew too well the fate of those who tried to leave Amelia King's kitchen without heartily partaking of her food.

Shutting out Sydney's incessant complaints, his thoughts drifted back to Nicolette and how quickly his time with her ended. There was no way he'd see her again unless he made the effort. From what he gathered last night, she wouldn't be receptive even if he decided getting in touch with her was a good idea, which he definitely knew wasn't. His heart and his libido said it was a super-duper idea, but neither of them had a habit of making good decisions.

Clint entered the room. Heath barely acknowledged him when he sat down at the table. Heath should make an effort to be better company for his brothers. Clint had driven over five-hundred miles. Alex was on the verge of marrying—again—and all Heath could think about were his own problems. Selfish bastard.

"Mom said you went with Nicolette to a ceremony for Rudy last night?" Clint said. "How was it?"

Out of the din of chatter, Heath realized this remark was directed at him. He halted in the act of forking a piece of egg. "I didn't go *with* Nicolette. I saw her there. It was a nice ceremony. Rudy would have been proud."

Clint didn't reply as he dug into his own breakfast. Apparently, the eldest King brother had issues of his own. He seemed not to be in a talkative mood, which suited Heath just fine. The room fell into silence, save for the sound of forks against plates until Alex rose from his chair.

"Excuse me, Mom. Breakfast was wonderful. I'm going upstairs to shower and change."

Amelia didn't turn as she responded, continuing to scoop bacon onto the paper towel so it could drain and stacking more pancakes onto the growing pile. "I've got breakfast for the girls. You can spend time with them while Zoe's setting up."

Amidst a bevy of shuffling noises and more chatter, Alex left, then Sydney. A few moments later, Amelia turned her spatula over to Clint and retrieved her crutches before also leaving.

Heath stood and carried his dishes to the sink, then headed to the doorway. Before he could escape, Clint's voice stopped him. "Hey."

"Hm?"

"What's going on with you? You're a hundred miles away. Everything okay?"

Didn't he wish. If he were a hundred miles away, he wouldn't be dealing with all the bullshit. Well, that wasn't entirely true. If he were a hundred miles away, or even a thousand, he would still know what his father had done, and he would still be pining for a woman he could never have. Heath decided to give his brother a condensed version.

"Yeah, everything's fine. Trying to adjust to all the changes. You know. A lot's happened lately."

A lot had happened all right, but Heath knew there was much more to come. The thought had his insides twisted up like a pretzel.

Chapter Four

Nicolette alternated between staring out her kitchen window at the too-slowly rising sun, to peering at the clock on the microwave as she waited until she assumed Heath was out of bed and she wouldn't disturb him.

Heath. Bed. *Damn.*

She swallowed against the sudden dryness in her throat. She'd slept in a cold, empty bed for so long that the image of lying next to a warm body—Heath's body—initiated a longing deep within her. She imagined opening her eyes to find him lying next to her, shifting against him and hearing him murmur in his deep, husky voice. Feeling her hands run over his chest...a tingling starting between her thighs...

Stop it! She could *not* think of Heath that way. She still wasn't over Rudy's death, and even if she were ready to start something up with a man, it could *not* be Heath. Not ever. Heath was her friend. Nothing more.

She sighed and took a sip of her coffee, then stood to pace restlessly across the kitchen floor. Sleep had eluded her last night, her stomach a tight knot of fear as she lay awake, staring at the shadows that played across the ceiling.

This was the first time the blackmailer made physical contact. In the four months since all this started, he'd left notes, made phone calls, given her instructions, nothing more. She'd made the drops as instructed—always at a new location—and never run into him. Until now. First the phone call to Louisa's home, now the scare in the parking garage. He was escalating. He'd asked for one payment a month in the beginning. Now he wanted his next payment two weeks after the last.

The money was drying up, and would soon run completely out. Rudy's life insurance wouldn't be enough to keep the blackmailer satisfied for long. Would he go through with his threat and kill someone she loved? Although, there weren't that many people in her life he could go after.

God. She'd never really thought about how alone she was. She hadn't felt the lack of family as deeply when Rudy was alive. He and Louisa had been all she needed. Nicolette had never been very good at cultivating friendships. She'd learned from her childhood to keep people at bay. The less others knew about her, the better.

How different would things be if she knew where her father was? Would he be a loving, protective kind of dad who would shield his little girl from all the unpleasantness? She hadn't seen him since she'd left for college, but the father she remembered had been like that, before the Incident. Afterward, he'd been morose and withdrawn, especially once her mother died.

She had no idea what kind of man he'd become. During her marriage to Rudy, she suggested more than once that they find her father. She wanted to reunite with him and make him a part of her life, but Rudy strongly discouraged the idea. Nicolette argued at first, but Rudy convinced her by pointing out that if her father wanted her to be a part of his life, he wouldn't have given up so easily when she stopped contacting him. Rudy suggested that perhaps, just as her father was a reminder to her of the misery her family suffered, maybe she was a reminder to him.

43

Nicolette eventually stopped bringing it up, but she never stopped thinking about it. Never forgot the man who'd bundled her up and taken her outside in the Wisconsin winter and scooped up snow to make snow ice cream. The same man whose face beamed with joy as he'd watched her struggle through her first piano recital. That performance had also been her last. Looking back, she knew it was a performance only a parent could have loved. She'd known, even then, how very much her father loved her.

That had been before the murder. Before he'd been wrongly accused of killing a young girl who lived in their neighborhood. The police eventually found the real killer and dropped all charges against Nicolette's father, but the charges hadn't been dropped in the hearts and minds of the community. Nicolette—in junior high at the time—had been tormented and ridiculed daily. Her father lost his job on some trumped up excuse. He'd found work delivering pizzas and barely eked out a living, but for all practical purposes, their family died the day of her father's arrest. Her mom had done so literally a few years later, but that was just a formality.

Nicolette knew what life was like for people suspected of doing something horrible. Using drugs wasn't quite on the scale with murder, but for a man in Rudy's position, it was enough to tear down everything he'd built. Everything Nicolette had helped him build, and she couldn't let that happen.

She didn't know exactly what the blackmailer would do if she didn't pay, but whatever it was, she couldn't take the chance. Nor could she continue to pay, not when the money was nearly depleted. She'd have to get help. In spite of the threats the unknown man had made, she could no longer do this on her own.

She knew what she had to do. Before she could

pick up the phone to call Heath, it rang. She gasped, then admonished herself for being so jumpy. She relaxed, recognizing Marla's number on the caller ID.

"Hey, darling, how are you this morning?" Marla said. "Lovely event last night, wasn't it?"

"Yes. I was so proud of Rudy."

"He would have been touched. Listen, are we still planning to get together about the Christmas party this afternoon?"

"Sure. I was going to meet you around two at the museum. Will that work?"

"That will be perfect. I'm getting nails this morning, so I won't be free until later anyway."

Getting nails meant having a set of long, meticulously painted, acrylic nails put on Marla's slim, elegant fingers. Nicolette held up her hand and looked at her own neglected, stubby-nailed fingers and cringed. Maybe before the party, she should *get nails* herself.

"Okay. I'll see you at around two."

In spite of her grief and fear, Nicolette was excited about the party. Nothing could compare to the joy she felt as she looked into the elated faces of the little children, some whose lives had no doubt been filled with untold despair. Even the teenagers couldn't hide their excitement, no matter how *cool* they tried to act. All of them had been through the same kind of hell. Not knowing if Mom or Dad would keep their job, their home. Not knowing where their next meal would come from. And, probably worst of all, the hell they faced in school. She, of all people, knew what it was like to be bullied and ridiculed by classmates. But, at least the home life was more private, not as many witnesses to the humiliation and despair of their existence.

Refilling her coffee cup, she glanced once more at the microwave clock. Eight a.m. Heath should be up by now. She couldn't wait any longer, even if it meant disturbing the entire household. If she didn't tell someone soon, she'd go nuts.

Lifting the receiver, she dialed Amelia King's house.

****

The phone in the next room rang. Heath's mother answered. Her voice lifted with excitement as she said, "Oh, my goodness, dear. So wonderful to hear from you. Yes. Yes, he's right here. Hold on." A brief pause, then, "Heath! Phone, for you."

"For me?" he called as he left the kitchen.

He found his mother at the foot of the stairs holding the cordless phone out to him. Before he could take it from her, she whispered loud enough for the person on the phone to hear, "It's Nicolette!"

Blood rushed to his head, and Heath paused a moment. He tried to tamp down the pounding of his heart as he brought the phone to his ear. "Hello. Nicolette?"

"Heath, hi. I'm so sorry to bother you. Is this a bad time?"

"No, not at all. Glad you called," he said, uttering the world's biggest understatement. "What's up?"

A long silence, then in a voice so soft he had to strain to make out the words, she said, "You know last night when you said you knew there was something wrong with me?"

"Yes."

"You were right, Heath. There's something terribly wrong."

A ball of worry tightened in his throat. "What is it? Are you okay?"

"I am. Right now, that is. But, I don't know... I'm not sure what's going to happen and..." She took a deep breath. "Heath, I need you."

God, how he'd wanted to hear her say that,

although she most likely didn't mean it sexually. It was a nice fantasy, but this was something serious. Something was wrong with Nicolette.

"Sure, what is it?"

"I'm in trouble. I need your help."

Right. I got that part. "With what, Nicolette?"

Heath looked at his mother. She'd been staring at him curiously, but turned away as if she hadn't.

"I can't tell you over the phone," Nic said. "Can you come here? To my house? I'm not sure if I should even..." Another deep breath. "Never mind. I'm sorry. Just forget I called."

"The hell I will!" His voice was harsher than he intended, and he caught his mother's disapproving frown before he turned his back to her and said more quietly, "If you're in trouble, I want to help."

"Are you sure?"

"Of course. What are friends for?"

Her voice now held a wealth of relief. "Thank you, Heath. Thank you so much."

"Be there in half an hour." He hung up the phone, the happiness welling in his chest inappropriate considering a friend was in trouble.

"What is it, Heath?" Amelia asked.

"Nothing I can talk about right now, Mom."

The doorbell rang, saving him from further explanation.

Amelia's face lit up, the phone call forgotten. "That must be Zoe and the girls!" She scrambled for her crutches.

"I'll get it," Heath offered. "By the time you trudge over there, they'll be in high school."

"Oh, you. Watch your tongue, young man."

Heath grinned and made himself walk to the door at a normal pace. As much as he wanted to meet his nieces, instinct demanded he speed to Nicolette's and rescue his damsel. For that, he'd need a white horse, right? He wondered what color

47

Clint's horse was. Probably not white. He'd have to settle for a burgundy Tahoe as his trusty steed.

When he opened the door, three little figures rushed past him so fast, he barely caught a blur of dark hair and fuzzy, blue hooded coats. He bit down a curse as a tiny shoulder came frighteningly close to his groin.

Looking up, he found an attractive woman—nah, attractive wasn't the right word, she was a knockout—standing at the door. A woman who, although his brain knew it to be true, his eyes told him it couldn't be Zoe Hillman. Zoe had weighed more than twice what this woman standing before him did. In spite of her weight, though, Zoe had always been pretty.

"Heath?"

He realized then that he was staring like a dumbstruck moron. "Yes. Sorry, Zoe. Come in."

He reached out to give her a peck on the cheek as she entered. Deftly, she corralled the three miniature cyclones who were now swirling around their grandmother. "Girls, come meet your Uncle Heath."

They stilled, and he wondered how long the lull would last.

"Hello," he said, not knowing whether to offer his hand to shake or to hug them. He wasn't used to kids, and he didn't want to scare them off, although he had a feeling not much could scare these little rascals. Mischief glinted in the three pairs of blue eyes that looked up at him.

"This is Macy, this is Michaela, and this is Mia." Zoe touched each of the tiny, dark heads as she introduced them.

Heath peered down at the three little replicas of his baby brother and felt a sudden rush of warmth, an invisible bond and a fierce compulsion to protect. Before he could get all misty, he said, "Well, they're

Kings all right." Then, realizing how that sounded, he turned to Zoe. "Oh, sorry. I didn't mean that like it came out."

She smiled, her eyes sparking with humor. "Not a problem. I know what you meant."

"They're beautiful."

"Thank you. They're a handful."

Heath shook his head. "I can't even imagine taking care of one, let alone three. You deserve some kind of medal."

She laughed. "I'm sure just being their mother is reward enough, although I'll admit there are times I question that theory."

One of the girls, Michaela, if he remembered right, said, "You're our uncle?" with the doubt of a prosecutor questioning a defense witness.

"I am," Heath said, squatting in front of them.

"He's my little boy," Amelia said.

Macy scowled. "But he's not even little."

"Not anymore," his mother said, her voice sounding younger than he'd heard it in years. "But he used to be as little as you. Even littler."

"Was he in your stomach like we was in our mom's?" Macy asked.

Amelia guffawed. "Yes. I suppose he was."

Zoe's face turned pink. "Come on, girls, let's go into the kitchen."

"Yes, let's," Amelia said. "Gramma made breakfast. You like pancakes?"

A cacophony of squeals rose, and Heath just had time to ruffle their soft hair before they ran into the kitchen.

His heart felt light as he headed to his truck. This trip was starting to improve. He'd met his adorable nieces and was already half in love with them, and he would soon see Nicolette. Never mind that she was in some kind of trouble. Last night, he'd gone to bed thinking those few moments with her at the ceremony were all he'd have. Now, he would steal at least a few precious more.

****

During Nicolette's third stint of peering out the window, her efforts were rewarded. Heath finally pulled into the drive. She watched him climb out of the car, watched the wind toss his dark hair into a sexy mess. But when he squinted toward the house, she let the blinds drop.

Her heart raced when the bell rang, and her hands shook as she swung the door open.

Beneath his wind-tousled hair Heath's golden eyes searched her face. "Hey, are you all right?" He spoke before she had a chance to.

"Come in. Please." She stepped back, catching a whiff of some kind of woodsy, masculine aftershave as he brushed past her. "I'm glad you came."

"You sounded like you needed me."

She led him to the living room and took his coat, a brown suede, still warm from his body heat. He wore jeans and a white knit pullover. Although his reasons for being there were not the most pleasant, it felt good to have him in her home. Odd, but good. Like, sexy good, and she wanted to lean into his warmth, his strength.

To keep from doing just that, she dropped her gaze and made herself busy with hanging his jacket on the coat rack.

"Have a seat. Coffee?" she offered.

"No, thanks. I'm good."

"I'll just go get mine, then. Be right back."

When she returned, Heath stood next to the fireplace, looking at a photo of Donovan, Marla, herself, and Rudy at one of the many benefits the four of them had attended together.

"This is that couple I met last night?"

"Yes. Donovan works at the charity. Marla is an up and coming politician. She's on the city council

50

and plans to run for mayor in the next election."

"Impressive. So, the four of you were pretty close? I never really heard you or Rudy mention them."

She took a sip from the large red coffee mug. "We've grown closer in the past couple of years. They've been great since Rudy died."

Heath moved over to stand in front of her, staring down into her face.

"So, why don't you tell me what's got you so upset?"

He was so close she could see the stress lines around his eyes. What had put them there? Maybe she shouldn't burden him with her problems. Not when he might have plenty of his own.

So that she'd have time to think—and doing that with him so near was proving to be impossible—she stepped back and headed toward the couch. Stopping beside it, she took another swallow of the coffee, its warmth and strong flavor helping settle her nerves.

"Why don't we sit?" she suggested.

Heath settled onto one end of the sofa and Nicolette perched on the chair caddy-cornered to it.

"You want to tell me what's going on?" His eyes narrowed as they once more searched hers.

That was the third time he'd asked without her revealing anything and she wondered how many more chances she had. Would he finally grow impatient, say to hell with her and leave? Maybe that would be the best thing, but it wasn't what she wanted.

Taking a deep breath, she opened her mouth to speak, then looked away, shaking her head. "I don't know if I can..."

Heath scooted to the edge of the couch and placed a hand on her knee, giving it a gentle squeeze. "Don't worry. Whatever it is, you can trust me."

"I know I can."

"You said you needed my help."

"I just don't know. I shouldn't drag you into this." She stared down at his hand on her knee. Having it there felt right, although a little unsettling. Tiny surges of electricity moved over her skin, even though her jeans barred him from actually touching her flesh. Suddenly, all she could concentrate on was the odd wonder of having Heath here. This intimate setting. The desire racing through her. She sighed and shook her head, tried to push those thoughts away. "I shouldn't drag anyone into this."

Hooking a knuckle under her chin, Heath lifted her face until she looked at him. "If you're in trouble, if you need help, you should tell me. You know I'll do whatever I can."

She stared into his eyes, once more losing her breath. Pulling away, she stood and paced, pausing to take sips of coffee as she did. Heath rose, but stayed beside the couch and didn't speak as he waited. She was grateful for his patience, that he was allowing her to work this out in her head before she explained.

She twisted a lock of hair between her fingers while she considered. This morning, she'd been sure she should do this, that Heath would help her and he'd want to be involved. But actually saying the words was quite different. Once she said them, there was no taking them back. Once Heath knew, there would be no 'unknowing.'

But did she really want to continue to carry this burden alone? Could she forgive herself if she kept silent and someone she loved was hurt, maybe killed?

Making her decision, she turned back to Heath, took a deep breath, then blurted out, "I'm being blackmailed."

Chapter Five

"You're being what?" Heath stalked to where she stood gripping the large red mug as if it might be her only hope of salvation. "Blackmailed?"

Her hazel eyes were rimmed with dark circles, their normal brightness dulled. Her face took on a pinched look, and she nodded jerkily. "A little more than six months after Rudy died, I got a phone call at work." She swept a handful of hair back from her face. "It was a man. He—uh—said he wanted money."

She stopped. Heath waited. When she didn't continue, he asked, "Money? Or else what?"

She lifted a hand, palm up. "Or he'd ruin my life. Ruin my charity. Rudy's charity. Hurt me. Hurt Louisa. You name it, he'd do it."

"What does he have on you?"

She shook her head. "Not on me. On Rudy." She stalked over to the patio door and stared out over the deck. "Rudy was apparently involved with drugs."

Heath tried to hide his surprise. She and Rudy both fooled around with drugs in college, but as far as he knew, they'd stopped long ago. Rudy had gotten back on them?

"I didn't know," she went on. "I swear. At least, not while Rudy was alive. Shortly after he died, I was cleaning out his side of the closet—" She stopped, took a deep breath.

"And?" Heath prompted.

Hesitating briefly, she turned away from the window and set her cup down on the end table. "I

53

found some paraphernalia. Then, when the caller said those things, I knew he was telling the truth. He knew too much about Rudy, and the information he gave answered a lot of things I'd wondered about during the past few years. Things I put out of my mind because I didn't *want* to know."

Heath hoped she wouldn't get angry with him, but he had to ask. "What about you? Have you done drugs since college?"

"No." Her head shook in vehement denial, and he couldn't gauge whether she was angry or simply trying to convince him. "Not at all. No way. Haven't touched them since college." She shrugged dismissively. "Even then, I just dabbled. I really only partook because Rudy did them. Maybe I should have known he wouldn't truly give them up."

"So why would drugs be a big deal now? Rudy's gone. It's not like he could go to jail."

"I know. But Renewed Hope's purpose is to get people off drugs. Get them clean, give them a new start. Rudy's charity has a lot of powerful, connected benefactors. If it got out that the founder of the charity was guilty of the very thing the charity spoke out against, it would fold. Benefactors would pull out. People who need us, who count on us, would suffer. Rudy's standing, his reputation would be ruined."

"How much are you paying the blackmailer?"

"Ten thousand a month. I've paid it for the past four. He'd been blackmailing Rudy. After Rudy died, the asshole waited for the insurance money to kick in, then called me." Tears filled her eyes. "The money will run out before long. He called yesterday and asked for another payment just two weeks after the last. He wants another ten grand this Friday. And now it's more than just phone calls, he—" Her lips quivered and she shook her head.

"He what?"

"Nothing. Never mind."

Heath took her elbows in his hands. "What happened, Nicolette?"

She pulled away from his touch. "Last night when I left the event, he was there. In the parking garage."

A stab of anger shot through Heath's chest. "Did he hurt you?"

"No. He grabbed me, threatened me. It was just more...violent than he has been. I'm afraid of what he might do when the money runs out. Yesterday, he called Louisa's house phone, just to let me know he knows all about me. I can't let him hurt her."

"We need to go to the police."

"No! Please, Heath. No police. He said he'd kill me. That even if he was arrested—and like he's reminded me more than once, I have no proof—Rudy's reputation would still be ruined. I can't go to the police."

She had a point. Heath would make sure the son of a bitch didn't get his hands on Nicolette, but until they had proof of the blackmail, it would just be her word against his. "That may be true, but it's not a good idea to cave to a blackmailer's demands. For now, though, keep doing what you've been doing. I'll figure something out."

"I know I shouldn't ask you to help me. It's my problem, and I need to deal with it. I just thought since you have that security firm, and since you were once a cop, you'd have experience dealing with this sort of thing. I figured you'd know what to do."

"Yeah. I mean, I can't promise anything, but I'll do what I can. I'll look into it, see what I can find out. I need you to tell me everything you know. We'll have to work closely together on this."

"I'll help in any way I can."

"We don't have a lot of time. I leave in less than a week." He couldn't imagine leaving her if this wasn't settled, if he didn't know she was safe, but he'd worry about that when the time came. "I'll do everything I can to make sure it's handled before I go."

She nodded. "Thanks, Heath. You're a good friend."

Heath looked toward the stairs. In order to protect Nic, he needed to be as close to her as possible. "How many bedrooms you have here?"

"Three. Why?"

"Anyone else live with you?"

"No."

"I'll be staying here with you."

Her brows rose. "Why?"

"To look out for you. If this guy came up to you last night, he could be escalating. I don't want to find out what he might do next. Plus, I'll need to get all the information from you that I can. There will be a lot of going over documents, checking into friends, associates, people involved with the charity, everything. We can get more done if we're staying at the same place."

"No. I don't think that's a good idea."

Did she think he had an ulterior motive? Just because he wanted to get her into bed, it didn't mean he would try anything. At least, he hoped he would be able to control his insanely strong attraction to her. "I need to be near you, Nic. Keep an eye on you. You're not safe."

She crossed her arms and rested them beneath her breasts, lifting one hand to her mouth and chewing the pad of her thumb. "What about if you were close, but not exactly here?"

"I don't get it."

"The other side of the duplex is empty. I keep it that way for visiting relatives, people who need temporary housing, that sort of thing. It's furnished. There's a connecting door. You'd be close enough to keep an eye out for me, and we'd have an opportunity to work together as often as we needed."

He nodded. "That'll work. I'll go back and let Mom know I'll be staying away for a few days." At her panicked look, he said, "I won't tell her why. I'll just tell her I have some things to take care of. Why don't you go with me, so I don't have to leave you alone?"

"No. It's okay. You're not going to be with me twenty-four/seven anyway. I feel I'll be fairly safe until the next drop, at least. If he doesn't get his money, then he might try something. In the meantime, he'll want me healthy."

Heath walked to the door. "I'll be back a little later today. While I'm gone, keep the doors locked. I want you to dig out everything you can about this. Notes, if the blackmailer left any. Write down times he's called, dig out any paperwork you might have that could be pertinent. I want you to pull phone records both before and after Rudy's death. Highlight any unfamiliar numbers."

"Okay. Yeah. Sure."

"I'd also like a photo of you, and one of Rudy I can carry with me." He wasn't sure if they'd be needed, but he believed in being thorough. "We'll go through all the paperwork and questions today, then I'll hit the streets tomorrow."

She walked him to the door and stepped onto the porch with him. She wore faded jeans and a button-down olive sweater that gave her skin a sickly cast in the winter light.

Her neighborhood was a quiet cul-de-sac with well-kept lawns. The Christmas decorations looked stark and forlorn in the cold gray morning. Lights trimmed Nic's duplex, but a thin, cardboard cutout of Santa was the only other decoration, like a half-assed attempt at gaiety by someone whose heart wasn't in it.

Standing on tiptoe, Nicolette braced her hands on his biceps and planted a kiss on his cheek. For a brief moment, the feel of her warm breath contrasting with the cool air caused his heart to stutter.

Before he could react, it was over, and she released him, "Thanks, Heath. Really."

He took her shoulders and stared down into her face, "Don't worry. You're not alone in this anymore. I'll help you find this guy, I promise."

She nodded and watched him from the porch while he headed to his car.

When he climbed inside the Tahoe, Nic went back inside. He pulled out his cell phone. He dialed the number to his security firm, and Burke answered with, "How's it going up north?"

"You wouldn't believe it, if I told you."

"Try me."

"I don't have time to go into all the details, but a friend of mine is in trouble. I'm going to have to do some investigating. I'll need you to send me a few pieces of equipment."

He gave Burke the list and asked him to overnight it.

"Damn, dude. You're itching to get on it, aren't you?"

"It's urgent. She's in trouble."

"She?"

Heath could hear the disapproval in the silence on the phone line. "Yeah, *she*."

"Are we talking about Nicolette?"

Burke didn't know exactly how deep Heath's feelings for Nicolette ran, but on a few regrettable occasions, fueled by melancholy and Jack Daniels, Heath had shared more than he would have liked.

"Yeah. But it's not what you're thinking. She's a friend. I'll do whatever it takes to keep her safe."

Burke promised he would get the package out

today. Heath hung up the phone.

Before starting the truck, he leaned his head back and squeezed his eyes shut. He'd vowed to Burke he'd do whatever it took to keep Nicolette safe. He only hoped to hell he could make good on that promise.

****

As Heath opened the door to his mother's house, he smelled the spicy scent of her baking and heard squeals of delight coming from the triplets. He smiled. That had to be one of the sweetest sounds he'd ever heard. Alex was a lucky man.

One of the girls, Macy he believed, stood on a chair next to the fireplace looking at photos. The other two chased one another around the coffee table.

"Hey, girls. Slow down," Heath said. "That's how accidents happen."

A giggling shout erupted from the one in front, and she didn't even attempt to slow her pace. Heath reached down, snatched the chaser up, and lifted her in his arms.

"Which one are you?" he asked as she stared back at him, her big blue eyes not showing any fear.

"I'm Michaela, silly." She pointed to her former quarry. "That's Mia."

"Okay. You and your sister need to chill."

"But we're having fun!" the still free one said.

"Yeah. It's all fun and games till someone loses an eye."

Mia screeched to a stop and turned her wide-eyed gaze to Heath. "What's gonna happen to my eye?"

Heath cringed, feeling like a heel. He hadn't meant to scare her. "Nothing, sweetie." He deposited Michaela on the ground and squatted until he was eye-level with them both. "It's just an expression. Uncle Heath was just kidding."

"Oh," they said in unison, but instead of resuming the chase, they plopped onto the couch. "Can you turn on cartoons?"

"If I can find any." Heath picked up the remote and powered up the TV, putting it on the channel guide. "Macy, you want to come watch?" He was pretty certain he had the name right. Process of elimination.

Without turning around, she asked, "Is this grandpa?" and pointed to a picture of Heath at his military graduation.

Heath found a cartoon channel and went over to Macy. "No, honey. That's me. This is your grandpa." Heath showed her a photo of his father in his army uniform.

"You look the same."

We were the same, Heath thought. His dad was the main reason he'd joined the military right out of high school. The main reason he'd done most of the good things in his life. And look at how things had turned out now.

He lifted Macy by the waist and set her down on the floor. "Why don't you watch TV with your sisters? I need to talk to Grandma. Where is she?"

"She's in the kitchen making stuff."

Heath grinned and ruffled her hair. "Cool. Be good, and I'll let you know when Grandma has a treat ready for you."

He exited to a chorus of 'Yays' and found his mother in the kitchen. The tantalizing smells grew stronger in there, and his stomach rumbled in anticipation.

Amelia smiled and shouted over the sound of the mixer she held, "Oh, hello, dear. So glad you're back. Is everything okay with Nicolette?"

"She's fine."

"Good. Did you bring her back with you? I'd love to see her."

"No. I won't be staying long myself."

She shut off the mixer and turned to him, her face showing disappointment. "Why not? Where are you going?"

"I have some things to take care of."

"How long will you be gone? You'll be back for dinner, right? The triplets are staying. Aren't they just the cutest thing ever? Can't believe I'm finally a grandmother."

Now for the hard part. "I'm actually staying somewhere else for a little while."

"What? You just got here. You're supposed to be with your family for the holidays."

"I know. But something's come up. I need to help a friend."

Her brows drew together. "Nicolette? Is there something going on between you two?" Her expression was hard to read, but she looked neither completely pleased nor upset about the idea.

"No, Mom. There's nothing between us. I just have some business to take care of. I can't really talk about it."

"Ah. One of those security assignments?"

"Something like that." He loved his mother, but sometimes her inquisitive nature bordered on nosiness. "I really can't say much. I hope you understand."

She sniffed, but nodded, turning away to pour batter into loaf pans. "I understand. I'm making you some pumpkin bread. You'll be back to pick it up before you go back to Oklahoma, won't you?"

"Mom." He sighed heavily. "I'll only be gone for a few days, and I'll be back to visit, even while I'm working on the case." *Case*. The word sounded wrong. This could never really be a 'case.' It was Nicolette. She was far from just a client. For one, she wasn't paying. For another, he seldom wanted to get naked with his clients, let alone declare his undying love for them. "Of course, I'll be back for Alex's wedding. And I'm spending Christmas with you."

She turned back, her face lighting with pleasure. "You are?"

"Absolutely." He kissed her on the cheek. "I'm going upstairs to grab my things."

"Maybe you could bring Nicolette with you sometime."

He grunted noncommittally as he headed out the door. He wasn't sure how much socializing Nic would want to do, especially with his family. That might be a little too intimate, too personal, for her.

"Invite her for Christmas!" his mother called out as he reached the staircase.

For a brief moment, the image of Nicolette gathered with the family in front of the tree flashed through his mind. Then another, he and Nic surrounded by their own children in front of their own tree.

Get that out of your mind. That would never happen. Not with Nic. His *friend.* He cursed as he threw his belongings into a duffel. What the hell. The rosy, picture-perfect family was just a fantasy, anyway. After learning a man like his father couldn't stay faithful, he had his doubts anyone could.

He said goodbye to his mother and was treated to three tiny, but surprisingly strong, hugs before he left. Throwing his duffel into the passenger seat, he climbed into the Tahoe and headed to Nicolette's.

When he was in sight of her house, his gut tightened. A police car was parked out front. It was an unmarked, but he knew the KCPD used Crown Victoria's and something told him this belonged to them. Had something happened to Nicolette? Heart pounding, he jammed his foot on the accelerator and squealed into her driveway.

Chapter Six

Heath was running up the stairs when the door opened. Two men in suits came out—one tall and black, the other stocky and Hispanic, wearing a perplexed frown beneath a thick mustache. Nicolette appeared behind them. Heath's legs weakened in relief.

By her face, he could tell she wasn't thrilled he'd shown up at this moment. She looked nervously from him to the two men. What the hell was going on?

"Is everything okay?" Heath directed the question to Nicolette, but she didn't respond.

"I'm Detective Patella, and this is Detective Berry," the Hispanic one said. "And you are?"

"Heath King." Heath shook hands with the detectives.

Patella looked back at Nicolette, then to Heath again. "You a friend of Mrs. Morgan's?"

"Yes. Is there a problem?"

"Just following up on a homicide investigation."

"Homicide?" Heath looked up at Nicolette, who looked away miserably but didn't speak.

"Her husband, Rudy Morgan. We're investigating his death. Maybe we could ask you a few questions."

"He doesn't know anything." Nicolette spoke for the first time. "He's not from here. He wasn't in town when Rudy had his...accident."

Berry studied Heath and slowly nodded. "Still. If you don't mind, maybe you could give us a few moments of your time?" He reached a hand out and lightly gripped Heath's arm. "We've bothered Mrs. Morgan enough for one day. Maybe we could talk to you in the car?"

Heath wasn't an idiot. They wanted to get him apart from Nicolette so they could compare their stories. But since he had nothing to hide and wanted to know what this was about, he let them lead him away, giving Nicolette a reassuring smile as he did.

He climbed into the back seat. Patella got in next to him while Berry slid into the driver's seat.

Patella spoke first. "Did you know Mrs. Morgan's husband?"

"Yeah. Almost all my life. We grew up together."

"So, you're from the area?"

"I was born in Kansas City, but moved away right after college. A buddy of mine in OKC hooked me up with a job." Heath didn't tell them that Burke had convinced him to enter the police academy in Oklahoma City. He didn't want to tell the detectives he was an ex-cop, they'd find out soon enough. He also didn't want to tell them he'd been anxious to agree with Burke's suggestion. Handling Rudy and Nicolette's marriage seemed a little easier from a distance. "Rudy and I remained friends all these years."

"And Mrs. Morgan?"

"I met her in college. The same time as Rudy." The inside of the car was stuffy, and Heath put his finger on the window button. "You mind if I crack this a bit?" When Berry nodded his okay and turned the key, Heath slid the window down a few inches. "So, what's this all about? I thought Rudy's death was an accident."

"She didn't tell you? How close are you and Mrs. Morgan?"

Not nearly close enough.

"We're good friends, but we live over three-hundred miles apart, so we don't see one another often. I haven't seen her since Rudy's funeral."

"So you just showed up today? She seemed to be expecting you."

Heath sighed. "I saw her last night. I live in Oklahoma City, but I'm here for the holidays, and I ran into her at an event honoring Rudy. I saw her again this morning, and she invited me to stay here for a few days." The two detectives exchanged looks and Heath said, "In the empty duplex next door."

"Why?"

"Why?" Heath repeated.

"Yeah," Patella said. "Why are you staying at the duplex? You're here for Christmas holidays, right? You got family here to stay with?"

For the first time, Heath said something that wasn't entirely true. Not particularly a lie, but he was definitely leaving out something. Now that he knew Rudy's death was suspicious, the blackmail could very well be pertinent to the investigation. But he'd promised Nicolette. She did, however, have a lot to answer for, once he finished with the cops. "My mother's house is overcrowded with all the family in. Plus, there's a lot of drama going on right now. You know how it is. Sometimes it's a little more than I wanna deal with. Nicolette had an empty place. She offered, I accepted."

"Before Mr. Morgan's funeral, when was the last time you were in town?"

"I was here not long after his accident. The next day. I came as soon as I heard."

"You weren't here the day of?"

"No."

"When was the last time you saw Mr. Morgan before the accident?"

Heath had to think on that one. Before Rudy's and his father's death, he'd come to Kansas City every few months. Once in a while, Rudy and

Nicolette, or sometimes just Rudy, came to visit. Rudy's accident had been right after Christmas. So, yeah, that was it, the last time he'd seen him had been the day before Christmas. He told that to the cops.

"Did you and Mr. Morgan have any kind of disagreement?"

"No. Hell, no. I know what you're getting at, and no. No problems at all between us. We were close friends."

"As close as you and Mrs. Morgan?"

Heath made an effort to hold back his anger. "I know what you're getting at. We're just friends."

"Never had an intimate relationship?"

"Never."

"Not even after Mr. Morgan's death?"

A memory of that time when Rudy had been in a coma flashed through Heath's mind, and he pushed it quickly aside, hoping his expression hadn't given anything away. "Not even then. Let me ask you something. Why do you think Rudy's death is suspicious? Didn't he die from his car accident?"

"Yes. But some of the evidence at the scene suggested foul play."

"What evidence?"

Patella smiled. "I'm sure you know we can't discuss that with you, Mr. King."

"I'd be willing to bet a lot of it's been printed in the paper. I wouldn't expect you to tell me any of the good stuff you're keeping from the media."

They looked at one another for a few seconds again, then Berry said, "There were no skid marks at the scene of the accident, which indicates he was unconscious when he went off the road. Supposedly, he was alone, but the passenger door was ajar, indicating someone had gotten out of that side."

When Berry paused, Patella took over, "There was nothing mechanically wrong with the car. No indicator of why the accident occurred."

"Is Nicolette a suspect?"

A slight hesitation, then Patella said, "She's a person of interest."

Heath knew they were leaving out some details, but just what they'd told him definitely sounded suspicious. The thought that someone wanted his friend dead was disturbing. The idea Nicolette could have had anything to do with it was ludicrous.

"There's no way she could have harmed her husband. She's not that kind of person. For God's sake, she loved him. She's not capable of murdering anyone, and damned sure not her husband."

"Everyone's capable of murder, Mr. King. All they need is motive and opportunity."

"And you think Nicolette had that?"

Patella shrugged. "We're trying to find out. Life insurance money. Marital difficulties." He paused and gave Heath a hard look. "A lover."

Heath heaved a sigh. "Nicolette didn't care about the insurance money, and they didn't have difficulties. No more than any other couple."

"You didn't deny she had a lover."

"I damned sure didn't say she did."

"Did she?"

Heath clutched the door handle. "I think this interview is over." As soon as he said it, he realized it made him sound guilty. If not of murder, then of cheating on his best friend. "She didn't have a lover," he added before climbing out of the car.

Patella got out, too. He met Heath as he rounded the car to head for Nicolette's door. "How long will you be in town, Mr. King? In case we have more questions."

"I'm leaving Christmas afternoon. But you're not going to find any evidence against Mrs. Morgan." He didn't pause as he made his way up the steps.

Behind him, Patella said, "Is that because there

is none, or because she hid it too well?"

Heath didn't respond. He heard the detective get back in the car as he lifted his fist to bang on Nic's door. She had a hell of a lot of explaining to do.

****

Nicolette paced, twisting her fingers together. Anxiety sat like a brick in the pit of her stomach. Heath was talking to the cops. Heath would know. Heath would think she—

A loud banging on the door made her jump. She looked through the peephole. Heath stood on the other side, scowling, looking like he was ready to bang again.

She opened the door, and he strode past her without an invitation.

She slowly turned to face him "What did they tell you?"

"A hell of a lot more than you did!" Tension set into the lines of his face, tightened his broad shoulders. "What the hell, Nic?"

"I'm sorry. I didn't know if it was important—"

"Not important?" He began to pace, too, but where her pacing had been nervous, his was furious. "First of all, you didn't tell me that the death of my best friend might be—no, *was definitely*—not an accident. Secondly, you didn't tell me that you," with that, he paused and jammed a finger toward her, "were a suspect. Thirdly, you ask for my help because of a goddamned blackmailer and don't bother to tell me that he's not your only trouble— that you're fucking being investigated by homicide detectives. For God's sake, Nicolette, what the hell were you thinking?"

She opened her mouth to reply, and a lump of tears formed in her throat. Heath had never been upset with her before. She didn't like it. Not one damned bit. On top of all the other things that had happened lately, it was just too much. She took a deep breath and shut her eyes, willing the tears not to fall. With all the other negative things Heath thought about her, she damned sure didn't want him to see how weak she was, how frightened.

Turning her back to him, she crossed her arms over her breasts. "You're right. I should have told you. I was just so ashamed. So worried about what you'd think. With all that's happened, I couldn't stand it if you believed them."

"Believed them?" His voice gentled. She heard him move to stand behind her, then felt his hands on her shoulders. "Believed the police? That you had something to do with Rudy's death?" He turned her to face him and took her hands in his. "I would never, ever believe something like that about you. I'll admit, I'm shocked and upset at the thought of someone purposely harming, killing, Rudy. I'm hurt that you didn't trust me enough to share that with me—"

"I do trust you, Heath. I—"

He stopped her with a finger to her lips. "I want you to know that you can trust me. But, please, no matter what it is, no matter how unpleasant, you have to promise that from this point forward, you'll tell me everything. Deal?"

She nodded. Her heart thumped at the feel of his fingers on her lips. She wanted to kiss them, to trail her lips down his hand, up his arm, to his chest, slowly making her way to his mouth, to those sensuous, firm...

The air in the room had changed, was charged with something electric. Heath didn't remove his fingers. Instead, he gently ran them along her lips, down her chin. She met his eyes. They'd darkened to rich amber as they gazed down at her, roaming over her face, then locking back onto hers. Her breathing was so uneven, the sound of it had to be audible in the silence. For several seconds they stood looking at one another, so close their bodies nearly touched.

What would he do if she moved a fraction of an inch closer? If she reached a hand behind his neck and pulled his lips to hers? If she pressed her body against his, gave in to the longing that surged through her? The longing she had no right to feel, the longing that had no place between her and Heath.

Sucking in a deep breath, she stepped back. Heath dropped his hand. He looked as shaken as she felt. She began to pace again, speaking rapidly so as not to acknowledge what had passed between them.

"I have your place next door all ready for you. If you want, you can grab your stuff and get settled in before we go over the paperwork."

Heath cleared his throat, but his voice sounded unsteady when he spoke. "I'd rather bring my stuff in later. First, I'd like to go over whatever you've gathered for me. That way, if I need more information from you, or if I feel there's something I should check out today, I'll have time before businesses close for the evening. Will that work?"

"Sure. I'll get the documents. It's nearly lunchtime, are you hungry?"

"Not really. I had breakfast before I came. Maybe we'll grab something in a little while. Unless you want to eat now?"

"No. I'm fine." Nicolette didn't think she could force down a bite of food if someone held a gun to her head. After the detectives' visit and that moment between her and Heath, she was a jumble of conflicting emotions; the anxiety brick in her stomach was double its former size. "Have a seat. I'll be right back."

When she returned, Heath was seated on the couch, one ankle resting on the opposite knee.

"There isn't much." She handed him the thin stack, in addition to the photos he'd asked for, as she lowered next to him. He uncrossed his legs and sat forward, bringing his knee so close to hers they almost touched. Again. She swallowed hard.

She waited in silence while he shuffled through the paperwork, sometimes pausing for a brief moment, other times seeming to read thoroughly.

He took a Tasmanian Devil Pez dispenser out of his pocket and held it out to her. "Want some?"

She raised her eyebrows inquisitively. "Pez candies?"

He gave a boyish grin. "My friend, Burke's son gave this to me when I quit smoking. I haven't had a cigarette in six months, but now I'm hooked on these damn things."

She laughed and shook out a few of the candies before handing the dispenser back to Heath.

"You highlighted anything that seemed unfamiliar to you, right?" he asked.

"Yes."

"I'll want to take some notes later, maybe ask questions about some of the calls that aren't highlighted. As a matter of fact, what I'd like you to do is make notes on all the non-highlighted phone calls, the name of the person the number belongs to, their relationship with you and Rudy, the type of business they're in, anything at all that comes to mind."

"Okay. That will take a while."

"You have a copier here?"

"Yes. You want me to make a copy of the paperwork?"

"Just the phone records. That way, you can be working on those notes while I keep one copy to work from."

"Will do. What else?"

He seemed to be running through a to-do list in his mind. "Where's his cell phone? There may be text messages or voice mail that won't show up in the report from the cell provider."

"I don't know. It was never recovered."

His eyes narrowed. "Did he have it with him the night of the accident?"

"Yes. I called him from home a little while before he—before the accident. He was in the car, and we spoke. The cops were able to verify the call, so they know I was here." She shrugged and brushed back a hank of hair. "I guess they think I had someone kill him. I don't know. It's all so crazy. The police think his missing cell phone is another thing that looks suspicious, but I would think it could have gotten lost in the wreckage, you know? The window was busted. It could have flown out and be lying somewhere in the area, but they just weren't able to find it."

"That's possible," Heath agreed, but he looked troubled. "I need you to write down numbers where I can contact you, or anyone else you think I need to talk to. A list of numbers and addresses for the charity, your cell, whatever you think I might need."

"Okay. I'll get that for you. Anything else?"

"Not at the moment." He frowned as if considering his next words carefully. "Nic, I do need to ask you something."

"Sure."

"I told the police that I knew you didn't have anything to do with Rudy's death, and I firmly believe that."

"Thanks." His confidence in her was heartwarming. It seemed lately she'd been the object of suspicion and rumors. It was nice to have a friend who felt otherwise.

"I also told them there was no way you had been unfaithful to Rudy."

She waited. And noticed he hadn't tagged on the phrase, *and I firmly believe that.*

Pain filled her heart. "Heath? Do you think I

cheated on Rudy?"

He didn't meet her eyes. "I didn't say I think you did cheat. But, as much as I hate to, I'm going to have to ask if you did. Not only could it be a big factor in why the police suspect you, it could also have something to do with your blackmailer."

"What?" Angry and hurt, she pushed to her feet and resumed pacing. Between her and Heath, she might end up having to replace the carpet. "I can't believe you'd ask me that." Shoving a hand through her hair, she shook her head. "I thought you knew me better than that. You're the only man who—"

God. She'd been about to say he was the only man she'd consider cheating with. She'd like to say that she wouldn't even cheat with Heath. After all, when they'd shared that moment during Rudy's coma, nothing actually happened, but as shaming as it was, she couldn't honestly say that under the right circumstances, she would be able to resist. Like, if Heath had pushed the issue back then, if she'd known of Rudy's drug use at the time. If, if, if...

Truth was, she couldn't say positively for sure that she would never have cheated on Rudy with Heath. But she damned sure didn't want him to know that. And she most definitely didn't want him to think she'd cheated with someone else.

"You're the only man I thought would never believe that of me," she amended, although not convincingly.

Heath stood. He walked over and halted her pacing with a hand to her arm. Nothing sexual about his gesture, it was meant as nothing more than friendly, but it still sent waves of warm desire through her body.

"Hey, I'm sorry," he said softly. "I do believe you. I had to ask, though. Do you understand why?"

She moved away from his touch, nodding. "I do. I'm sorry I reacted that way. Things have been so

73

crazy though. I'm afraid I'm a little on edge."

"I can imagine why you would be."

"I want you to know I never cheated on Rudy. Not once. That's why I wanted you to stay in a separate place. I don't want to give the police any reason to suspect I was unfaithful. They might even believe you and I killed him. For the insurance money, or so we could be together."

"Good point. Something I don't understand, though, is why the police haven't uncovered Rudy's drug use in their investigation. They're usually pretty thorough. As far as you know, have they?"

"It seems they haven't. I guess he kept it hidden well. After all, even I didn't know about it."

"If you tell them, it might get the heat off you. His death could have been drug related, and that information might turn the investigation in another direction."

"I thought about that myself, but I'm not sure it would be worth it. His death likely had nothing to do with drugs. I'm not even sure it was murder."

"You still believe it was an accident?"

She shrugged. "I really can't imagine anyone wanting to harm Rudy. If they did, I want them caught and punished, but I just don't think revealing his drug use and smearing his name will make that happen."

Heath nodded. "Okay then, for the time being, we'll play it your way. But, I'm telling you right now, if I uncover anything that points to a drug-related killing, anything that will help get you out from under suspicion, I won't hold it back from the authorities."

She thought about that. A much as she would hate for Rudy's skeletons to see the light of day, if it helped bring his killer to justice—providing there was a killer—or if it kept her from being charged with his murder, she'd have to agree it was necessary.

"Okay," she said. "I can live with that."

"It'll all work out, Nic." Once again, he took her hand, and once again, it had an effect on her. It occurred to her they might have to back off on the touching thing. She wasn't sure how much of this she could withstand without doing something she might regret.

****

Heath pulled onto the shoulder of Highway 152 and North Hampton. It was the first time he'd visited the scene of Rudy's car wreck.

Up until now he had no reason to. He'd thought it was an accident and didn't want to view the scene where his best friend's life ended. Rudy hadn't actually died at the scene. He'd spent two weeks in a coma from which he'd never recovered. But for all intents and purposes, Rudy had died here.

Someone had erected a makeshift memorial, a white cross with a photo of Rudy in the center. An array of flowers lay at the base of the cross. Bright yellow, red, and pink blooms contrasted against the bed of white snow. The other flowers had likely been there a while and were dead, some had been blown and scattered several feet in all directions.

A few cars whizzed by, but very few. It was easy to see how an accident out here in this somewhat remote location would go un-witnessed. Also easy to see why it would be a choice location to commit murder.

The wind picked up, flakes of snow blew into his face. He hunkered down in his jacket, wishing he'd worn his heavier coat since he'd likely be outside for a while.

He'd left Nicolette's without unloading his things. He needed a breather. Seemed he'd spent the past few days fleeing from painful situations. At his mother's, it had been the memory of the father he'd trusted who'd betrayed him. At Nicolette's, the memory of his best friend and the news that he might have been murdered. Mostly, he wanted a respite from the pain of being so close to Nic, yet not able to have her. The pain that came from the guilt of wanting his best friend's widow so badly it was a physical ache.

It was kind of strange that he was too much of a coward to face those things, yet he'd stared down the enemy on a battlefield and hadn't even considered backing down. Not that he'd been thrilled about war, but at least he'd handled it with a modicum of bravery and determination. How pathetic was it that he feared his feelings more than he did the likelihood of dying?

He walked slowly along the highway in the direction Rudy's car traveled. The cops had been right. No skid marks. Any signs of the car, or its deadly trip down the incline, had long since vanished. Weather, new grass growth, and investigators, had changed the landscape immeasurably.

He looked over the steep incline at the area of Rudy's final resting place. Not far away was a baseball field where he and Rudy had played on a ragtag team the neighborhood boys had put together. His brothers had played, too, even Jesse.

Hell, she could hit as well as any boy on the team, and she could throw almost as hard. They'd played touch football in that same field. Heath remembered one game where Rudy and Jesse had ended up in a heap on the ground and Rudy had taken just a little longer than he should have to untangle. Heath was certain Rudy had a crush on Jesse, although he'd never admitted it. No way could he admit something like that. Jesse had always been one of the guys. It would almost have been like admitting to having a crush on a dude.

Heath laughed at the memory. The laughter died as suddenly as it had come and sadness filled his soul.

Never again would he play sports—although at their age, the playing had morphed to watching—with his best friend. Never again would they harass one another in that good-natured bordering on mean-spirited way that was standard in the world of the male species. Heath still couldn't process that Rudy's death, which he'd thought had been a tragic accident, might have been murder.

He made his way cautiously down the steep incline, slipping occasionally on the frozen grass. At the bottom, he surveyed the surrounding area, looked back up toward the highway. Steep, but not deadly steep. A car could go off the incline without necessarily ending its journey in a serious, let alone fatal, crash. From what he understood, Rudy had suffered head trauma in the accident, which put him in the coma that eventually killed him. But how had he suffered head trauma that severe? Heath was certain Rudy wore a seat belt. He always did.

So how had going off this incline caused his death? And why had he gone off the incline in the first place? Was he driving so fast he lost control? Even so, why hadn't he tried to stop? Heath couldn't recall what the road conditions were like at that time. It was January and they'd gotten some bad weather the December before, then again late in January, but Rudy's accident had been around the second week of the new year. Heath couldn't remember icy roads at that time, and unlike Oklahoma City, the Kansas City area was fairly well-equipped for inclement weather, and road conditions were seldom hazardous.

Which would all tie in with the police's theory that Rudy's accident was no accident.

Did the murder have anything to do with the

blackmail? Heath didn't have the same access to information and evidence the police did. He'd feel better if he could share everything he knew with them, but he'd made a promise to Nicolette. And she was right. The blackmailer had threatened her life. The police may or may not believe her and even if they did, there was a good chance they wouldn't be able to find out anything more than Heath could. They might have more means at their disposal, but when it came to protecting Nicolette, they damned sure didn't care as much as Heath.

He spent more than an hour looking for Rudy's lost cell phone, or other clues the police might have missed. As expected, he found nothing. Not only had too much time passed, but the investigators had no doubt been thorough.

What the hell had happened to Rudy's phone? If he found it, would it provide clues to what had happened to Rudy or to the blackmailer? More than likely, the answer was yes, which also probably answered why the phone was nowhere to be found.

Chapter Seven

"The room is beautiful!" Marla exclaimed.

They'd rented a room at a local museum. Each year, they held the event at a different location, and so far, this place was Nicolette's favorite. In addition to the room being perfect, the museum brimmed with Missouri history and displays that both children and adults would enjoy.

"It is gorgeous." Nicolette twirled around, surveying the space from all angles. In her mind's eye, she was already picturing the tree and the Santa with a line of children waiting to climb on his lap. She could also picture the older kids. They would try to play it cool and pretend they thought it was lame, but their eyes would give away their excitement when they opened their gifts.

Her heart swelled with the first real rush of Christmas spirit she'd experienced this year, but quickly turned to pain when she thought of Rudy and how this would be her first charity party without him.

"Hey, you okay?" Marla's ice blue eyes searched Nicolette's face. "You look like a kid in a candy store one minute and a death row inmate in the next."

Nicolette forced a smile. "Just thinking about Rudy. He loved these parties so much. They meant the world to him."

"I know," Marla said softly. She looked away and began rummaging through one of the boxes filled with decorations. Tugging out a string of garland, followed by a plastic grocery bag of candy canes and bows, she said, "Better get started. This room isn't going to decorate itself."

Nicolette dug into another box and found lights and bulbs for the tree. Donovan would be here later to help erect the twelve-foot tree, so for now, she set those aside.

They continued to open box after box, and before long, the room began to look like a winter wonderland.

Marla paused and wiped her brow on her sleeve. She put her hands on her hips and examined their progress. "I think it looks great."

"It does." Nicolette brushed a hand full of hair back from her face with a nod. "We've worked our tushies off but I think it's gonna turn out perfect. The kids will love it."

"Yep. But we deserve a break." Marla pulled a coin purse out of her handbag. "I'll run to the vending machine and get us a Diet Pepsi."

"Sounds good. Thanks."

Nicolette sank into one of the settees arranged near the spot where the tree would stand. Marla returned with their drinks and passed a can to Nicolette as she settled in a chair across from her.

Marla peered at her shrewdly, then smiled with a wicked glint in her eye. "That Heath guy, he's something, isn't he?"

At the unexpected mention of his name, a slow flutter started in the pit of Nicolette's stomach. She forced a nonchalant shrug. "Yeah. He's a good friend."

"Friend? Guy looks like that, he should be much more than a friend. He's hot."

"Oh, well. I never really thought of him that way," Nicolette said, then wondered if her pants would catch on fire.

"How could you not?" Marla asked, her eyes rounded in surprise.

"Because. Rudy and I have known him since college. He's like a brother to me. He was Rudy's best friend."

"Maybe so." Marla's tone turned serious. "But Rudy's gone now. I'm not sure how you feel about him, but the way Heath looked at you, he's not thinking about what good friends you guys are."

Nicolette took a gulp of the soda and shook her head. "You're crazy. Heath never thought of me in any way other than friendship." *Except maybe for that one night just before Rudy died. But then, I was the aggressor, and Heath was the one who had stopped anything from happening. There, Marla, what do you think about that?*

Marla reached out a hand and patted Nicolette's knee. "I doubt that. I'm pretty good at reading people. Maybe Heath's not who you should use to heal your grief, but don't close yourself off to opportunity, okay? Remember, Rudy's the one who died, not you."

Nicolette nodded and stood, signaling an end to the conversation. She finished her Diet Pepsi and tossed the can in the bag of trash they'd accumulated. Going to the one remaining box of decorations, she bent inside and took stock of what was left.

"Hey, didn't we pack a few of those singing, dancing Santas?" She rose and turned to Marla. "I can't find them."

Marla rolled her eyes. "If my Christmas wish came true, someone chopped them into tiny pieces and buried them where they'll never be found."

Nicolette laughed, then triumphantly brought out one of the three Santas from the bottom of the box. "Guess your wish didn't come true, Scrooge." She flipped the switch on the plastic stand and Santa started shaking his hips while the tinny sound of "Santa Claus is Coming to Town" issued from his smiling lips. Marla groaned as Nicolette lifted out his two companions and had the trio happily belting out three different tunes.

****

It was nearly six in the evening by the time Heath returned to Nicolette's. Once more, a strange car sat in the driveway. This time, a Mercedes. Not the cops.

Nic answered his knock. She'd changed from the jeans and sweater into a white, long-sleeved shirt-dress that came to just above her knees. She looked casual and elegant all at once. Heath wanted to pull her against him and run his hands along her backside, feeling her warmth through the soft, cotton material.

Her face still held that pinched look as she stepped back to let him inside.

The couple he'd met the night of the benefit sat on the couch in the living room. They stood when Nicolette and Heath walked in, and Heath shook hands with them.

"Heath, you remember Donovan and Marla Sussman. They're having dinner with us this evening," Nic said, as though she and Heath already had dinner plans together.

"Great." Heath tried to make his voice pleasant, although it wasn't great at all. He wanted to be alone with Nicolette. He told himself it was so they could go over notes she might have made on her copy of the phone records.

"Nice to see you again." Donovan settled back onto the sofa, careful not to spill the drink he held. From the color, it appeared to be whiskey. "Glad to meet a friend of Rudy's. Marla and I thought the world of him. Think the world of our little Nicolette here."

"Yes," Heath said, looking at Nicolette, who stood in the center of the room, hands clasped in front of her. "Who doesn't?"

Nicolette's eyes met his. She smiled, and the haunted look went away for a few seconds. Heath pretended it didn't make his heart skip a beat as he smiled back.

For dinner, Nicolette served a chicken casserole with salad and crusty French bread.

"Sorry, it's not much," she apologized. "I sort of threw it together last minute."

"It's great," Heath assured her, shoveling a forkful of casserole into his mouth.

"Rudy spoke of you often," Donovan said. "It's a shame we never met while he was alive. You golf?"

"Yeah, but not all that well."

"Then I definitely wish we'd have played a round together." Donovan laughed. "I might have finally won a game."

"Donovan's been a life-saver since Rudy passed." Nicolette favored Donovan with one of her dazzling smiles. "I don't know what I would have done without him."

"So, how did you and Rudy meet?" Heath asked.

"We met on the golf course a few years ago. My buddy canceled out on me, and Rudy invited me to join him and a couple of his guys so he'd have a foursome. We hit it off. Not long after, he brought me into the charity."

"Rudy did love to golf."

"I found out we had a great deal in common. Golf, fishing, a desire to help others." He frowned. "We became very close in the two years we'd known one another before Rudy's death. Marla and I both feel the loss deeply."

Heath looked at Marla. Her eyes were moist, her mouth drawn into a sad frown. Donovan cast her an unreadable look, and she seemed to shake off her mood, then swiped at her eyes.

"I'm sorry," she said with a small smile. "His

death was difficult on everyone who knew him."

But a little more difficult on Marla than her husband, it seemed. Interesting.

"Yes, yes it was." Donovan nodded, then in an obvious attempt to lighten the mood, he said, "Rudy and I also shared a love for beautiful women." He winked at Nicolette and squeezed his wife's hand.

Marla flashed a brief smile then turned her attention back to her plate, unobtrusively slipping her hand out from under Donovan's.

Heath wondered if the subtle rejection was indicative of trouble in the marriage or if he was reading too much into it. It was his nature to be investigative, and with everything that had gone on lately, he was becoming suspicious of everyone.

Finally, after dessert and coffee, Donovan stood and announced it was time to leave. Heath thought it was way past time, but he didn't voice his opinion as Nicolette saw the couple to the door.

"I'm sorry I sprang them on you," Nicolette said when she returned. "They stopped by, and I thought it would be rude not to ask them to stay for dinner."

"No problem. They seem nice."

"They are. I've gotten very close to them. I suppose Marla's my best friend now. I've lost touch with a lot of the friends I had in the early years of my marriage. And I've lost touch with the few people I knew in Green Bay. It's difficult to maintain a friendship over so many miles."

"I know. Had it not been for my family being here and all the trips, Rudy and I might have drifted apart."

Nicolette smiled. "No. That would never have happened. As close as you two were, you could have maintained a friendship from separate continents."

Heath grinned at that. She was probably right.

"Marla seemed quiet all evening," Heath said. "Is that her normal demeanor, or was she upset about something?"

Nicolette shrugged. "She seemed more reserved tonight than usual. Actually, she's been that way for the past few months. She hasn't confided in me. I don't know if it's marital difficulties, or what. She's had a hard time with Rudy's death. The four of us were really close."

"Rudy was a good guy. Everyone he met cared about him."

Nicolette's face drew into the pained look again. "If the police's theory is correct, not everyone."

A pall hung over the room as he considered the enormity of someone wanting Rudy dead. Unthinkable.

In the silence, Heath wandered over to a cocktail table that held a Santa's workshop crystal figurine he'd bought for Nicolette one Christmas before she and Rudy married.

He picked it up, hefting the ridiculously heavy knick-knack in his hand. "Wow, can't believe you still have this."

She smiled. "I put it out every year. It's my favorite gift I've ever gotten."

He turned to her and lifted his brows. "You're kidding!"

"No. I love it. Makes me think of the old days." Her gaze turned pensive, and she gave him a small, sad smile.

Heath replaced the figurine, then moved to a shelf that held a group of photos. There were pictures of Rudy and Louisa, some with Nicolette and some without. There were others of people Heath didn't recognize. He picked up a photo of the wedding party. Rudy looked like the happiest man on earth, as well he should. Nicolette was smiling and beautiful. Standing next to Heath was the maid of honor, a girl whose name he couldn't recall in spite of the flirting they'd engaged in. That, he recalled vividly. He'd drank too much and tried too hard to pretend he didn't care that the woman he loved had just pledged her undying devotion to his best friend.

"That's a great picture." Nicolette walked over and stood beside him. "The reception after was lots of fun. Remember when Rudy did the Macarena?"

Heath laughed. "I think the alcohol had something to do with that."

"Maybe, but he was a goof ball even when he was sober."

"True. We had a lot of good times in college."

Nicolette nodded. "Funny how well we all hit it off right away. In the beginning, I never dreamed I'd end up dating, let alone marrying one of you."

"Yeah. You guys had a great marriage. I guess you picked the right one."

Her eyes latched on to his, and she said softly, "I never knew I had a choice."

Heath held her gaze, suddenly finding it difficult to breathe. His eyes drifted to her lips, and he wondered what she'd do if he kissed her.

****

Nicolette's face heated. She couldn't believe she'd said those words. Heath stared at her, his expression unreadable.

She swallowed nervously, trying to think of a way to fill the silence. Heath broke the spell himself by moving away and replacing the photo on the table. When he was a safe distance away, he asked, "Did you get a chance to make those notes on the phone records?"

So, he was back to business. Cool. That's the way it should be. "Yeah. Let me go get them."

When she returned, Heath lounged in the easy chair, one jean-clad leg crossed over the other. His shirt was open at the neck and a few dark chest hairs peeked out.

Sexy. God. He's still so sexy.

Nicolette handed him her copy of the phone records with the familiar numbers highlighted. He studied it, along with the paperwork she'd already given him, then thumbed through the pages, seemingly unaware of the effect his nearness was having on her.

He withdrew one of the blackmailer's notes. She remembered that one. It was the first. She'd found it on top of her desk at the office. At first, she thought it was a joke. The follow-up phone call made her realize it wasn't. She couldn't mistake the threat in the caller's voice.

Heath's jaw clenched as he read the note. "Bastard."

"Yeah. Tell me about it." She pointed to the other papers. "Like I said, not much there. The other notes. Bank statements. Rudy's calendar for the few months before his death. Not sure it will be any help."

"It's a start. I wish you hadn't handled the notes. Did anyone else besides you touch them?"

"No. No one else knows about this. They came in envelopes."

"You have those? We can check for DNA, although only if it ends up going to trial. I have no way to compare, nothing to compare it to. Not to mention, DNA tests take a long while to get back."

"I didn't keep the envelopes."

He sighed heavily, and she knew he was irritated with her. It was stupid, even she'd admit that, but she hadn't planned on it going to trial. Still didn't. She didn't intend to tell the authorities. Or anyone other than Heath, for that matter.

"Do you recall any strange, new people Rudy began associating with, maybe right before his death?"

"No. Not that I know of."

"Did you notice a change in his behavior? Sums of money vanishing that he couldn't explain?"

"No. Not really. I mean, now that I know what he was doing, I think back on times that I wondered if he was hiding something from me. Nothing specific pointed to drug use, especially not heavy drug use. The thought that he was having an affair crossed my mind, but I never had any proof, any real reason to suspect. Then, after the blackmailer called, it all started to make sense. I even realized Rudy's mood had been a little, I don't know...off from time to time."

Heath stood and went over to his duffle bag. Opening it, he pulled out a notepad and pen. He returned, this time settling on the couch next to Nicolette. He scooted forward and laid the paperwork on the coffee table, then made notes on the pad as he sifted through the stack.

"Do you have a way of checking fingerprints?" Nicolette asked.

"I do. I can eliminate yours and mine, see if there are any unknown, but any blackmailer that's worth a damn wouldn't leave fingerprints."

As he continued making notes, she fell silent, watching as he bent his dark head over the table, watching the muscles in his forearm jump as he wrote. After several minutes, he dropped the pen and leaned back into the couch, kneading his neck with his fingers.

"Here," she said, taking his shoulders and turning him around where she had access to his neck. He was compliant as she massaged him. She tried to ignore how warm his skin felt, how touching him sent tingles through her body.

"That feels good," he murmured.

"Thanks," she said breathlessly.

"No. Thank *you*." He groaned, and her fingers stilled. She sucked in a breath and closed her eyes as a warm, yearning languor spread through her body.

He shifted to face her, and she dropped her hands. His eyes roamed over her face and settled on her lips, then rose once more to hers. His were an intense golden hue and sparked with an inner flame.

"Want me to do you?" he asked.

Her eyes rounded, and she caught her breath. "What?"

His lips spread into a slow grin. "Give you a neck rub."

"Oh." She laughed shakily and ran a hand through her hair. "No. That's okay. My neck's fine." She couldn't imagine how she'd handle having his warm strong hands roaming over her skin.

"Okay then." His voice was brusque as he stood. "I guess you can show me where I'll be staying."

She nodded and stood also. Her legs weren't quite steady as she led him toward the door connecting their units.

****

The door Nicolette opened led directly into a bedroom. Heath dropped his duffel on the bed and followed Nic while she showed him the other rooms.

This side of the duplex looked exactly like Nic's, other than the décor. There were minimal furnishings, a couple of paintings on the walls, and a bouquet of fake flowers on a side table.

"Here." Nic handed him a key. Their fingers briefly touched before she pulled back. Just like she hadn't wanted him to rub her neck. She wanted to avoid touching. Was it because she'd felt the same thing he had while she was massaging him? And when he'd almost kissed her?

Not likely. After all, women didn't get boners, did they? Geez, he was pathetic. A friend offered an innocent neck rub and he acted like she'd given him a hand job. He shook his head to clear his thoughts.

"There's another bedroom upstairs," Nic was

saying. "There are clean sheets on both beds and blankets. Clean towels are in the bathroom cabinet." She moved to the kitchen, and he followed. "I wasn't expecting guests, so there's not much to eat here. There should be some beverages in the fridge." She opened the door to inspect and nodded. "Beer, bottled water, sodas. A few condiments." She opened one of the cabinets. "Some canned goods, but not a lot to choose from. I can shop for you tomorrow, if you'll give me a list. I know there's coffee here for in the morning, but if you want breakfast, you'll have to come next door or grab something out."

"I'll take care of that. Mom wants me to come out to the house for breakfast. I won't bother you in the morning, unless I have more questions. I made a few notes, some things to follow up on so I'll be gone a good part of the day."

"Okay then. I guess you're set."

"I guess I am." On impulse, he said, "Would you want to go with me in the morning?"

"To investigate?"

"No. For breakfast. Mom said I should invite you over."

She smiled. "That was sweet of her. Tell her thank you, but I have to go into work early tomorrow. Maybe some other time."

"Right. I'll tell her." He almost invited her to Christmas then, but he didn't. He didn't want to seem needy or insinuate that he thought there was something more going on between them than a friend doing a favor for another friend.

"Well, goodnight then," she said. "Call me if you need anything. Or just knock on the door we came through. Otherwise, I guess I'll see you tomorrow evening."

"Sounds good. If I have any questions throughout the day about the investigation, can I call you at work?"

"Yeah. Sure. Just call my cell phone."

He watched her walk away and disappear through the door. His body tingled as if her soft fingers still touched his skin.

Chapter Eight

Nicolette wandered through the house. Silence closed in around her. The emptiness seemed more pronounced now that Heath was gone. She went to the wedding photo he'd been looking at. It was her favorite. Heath looked devastatingly handsome in a white tux and black silk shirt with a black tie. She remembered, even on the day of her wedding, feeling a twinge of jealousy that Juliette was the one who got to walk with Heath down the aisle, was his companion for the evening. Juliette and Heath had flirted like crazy. Nicolette always wondered if they'd slept together, but never asked either of them. She didn't want to learn that they had.

In the bathroom, she brushed her teeth and slipped into her pajamas, then went to bed. Once there, she tossed restlessly for what felt like hours. She looked at the clock. A little after eleven. She hadn't been in bed all that long, but she didn't feel like she'd ever fall asleep.

Throwing back the covers, she climbed out of bed. Maybe warm milk would help. Something had to. She couldn't stop thinking about the blackmailer, wondering if it was a mistake to bring Heath in on this. What if he ended up getting hurt? Or, what if he told someone, and the details of Rudy's past leaked out?

No. She didn't have to worry about that. She could trust Heath. And he wouldn't get hurt. He knew what he was doing. He was in the military and had been a cop for several years. Now he had his started here and went up own security firm.

Yes, Heath could take care of himself. He was smart and would probably figure out who was behind this, but then what? They still couldn't go to the police. How would they stop the guy, short of killing him, even if Heath uncovered his identity? Maybe if Heath gave him a good scare, let him know they were onto him, he'd just go away. Especially since he'd made quite a profit in the past few months.

She moved through the dark house. In the kitchen, she made do with the night light plugged into the outlet. The house was chilly. Nicolette shivered, wishing she'd put on her robe.

She put a cup of milk in the microwave. As she waited for it to heat, she glanced out the window that looked out over the backyard. Although it was well after dark, the bright snow lit up the night. A figure moved across her yard, and her heart started beating so fast and hard it was almost painful.

Dear God. Someone was out there. Should she get Heath? The ding of the microwave made her jump. Taking the mug from the microwave, she peered out the window once more. The intruder moved close enough that she recognized him. Heath! Her relief was so strong she nearly wept.

She watched him move around the semi-dark yard in confident strides. He was checking things out. Making sure she was safe. Protecting her.

She gripped the warm mug between her hands and sipped cautiously. In addition to her fears and uncertainties about the blackmail and Rudy's murder, she had to be honest and acknowledge the biggest concern of all. How could she keep herself from falling in love with Heath all over again?

****

Heath, his brothers, and his future sister-in-law gathered in the kitchen for breakfast, his mother busy at the stove. Her efforts sent the tantalizing aroma of sausage in the air. Heath sniffed appreciatively.

The waffle iron dinged, signaling one of her mouth-watering waffles was up for grabs. As Clint went for it, Heath tried to cut him off by shoving his empty plate in Clint's path.

"Mine. Back off." Clint lightly hit Heath on the arm to deflect his aim.

Heath grinned and tried to shoulder his older brother away. "Gotta move faster, Clinty."

Clint gave a mock scowl. "Don't touch that waffle, Candy."

Heath rolled his eyes at the childhood nickname, and didn't bother to remind Clint he'd gotten his name from Lee Major's character on the Big Valley series, not the candy bar. Heath had spent most of his life pointing out that fact, but his brothers insisted on calling him Candy because they liked to torment him. Although Heath always despised the nickname, his spirits lifted with the good-natured banter. He growled at Clint, but moved aside and let him have the waffle.

When his turn finally came, he helped himself and held his plate out for his mom to add a few sausage patties, then joined the others at the table.

He eyed his younger brother and his fiancée, noting the almost tangible tension between them. Not exactly the affinity he'd expect from a couple pledging to spend the rest of their lives together, but then, in the short time he'd known Sydney, he'd discovered that she managed to inspire tension in everyone around her.

Thoughts of Nicolette surfaced, and he wondered how she'd fit into the King family picture. Pretty damned well, he concluded. His family already liked her. Once they got to know her better, they'd love her. Too bad Heath wasn't allowed to, or

94

at least not in the way he wanted.

He shoveled food down faster, suddenly anxious to launch his investigation. Someone was threatening Nic. If he couldn't make her his, the least he could do was protect her.

As any friend would.

He looked at his mother, still working at the stove. Between bites, he said, "So, Mom. Why the insistence we come for breakfast?"

She placed a skillet of eggs on the table. The three brothers took turns heaping their plates. Sydney nibbled on dry toast, ignoring the sumptuous feast.

"Well, boys, it seems to be the only time I can get my family in one place at one time." Amelia settled into a chair at the head of the table and, one by one, favored her sons with a look that meant she'd not be challenged. "Keeley's coming by today. She called late yesterday afternoon. Asked if I minded. I've invited her over, and I want to tell you all, at the same time, I won't tolerate any shenanigans. You'll behave. Treat her like family."

The food in Heath's mouth seemed to congeal in mid-chew. He managed to swallow but pushed his plate away. That was the last thing he'd expected, or wanted, his mother to say. He'd known of the likelihood that the interloper would be forced on him at some point, but he certainly wasn't ready for it to happen yet.

"I'll have to reserve the pleasure for another time," he finally said. "I wasn't planning to come back today."

His mother cast a searching look his way, as if trying to detect whether he was being a smartass. She didn't comment, and he didn't elaborate further, didn't add that, if it were up to him, he'd *never* meet Keeley Jacobs.

Sydney snarled, "Isn't that just peachy." She

stood abruptly, ran her hands down her skirt, then turned a venomous gaze to Alex. "I'm going into the city for a while. Remember what I told you."

What had she told him? That, in actuality, she was a demon and the ceremony would have to be held beneath a full moon, while her minions sacrificed a virgin? At least that would make the wedding interesting enough to give Heath a reason to be there.

Alex watched his fiancée storm from the room and shook his head. "She's just stressed about the wedding."

"You're the one who should be stressed," Heath said before he could stop himself. "You've got to wake up to *that* every morning for the rest of your life."

At Alex's stricken look, Heath wished he could take it back. His mother scowled at him, but didn't comment. He was certainly scoring a lot of points with her today. At this rate, she'd be glad he wasn't staying here this week.

Before either of his brothers could weigh in, Amelia turned to Alex. "Now, Alex, I need you to run me over to Margery Thomas's house before Keeley arrives. I'm on the Kappa's Annual Association Meeting committee, and I need to go over venue details with her." With that, she stood and limped toward the door.

When only he and Clint were left, Clint said, "What's going on with you?"

Clint's question brought him out of his reverie, and he looked up with a frown. "What do you mean?"

"I mean you haven't been yourself. What's bugging you?"

Heath stared out the window at the festive holiday display in the front yard. He tapped his fork on the plate and muttered, "Friend of mine's in trouble."

"Is she pretty?" Clint said with a grin.

Wondering how much he should reveal, Heath decided to give his brother something. Heaving a sigh, he leaned back in his chair. "It's Nicolette."

Clint remained silent as he processed the information. His brother knew Heath had a thing for Nicolette in college. What he may not know is that the 'thing' hadn't ended when Rudy won the girl. After a few moments, Clint gazed steadily at Heath. "So not just any woman."

Heath didn't respond, but the expression on his face must have portrayed his consternation.

"Careful there, little brother," Clint said, "that 'friends' thing can get a little tricky."

No shit. Like they all hadn't noticed the new way Clint looked at their surrogate sister, Jesse. "I suppose you'd know." Heath experienced a modicum of perverse satisfaction when Clint's amused look became a scowl. Going in for the kill, he said, "You've been spending a lot of time with Jesse."

Clint gave a reluctant nod. "Yeah."

Heath smiled at Clint's discomfort and offered a bit of wisdom he'd gleaned from his own disconcerting mess. Plus, he felt it was only fair that he issue a warning. After all, he'd have to whip his older brother's ass if Clint toyed with Jesse and ended up hurting her. "Be careful there, big brother."

Clint seemed to be digesting the advice, but before he could reply, Heath stood. Time to head out. He had a woman of his own to protect.

His own. Right. She wasn't his own in the sense he wanted her to be, so he'd have to make do with what he had. Which, right now, was the opportunity to be near her. As he carried his plate to the sink, he threw over his shoulder, "Well, I've got some things to do. I'll talk to you later."

Clint nodded, and Heath left him deep in

thought. The house was empty. Good. That meant he wouldn't have to suffer through any more probing questions as he made his way out the door and into the cold December morning.

****

Heath drove a few miles down his mother's road to an abandoned farmhouse. The small farmhouse was gray now but Heath remembered it being bright yellow. He couldn't recall who had lived there, but knew no one had in years. The grass was dead now, but in the spring it would grow to nearly chest high before someone—either the unfortunate owners or the city—would cut it down.

The driveway almost wasn't there, but two barely discernible trails were left. Heath pulled onto them, then parked behind a row of bare trees. As he'd done with almost every ancient structure he'd seen since he was a small boy, Heath wondered if the James Gang had ever hidden here. All his life, he'd been fascinated by their story and had convinced his parents to take him out to see the James farm twenty miles away in Kearney as often as he could. They'd seemed somewhat amused and a tad concerned that their middle son was so enthralled with a notorious outlaw like Jesse James.

Leaving the Tahoe running, Heath slid the seat back to give him more working room and picked Nic's folder of paperwork off the front seat. He would have to investigate without letting anyone know he was investigating. Pretty tricky when he had to ask questions.

A number Nicolette marked as unfamiliar popped up frequently in the months preceding Rudy's death. Heath dialed the number.

A male voice answered, "Salarber's Cut and Style, Ted speaking."

A barbershop? Heath didn't know what else to do other than make an appointment. Damned sure could use a cut anyway. "Yeah. Can I get an appointment? Today if possible."

"Let me see. Hmmm. Yeah. We have some openings today, it being Wednesday and all we're not that busy. Haircut only?"

"Yeah."

"Anyone specific you want to see?"

Preferably the person who is blackmailing Nicolette, or the one who did drugs with my best friend. Definitely the one who made twenty-seven phone calls in two weeks to a guy who is now mysteriously dead.

"No. Not really. I've never been there. How many barbers do you have?"

"Barbers. I like that. Don't hear it much anymore. Now we're *stylists.*" He infused the word with disdain. "We have seven stylists. If you don't have a preference, I'll just put down your time and whoever is free can get you. When you wanna come in?"

Heath looked at his watch. It was just now after ten. "Around eleven too soon?"

A pause. "Will eleven-thirty work?"

"Sure." Heath gave his name and took down the address, then called Nicolette at Renewed Hope.

After going through an automated maze, which eventually allowed him to punch in the first three letters of her last name, Nic's voice came on the line. "Nicolette Morgan. May I help you?"

"Hey, Nic. It's me."

"Heath—what's up?"

She sounded happy to hear from him, and for a moment, he let the pleasure of that thought wash over him. Then he took a reality check and reminded himself she was anxious to find out who was wrecking her life, not just pleased that he called.

"Listen, did Rudy get his hair cut at Salarber's Cut and Style?"

"Yes. Why?"

"There were a lot of calls from the shop on Rudy's cell phone records. I can't imagine he'd need that many consults on a haircut. Do you know which of the barbers he used?"

"No, I don't recall him ever mentioning a name. Before he started going there, he'd had the same barber for years, Don Valeska."

"Yeah. I used to go to him, too. He retired."

"Right. After that, about a year and a half ago, Rudy ended up going to Salarber's. He never mentioned who cut his hair. Do you think the blackmailer works there?"

"Even if those calls are from the blackmailer, he could be anyone in the shop. Hell, even a customer who used the shop's phone."

"You wouldn't think the blackmailer would take a chance on being overheard in a public place like that."

"True. But you never know how these people think. Of course, it could have nothing to do with that. Maybe whoever called him from the shop had to do with the drugs and not the blackmail."

"You mean like his dealer?"

"Maybe. Either way, I'm going to check it out. I'll stop by and see you at work when I'm done. I should have some kind of update for you then."

"Great. I'll see you a bit later, then."

Was there a note of more-than-businesslike anticipation in her voice? Then again, given the jumble of his thoughts, it could just be a projection of his own desires.

****

Salarber's Cut & Style was located in North Kansas City, just a few miles from Nicolette's house. Before going in, Heath studied the cars in the parking lot. Most likely the ones in back were employees, and the ones near the front door were customers. He jotted down the make, model and license plates of all of them, just in case. The person he was looking for could be a customer or an employee. Or no one to do with Salarber's at all.

The place was larger than Heath expected, especially when he went inside and saw the rows of chairs at either end of the long room beyond the lobby. The distasteful smell of perm solution hung in the air. Don would have been horrified at the thought of giving perms in his shop. His had been a two-seater that only catered to men and still had a barber pole outside.

Heath remembered the first time his father had taken him there when he was eight. Heath had been thrilled when the men included him in their conversation, and his dad showed off Heath's knowledge of major league baseball by quizzing him endlessly for the audience; the other barber, and two customers, one getting a shave, the other waiting for a cut. After that, Heath and his dad and his brothers made regular visits, every four weeks to Don's shop. The guy talk and cigar smoking made the King boys feel grown up, and it was a highlight of Heath's childhood. Some of the men swore like there weren't even kids in the room, although once in a while they would mutter, "'Scuse my language." When he and Rudy were twelve, Rudy started coming along too.

Heath cleared his throat and looked around for someone to help him, before he got all misty about memories that were as false as the breasts on the girl who approached, a friendly smile on her too-pink lips. Her hair was multi-colored, pinks and purples, and her shirt rose up, showing a belly button ring. "Can I help you?"

"I have an appointment at eleven-thirty."

"With?"

Heath shrugged. "No one in particular."

"First time, huh?" She smiled and touched her

bottom lip with her tongue, exposing a piercing. Heath cringed. Tongue piercings always looked more painful than sexy to him, although he'd heard how much better oral sex was when—

For God's sake. He reigned in his thoughts. Too long without sex. Too much time around Nicolette. Bad combination.

"First time here, yeah."

She frowned as she ran her long pink fingernail down a sheet. While she was trying to perform a task that appeared as difficult as unraveling the mysteries of life, a largely built man with a protruding gut and frizzy, receding hair entered the lobby area. "You the fella who said *barber* on the phone?"

Heath grinned. "Yes. That would be me."

"I'm Ted Welling, the owner." He looked at the girl. "I'll take him, Gertrude."

Gertrude. Heath would not have guessed that.

Heath followed Ted past rows of chairs, half of them filled, and a few empty, with bored-looking stylists, some men, some women, standing near them. One fussed with the items that lay on a shelf beneath the mirror. *Fussing* wasn't a word that usually came to Heath's mind, but with this particular guy, that was the only word that fit. He was slender and dressed all in bright blue shiny stuff with heavy Adam Lambert makeup. His white-blonde hair lay to one side and hung over his ear, while the other ear—one with a dangling silver earring—was left exposed.

Ted led Heath to a chair toward the back, and when he was seated, Ted shook out a cape and secured it around Heath's shoulders.

"How much you want off?" He grinned. "Or you just want me to style it nice and purty?"

Heath grinned back. "I want it fairly short, but not shaved."

"Got ya."

Ted picked up a pair of shears and got to work at the back of Heath's head. As he did, he kept a running conversation about everything from the shitty weather, to politics, to the Chief's lousy franchise, to how bad it sucked to have to run a business this way to make a living. "You know, it's all that metro-sexual stuff. Guys these days want to look feminine. Crazy thing. Young women seem to like it, though."

"Yeah. Guy who cut my hair most of my life ran a man's man shop." Did that sound sexist? Maybe, but he needed to segue into asking about Rudy, and no one who would care was within hearing distance. No harm. No foul. "You know it? Don's Barber Shop over on Barry Road?"

"Yeah. He retired, right?"

Heath nodded. "About a year and a half ago. I'd moved out of state, but my buddy was still going to him. You might know my friend. He started getting his hair cut here after Don closed his shop. But he passed away back in January. His wife recommended you."

"What's his name?"

"Rudy Morgan. You know him?"

In the mirror, Heath saw Ted squint at the side of Heath's head as he moved around to start on the hair there. "Everyone around here knew him. In the news a lot. Big philanthropist. I knew him because he sent a few people my way. Mostly clients, but I hired a couple of his guys."

"Recovered drug addicts?"

"Yep. I figured if a guy like Rudy believed in them, who was I not to give 'em a chance, you know?"

"How'd they work out? Any of them still with you?"

"Yeah. One was a gal. She's a real sweet thing.

Does a great job, too."

"So, are they here now? Which ones are they?"

Ted's hands stilled and he scowled. "Don't think I should tell you that. Why you asking so many questions, anyway, pal?"

Heath considered deceiving him but didn't see the point of withholding the truth, at least not all of it. "I guess you heard that Rudy's death is being investigated as a homicide?"

"Yeah. Cops have been in here a few times."

They would have gone over the phone records, too. Not likely they'd come in to interrogate a victim's barber without good reason. He wondered if they'd learned anything. Whether they had or hadn't, it didn't mean Heath would. Worth a shot, though.

"I was his best friend," Heath said. "I'm not a cop, but I run a security firm in Oklahoma City. I'm here visiting family for the holidays, and when I heard Rudy's death was suspicious I thought I'd do a little digging myself. I'd like to find out what happened to my friend."

Ted continued to scowl but had paused in the process of cutting Heath's hair. Heath could picture being thrown out and having to hunt a place to finish the job, looking like a freak with his half-cut hair. Finally, the shears started again, and so did Ted's mouth.

"I don't know anything about how he was killed, and I'd swear on a stack of Bibles no one here had anything to do with it. I've got some oddballs around here but no killers."

Heath held his response when a young guy, wearing a smock and listening to an iPod, came into earshot. At the places where Heath usually got his hair cut, the barbers always swept up their own hair. Business must be pretty good if Ted was able to keep someone on just to clean up after the stylists.

Heath waited until the man and his broom moved away.

"Not saying anyone here killed him. Just trying to learn as much about him as I can. Hoping it leads me to some facts I can share with the police that might solve his murder."

Ted nodded and the scowl disappeared. "My cousin was killed when I was a kid. They never found her killer. She was only sixteen. Hard thing to live with." He moved to the other side of Heath's head, efficiently snipping as he spoke. "Don't think you're going to find anything here, but I'll do whatever I can to help."

"Even give me the names of the people you hired from Renewed Hope?" As soon as he asked, he realized he could get that info from Nic. Better to make a friend of Ted and not ask for more than he was willing to give. "Never mind. Tell you what, how about you just tell me who Rudy's barber was. If he had a regular."

Ted smiled. "There's that word again. Barber. Did you figure out what the deal was with the shop's name?"

"The shop's name?"

"Yeah," Ted said. "Salarber's. Think about it."

Heath thought about it for a few seconds, then grinned. "It's a combination of salon and barber?"

"That's right." Ted laughed. "Sort of my little inside joke. You're pretty sharp to figure it out that quick. I think you'll figure out what happened to your friend, too." He straightened and pointed over Heath's shoulder. Heath twisted and found Ted was indicating the shiny blue guy. "Noah cut Rudy's hair."

"The guy with the white hair and blue clothes?"

Noah twisted a lock of hair in his fingers and stared at himself coquettishly in the mirror.

"Yeah." Ted shook his head and sighed. "Doesn't

look like he's too busy. Soon as I'm done with your hair, you can talk to him."

After Ted took Heath back up front so he could pay for his haircut, Ted motioned for Noah, and the guy sauntered to the lobby.

"This here's Heath King," Ted said. "He wants to talk to you about Rudy Morgan."

Something fearful flashed in Noah's silver-blue eyes before they grew wet with tears. "You're a friend of Rudy's?" Noah asked as he shook hands with Heath.

The guy's palm was damp. Nervous? What reason did he have to be nervous? Unless he had something to do with blackmail, or maybe murder?

Chapter Nine

Noah and Heath sat in the cushioned chairs of the lobby. Heath studied the guy, who crossed and uncrossed his legs repeatedly, then fiddled nervously with his hair.

Could he be a murderer? The guy just didn't seem the type. But then, if there was a definite 'type' for all criminals, solving crimes would be easy.

"I have a few questions, if you don't mind," Heath said.

"No. I don't mind." Noah's gaze darted nervously around the lobby, and he checked his watch. "I hope this won't take long. It's almost my lunch, and I'm meeting my girlfriend at Cracker Barrel."

"Girlfriend?" Maybe he meant 'girlfriend' the same way a girl meant girlfriend. Because if this guy wasn't gay, neither was Elton John.

"Yes." He sat up straighter, seeming offended. "My girlfriend. Ugh." He rolled his long-lashed eyes. "You thought I was gay, didn't you?"

"I'm sorry. It's just that..." Heath held out a hand then let it drop in his lap, at a loss for words.

Noah shrugged. "I get that all the time. I just like to express my moods with my ensemble. Tomorrow, you might come in and find me dressed like a construction worker."

Or *under* a construction worker. Heath cringed at his stereotyping and lack of political correctness. He didn't give a damn about this guy's sexual orientation or his wardrobe. Time to get back on track.

"How well did you know Rudy Morgan?"

Again, the eye-dart thing. A dubious suspicion came over Heath. If this guy were bisexual—and Heath had a hard time believing he was totally straight—did that mean that he and Rudy...

Nah. No way. Heath was beginning to learn that his lifelong friend had some secrets, but sex with men was definitely not one of them. Heath needed to look at this in a totally unbiased manner and not get tripped up in appearances. Deal with the facts, only the facts.

"I've done his hair for, oh, I don't know..." Noah crossed his legs and clamped his hands around his knees, then studied the ceiling for a while before saying, "I think since about six months before he died."

"Was that the extent of your relationship? A client and a stylist?"

"It was."

"You two didn't socialize at all?" *Didn't do drugs together, perhaps?*

He'd have to find out if Noah was one of the employees who came from Renewed Hope. If so, it was a pretty good indicator he might still be on drugs, and his nervousness could be due to the drug use he and Rudy shared.

"No. No socializing. I'm straight. Rudy was straight." Again, that offended tone.

"I didn't insinuate you had an intimate relationship with him. Just wondered if the two of you ever went out. You know, double dates or something?" Heath let his face show innocence.

"Oh. No. Nothing like that." The nervous eye dart started again. "No socializing." Which meant there was some kind of socializing. And if he was trying to hide the socializing, it obviously wasn't the kind he could talk freely about, the kind he wanted known. Had to be the drugs.

"Thanks, then." Heath stood, and Noah leapt gracefully to his feet, seemingly relieved. He seemed so relieved, Heath wouldn't have been surprised to see him do one of those toe-spin things ballerina's did. What was it called—pirouette or something?

Noah scurried away, out the door to meet his lady love. Ted wasn't around when Heath left, so he said goodbye to Gertrude and headed to his Tahoe, rubbing a hand at the irritation on his neck. The cape was never enough protection, and as was the norm, tiny hairs poked into his skin, driving him nuts. He needed to shower them off, but he'd go see Nicolette at work first. He had to find out what, if anything, she knew about his new pal, Noah.

****

Nicolette fiddled with the football-shaped Packers paperweight on her desk as she waited for the Willow Bend apartment manager to come on the line.

"This is Benita Rogers," a raspy, barely recognizable as female voice said.

Nicolette released the paperweight and picked up Toddrick West's file. "Hi. I'm Nicolette Morgan with Renewed Hope Charity. I'd like to come and look at one of your units as soon as you're available."

"You want it for one of them drug heads?"

Nicolette took a deep breath. "One of our recovering clients is ready to be placed, yes."

"He—or is it a she?—gonna shoot up in the place? Have a bunch of drug deals going on?"

Nicolette once more gripped the paperweight, trying to be patient. She could actually understand the woman's hesitation, but it still irked her to know the sort of resistance people who left Renewed Hope faced.

"He's been clean for ninety days. We require employment and weekly drug testing. He has been working at the same job, at a factory, for two months now. If he loses his job or fails a test, then we no longer help him, although we will see that he moves out of your apartment without trashing the place."

"Then I got a empty unit on my hands again."

"How many empty units do you currently have?" Nicolette was taking a gamble, but she'd bet potential residents weren't lining the streets or rushing in to place their name on a two-year waiting list.

After a long silence, the woman said, "You can come by any time, but if it's between seven and nine don't bother me. Just go on up and look at number 3A. It's the one that's closest to being ready to rent. Key's under the mat."

"You keep keys under the mats of all your empty apartments?"

She chuckled, and the sound turned into a fit of raspy coughing. "Key word, *empty*, princess. What the fuck they gonna steal?"

Nicolette's face heated in anger and she opened her mouth to respond, but Benita had already hung up. "Damn her," she muttered as she slammed the phone back in its cradle.

"Temper, temper."

Nicolette looked up to find Donovan standing in her doorway.

"Oh, sorry." Her face heated even more, this time from embarrassment.

"Problem?"

"No." Nicolette shook her head, feeling foolish. "Just a crabby landlady. Normally, it wouldn't faze me, but I've been a little on edge lately."

Donovan moved further into the room. He wore a navy suit with a light blue shirt and a pencil thin navy blue tie. His sandy blond hair was slicked down, its usual disarray tamed.

"Wow," she said as he took a chair across from her desk. "If I knew how to whistle I'd be doing it now. Why so spiffy? Hot date with Marla?"

"Noooo," he said. "Don't you remember? Hot date with the CEO of Tighe Industries."

Nicolette slapped a hand to her forehead. "That's today?" Tighe Industries was a manufacturer of electronics equipment and a highly successful corporation. The owner's son died of a drug overdose a few months ago and after pulling himself out of his grief, the father had contacted Renewed Hope, wanting to discuss a sizable donation. Donovan handled the financial matters for the charity and had set up a lunch with the CEO.

"Yeah, it's today. You forgot?"

"I did." Nicolette sighed and stood. "I'm sorry. I guess I haven't been on my game lately."

Donovan came around to stand next to her and took her hands in his. "That's no surprise, sweetheart. Don't beat yourself up. You lost the love of your life in a horrible accident." He paused, shook his head. "Or maybe not an accident. You're taking care of your disabled mother-in-law, trying to run the duplexes and the charity, now the holidays are approaching." He peered down at her. "And an old friend's back in your life. Someone who no doubt makes you think of Rudy every time you look at him."

Something about his tone said there was more to his statement than his words revealed. "I think about Rudy all the time anyway."

She pulled away and paced over to look out the window. Outside, holiday shoppers hurried along the sidewalk, and bumper-to-bumper traffic signaled another hectic day in downtown Kansas City.

"Yeah, but there's something about this Heath guy," Donovan said. "I mean, don't get me wrong. I like him. But I can't help but wonder..."

Nicolette's shoulders tensed but she didn't turn to look at him. "Wonder what?"

"If maybe there's more to this than just an old friendship. You two seem awful close."

Nicolette answered carefully, wanting to make sure her voice didn't betray her emotions. "He was Rudy's best friend. I've known him for fifteen years. Of course we're close."

"Can I ask you something?"

Nicolette gave a humorless grin. "Can I stop you?"

"Is there something more than friendship between you and Heath?"

Although it was none of his business, Nicolette felt like she owed Donovan an explanation. She wasn't sure why, unless it was because he was also Rudy's friend and had been instrumental in the success of the charity. "No. Nothing at all. We're just friends." *Unless you count the almost kiss we shared, the burning desire I feel each time I'm within ten feet of him.* "Why do you ask?"

She turned when he didn't answer right away. He was staring down at the floor, hands in his pockets. His posture told her he was troubled about something.

"What is it, Donovan?"

He raised his head. "I just want to make sure you don't do anything foolish. Anything to jeopardize the charity and all Rudy worked for."

"What are you saying?"

"There seems to be something between you two. I can't put my finger on what it is exactly, but I sense a deeper relationship than just friends. I'm going to be blunt. Have you been to bed with Heath King?"

"No! I have not. It's really none of your business if I have."

"I'm sorry, but I have to think about how it would affect the charity. I can't stop you of course, but I feel it's my duty to warn you of the ramifications of a relationship."

"It's been almost a year since Rudy died. I'm thirty-two years old. Am I supposed to live the life of a lonely widow, grow old and die alone?"

As soon as she said the words, she realized that, in some ways, the answer was yes, even in her mind. She didn't think she would, or should, ever get involved romantically with another man. Most definitely not Heath.

"Of course not, Nicolette. I want you to be happy. I want you to find someone. I really do. But come on, do you really think it should be your dead husband's best friend? What do you think people would say if that happened?" Without giving her time to answer, he continued, "They'd say you two had been carrying on the entire time, behind Rudy's back. Wasn't Heath here when Rudy was in a coma?"

She nodded miserably.

"Didn't he stay in the house with you?"

Another nod.

"There you go. People will say you were doing him while your husband lay dying. And by people, I'm including the police. Do you really want them assuming you wanted to be rid of Rudy so you could be with another man?"

Nicolette's impulse was to childishly cover her ears with her hands and block out his words. She didn't want to hear Donovan say the exact same thing she'd been thinking since Heath walked back into her life. Even if it was true.

"Stop it, okay? I get it. You're right. It's not necessary to warn me. There's nothing between me and Heath and never will be. He's like a brother."

The word *brother* nearly stuck in her throat. She'd never had a brother, but she was certain she wouldn't want to do the things with him that she wanted to do with Heath. Warmth spread through her body at the thought.

"You sure?" Donovan asked.

"I'm sure. For God's sake, even if it weren't for what the people involved with the charity would think, not to mention Louisa, all of Rudy's friends, my family, like you said, I have the cops breathing down my neck. Screwing around with Heath King would definitely add fuel to their fire, and that's the last thing I want."

"Good." Once more Donovan took her hands in his. "I love you, Nicolette; I want you to be happy. I just hope you can find happiness with someone other than Rudy's best friend."

"I know, you're right. But, you have to understand that ultimately it's my life, my decision. I don't like being told what to do. So, while I appreciate the advice, I'd like you to let me run my life as I see fit."

"Sure. Sorry if I overstepped my bounds. I'm just concerned." He put his arms around her and hugged her. She let him, relaxing and returning the hug.

A throat clearing at the door made them both turn. Her 'brother' stood in the doorway, looking sexy even though he had that fresh haircut thing that always took a few days to look right. But in his faded jeans and putty-colored Henley beneath the brown suede jacket, he looked ten times more handsome than Donovan in his finest suit. Her heart sped up as she disentangled herself from Donovan's arms.

"Heath. Hello."

His eyes went from her to Donovan, where they stayed for a few seconds before returning to her. "Is this a bad time?"

"No," Donovan answered for her. "I was just leaving for a lunch appointment."

He went to the door and stuck out his hand. Heath took it and they shook.

"Nice to see you again," Heath said.

"Same here." Donovan nodded and clapped Heath on the shoulder. "Gotta run. You take care of our Nicolette, here."

****

Heath watched Donovan Sussman walk down the hall, not liking the heavy feeling he had in his chest when he thought about seeing Nicolette in the man's arms. He recognized the feeling as jealousy and it sucked. It was ridiculous and petty. Not only did he believe Nic and Donovan were just friends, he had no right to be jealous of any man who touched her, even if it was in more than just a friendly way. So why the hell did the thought tear his soul apart?

"So, did you learn anything useful?" Nic asked. She wore a bronze-colored blouse and black slacks. Her hair was pulled back, accentuating the thinness in her face, making her cheekbones even more pronounced. She'd lost too much weight, but she was still beautiful.

"Not a lot, but I do have a few questions for you."

"Okay." She offered him a tentative smile. "I see you got your hair cut. At Salarber's?"

"Yeah. I figured it was a good cover. I could sniff around and get a much-needed haircut. "Once more, his hand went to the back of his neck where the hairs were starting to feel like a colony of ants had invaded his skin.

Nicolette walked close to him and lifted her hand, running her fingers lightly along the sides of his hair, then around to the back. "I like it, but I kind of miss the long-haired, bad boy, hippie look."

He grinned, although it was difficult to draw a full breath with her touching him. "I didn't know that was what I had going on."

"You did." She dropped her hand and moved away. "Did your undercover op into the salon accomplish anything?"

115

"I'm not sure yet. Do you know anything about a guy named Noah?"

She frowned, then shook her head. "Who is he?"

"He's the guy who cut Rudy's hair. Rudy never mentioned him?"

Pacing back to the desk, she thought for a moment before speaking. "No. I don't think so. Is there something suspicious about him?"

"He seemed nervous, like he was hiding something."

"You think he's the blackmailer?"

Heath recalled Noah's thin, fearful face, his bony body and non-intimidating demeanor. Although anything was possible, he said, "No. I don't think so. Maybe he was someone Rudy did drugs with."

"I hate knowing Rudy was on drugs. No telling what kind of seedy places he went to and seedy people he hung out with just to satisfy his craving."

"Drug users can be anyone from street thugs to scientists to millionaires," Heath reminded her, which always amazed him. It would seem someone with intelligence would know to stay away from the stuff.

"I know. So, what next?"

"Ted, the owner, said you'd sent a few of your people to get jobs at his shop, but he wouldn't give me their names."

"I'm glad. Part of what we do is protect their anonymity."

"I understand that, but I'm trying to protect *you*. The only reason I didn't press him for the information is because I figured you'd give it to me willingly."

She hesitated. "Their anonymity is critical to the program. If they thought I'd betrayed them..."

"Nicolette, for God's sake, I'm trying to save your life here. You think I'm going to run to the nearest newspaper and ask them to print an article listing the names?"

She sighed. "Of course not. I'm sorry." She went to a filing cabinet and came out with a folder. Taking it to her desk, she flipped through it. "Noah wasn't one of them. But here." She grabbed a neon pink sticky note and jotted on it, then passed it to Heath. "There were two men, one woman. Recognize any of the names?"

"No. No one I spoke with while I was there, but this gives me a starting point. Thanks." He folded the note and stuck it in his jeans pocket. "Listen, I have to run to the FedEx office and pick up a package, but before I go, can I use your computer real quick?"

"Sure. I have some things to take care of. Help yourself to my office, and I'll be back in a few minutes."

"Great. Thanks."

Heath sat in her chair and watched the gentle sway of Nicolette's hips as she left the room. Those same hips had rested where his were resting now. A slight movement in his groin had him shaking his head and admonishing himself to get back on task. He went to the DOC web site and typed in Noah Forsythe. Bingo. Convicted of minor drug possession in '04. Out on parole since. Ted Wellington had to know that. Apparently, he was a sucker for a hard luck story.

Heath tapped a pen on the desk as he stared at the screen. So, Noah had a history of drug use. He wasn't in the Renewed Hope program, so he may or may not have to submit to regular drug screens. If he was on parole, he most likely did, but a lot of times those things fell by the wayside, especially when the convict had been out of prison for a while. Based on his actions when Heath questioned him Noah was keeping some kind of secret to do with Rudy. If not the blackmailer, then he was almost certainly a drug buddy. It would pay to keep an eye on Mr. Forsythe.

Nicolette came back in just as he was finishing. "Any luck?" she asked.

"Yeah. Got what I needed. I'm going to head out and take care of a few more things."

She nodded. "I'll see you back at the house?"

He did his best to ignore the warm feeling those words evoked. "Sure thing."

"Great. I'll be there in a few hours, but then I've got something to do later this evening."

"Anything you need help with?"

"No. But you're welcome to come along. I just have an apartment to look at."

Heath lifted his brows. "You moving?"

"No. Looking at it for a client."

"I may tag along, if you're sure you don't mind."

"I'd like the company."

"Okay then, it's a date." Heath felt a silly smile trying to break through. He did his best to fight it off, but wasn't sure he succeeded.

Heath picked the package up from the FedEx office and waited until he was back in the Tahoe to rip it open. Burke had sent everything he'd asked for.

Good. He could install the devices right away.

Then it occurred to him he hadn't even told Nic about the surveillance equipment, or that he was tapping her phones. How would she take the news? Would she be pissed, or would she understand it was a necessary step to find out who was making her life a living hell?

Judging from her reaction when he'd asked for the names of the people she'd sent to the barbershop, she wasn't crazy about invasion of privacy. He was pretty sure she was less crazy about blackmail and murder, so she'd better just go along with it.

He called Nicolette's cell. When she answered,

he said, "I'm heading back up there. I have something I need to do at the charity."

"I've already left. What is it you need to do? I'm not sure if anyone's still there, but I'll turn around and go back if you need me to."

"If you've already left, it can wait till tomorrow. I also need to do it to your cell and home phone."

"Do what to them?"

"I'm going to tap your phones."

"Heath, I don't think—"

"Nicolette, please don't fight me on this. You asked for my help, and I want to be able to catch the call the next time the blackmailer phones. I have to tap your phones."

"I'm fine with my cell and home, but the charity just seems wrong."

"Has he ever called you there?" Heath waited for an answer and heard nothing but silence. "Nic? He has, hasn't he?"

She sighed. "Yes. Yes, he has."

"Then I'm going to tap your phone there, too. Look, I'm only going to listen to your calls, not the other employees, and I would never do anything that would hurt you. You know you can trust me on that, right?"

"Of course, I do. I'm sorry. I shouldn't be questioning you. You're doing me a huge favor."

"You know I'd do anything for you."

Silence again, then her voice thickened with emotion. "Thanks, Heath. See you at home."

Chapter Ten

While Heath waited in the driveway for Nic, he booted up his laptop and entered Noah Forsythe's name in the search engine, along with *Kansas City*. Nothing came up. He tried *Ted Wellington*.

An article from the Brady County Gazette appeared on the screen. It was about Ted opening the shop, and it went into detail about his past. He had received a purple heart in the Gulf War. Heath sat back and stared at the screen. A guy like that most likely wasn't involved in the blackmail or Rudy's death.

He plugged in the other names on the sticky note, but didn't learn anything about the people listed. Shutting down the computer, he drummed his fingers on the steering wheel while he waited for Nicolette to arrive. He could go on in to his side. He had a key, but he wanted to know the second she arrived so he could get those taps on her phones.

The neighborhood was nearly deserted. It was early afternoon and adults were likely still at work, and kids were likely reluctant to play out in the frigid temperatures.

Back in his day, this kind of weather wouldn't have stopped him and his buddies, but kids had gotten a little soft it seemed. They'd rather be parked in front of a video game than explore the dangers of sledding down a snow-covered hill on a thin piece of cardboard.

At the end of the block, a couple of kids were outside. They were trying to build a snowman, but the snow wasn't sticking for them. After a few minutes, they gave up and began lobbing snowballs at one another. Snow was falling more heavily; the blizzard conditions reported by the local meteorologists seemed likely.

That was another reason he should accompany Nicolette when she went to check out the apartments. He didn't want her out in a snowstorm alone.

Movement on the side of Nicolette's duplex caught his attention. He leaned toward the windshield for a better look and saw a man climbing a ladder that leaned against the building. Heath wiped frost off the window with the sleeve of his jacket and took a closer look.

The man slid open a window. Nicolette's bedroom?

Son of a bitch.

He vaulted from the truck and rushed to the ladder. Grabbing it by the rungs, he shook violently. The surprised occupant shouted, "Hey, what the..."

Mutual recognition dawned.

"Heath?" Jerome Badgett asked in bewilderment.

"Jerome! What the fuck do you think you're doing? Get down from there. Now!" Heath shook the ladder again.

"Hey, man. Take it the hell easy. Chill."

"Get your ass down here now. You can either come down the easy way or the hard way, but you have two seconds to decide."

Heath gave the ladder another forceful shake.

Jerome scrambled down. When he reached the bottom, Heath grabbed him by the collar and slammed him to the ground, landing on top of Jerome as he rolled to his back.

"Shit! That hurt." Jerome blinked up at him. "What the hell you doing? Are you crazy?"

Heath gripped Jerome's collar, still straddling him. "What the hell were you doing up there? Was that Nicolette's bedroom?"

"Yeah," he gasped.

Heath lifted him slightly, then shoved downward. Jerome's head knocked against the ground, not hard enough to render him unconscious but hard enough to get his attention. "What were you doing looking in Nicolette's bedroom?"

"Hey, dude, I work here, remember?"

Actually, Heath had forgotten. Jerome had mentioned he was Nicolette's maintenance man when Heath bumped into him at Juniper's Café. But that didn't make a hell of a lot of difference. Jerome also said, in so many words, he wanted in Nic's pants.

"So that gives you a right to be crawling into Nicolette's bedroom?"

"I wasn't, man. I was fixing her window."

"Fixing her window?"

"Yeah, man. She called and said cold air was pouring in around it. I was just checking to see if I could caulk it or if it needed replacing."

Shit. Heath was starting to realize he'd made an ass of himself. Good thing Nic wasn't here to see it.

"Heath? What do you think you're doing?"

Double shit. He looked up into Nicolette's furious face.

He climbed off Jerome and helped him to his feet. Jerome grabbed his back and groaned in exaggeration.

Oh, *please.*

"He just attacked me," Jerome said, his voice quivering. "I don't know what the hell his problem is."

Nic's brows rose questioningly. She crossed her arms and tapped her foot on the ground. Waiting.

Heath shrugged, feeling more foolish by the

second. "I saw him at your window. I thought he was...up to something."

"Ah," she said. "You saw my maintenance man with a ladder and a tool belt working on my window, and you automatically suspect he's up to no good. I get it." She rolled her eyes and stalked over to Jerome, taking his arm in her hand. "Are you okay?"

He sniffed and shot a triumphant look at Heath. "My back hurts. My head, too. And I'm freezing. Would you happen to have some coffee or tea or something? I need to warm up before I head back home."

"Of course."

Nicolette led Jerome around the house and up her steps, totally ignoring Heath. He gritted his teeth and stalked over to the SUV. Reaching inside, he snatched up the FedEx box he'd left on the seat.

Here he had been freezing his ass waiting for Nicolette so he could tap her phone and *protect* her as soon as possible, yet she'd chosen to fall for Jerome's bullshit act and delay Heath from doing his job. Swear to God, that woman was starting to try his patience. As soon as she finished her Florence Nightingale bullshit, he would have a serious talk with her. One more time she opposed his methods or got in the way of him doing his job, she was on her own. To hell with her. He was helping her for *free*, and she bucked him at every turn.

Of course you're helping her for free, you ass. She's your friend. And you love her. You're not exactly a pro bono knight in shining armor. You want in her pants. Plain and simple.

"Fuck," he muttered as he turned the key to the duplex and slapped the door open. Once inside, he punched Nicolette's number into his phone.

"Yes?" she answered, her tone cold.

"I need to take care of some things if you're finished kissing little Jerome's boo-boos."

"Booboos *you* gave him. I'm glad you think it's so funny to rough up an innocent man."

He sighed. "Look. I'm sorry about Jerome, but you have to understand I'm trying to do my job. We need to talk and take care of some things. I'm heading over there, so you need to send your patient on his way, providing of course, he can still walk."

Her frustrated growl came over the line, but Heath disconnected the call before she could say more. He took the contents of the FedEx box and marched next door.

When Nic opened the door, Heath could tell by the set of her jaw that she was still angry with him. She stepped aside to let him enter. The loud bang as she closed the door would have tipped him off to her mood, even if her expression hadn't.

Jerome was nowhere in sight. "Jerome leave?"

"Yes," she said, her lips set in a grim line.

Apparently Jerome hadn't been too incapacitated to walk, but Heath figured that thought was best left unexpressed. Since the best defense was a good offense, he said, "Look, I'm sorry, but you have to understand I'm trying to help you. I'll do whatever it takes to get the job done. You can't question every little thing I do."

"Every little thing? You mean like invading my clients' privacy and punching out my employees?"

"I didn't punch him."

"Ah. My mistake. By manhandling him like some out of control UFC fighter and slamming his head on the ground?"

"But I didn't hit him."

"You hadn't hit him *yet.*"

He gave her the grin that more than one woman had told him was irresistible. "Right. *Yet.*"

The grin must have lost its power. She stalked across the room and threw her hands in the air. He followed her and set his equipment on the coffee table.

"I don't get it," she said. "What were you thinking? You could have hurt him badly."

"I need your phone."

"What?"

"I need your cell and your home phone." He held up one of the transmitters. "I'm going to bug them. Tomorrow, I'll install one in your work phone."

"Are you not even listening to me?"

"I am. But you don't seem to be listening to *me*." He tossed the transmitter back into the box and stared at her, arms crossed over his chest. "You don't seem to understand how serious this could be. We're dealing with a blackmailer at the very least. Possibly a killer. I told you. I'm going to do what it takes to protect you."

"I don't know how you could think it was Jerome. You've known him forever. He's been great to me since Rudy died."

Heath shook his head. "He's been great because he has a thing for you. Not much of a leap from stalker to blackmailer."

"You don't know what you're talking about. He doesn't have a *thing* for me, and he's not a freaking stalker. He's my maintenance man."

"Look. We have no idea who's doing this. Until this guy's caught, we have to suspect everyone. Why can't you realize I'm trying to help you?"

Sighing, she brushed her hands through her hair. "I'm sorry. You're right. I know you're only doing what you think is best. I'm sorry. Forgive me?"

He reached down and picked up the transmitter again. "If you let me put this in your phone."

"Okay, fine." She walked over to her purse. Digging inside, she pulled out her cell and handed it to him. "Go for it, Inspector Gadget."

He laughed and took the phone from her. When he'd installed the transmitter in her cell and her home phone, he explained, "Your conversations will be recorded. If he calls, tell me right away, and I'll listen to the recording. I promise I'll only listen to *his* calls."

"Okay. Do what you have to do."

"I'll do whatever it takes to protect you, Nicolette." He moved closer and looked down into hazel eyes that had flashed green fire only seconds ago. Now they looked sort of…soft. "You understand that's my number one priority, right? That's what I'm here for."

She nodded. "I know. And I appreciate that."

Tingles moved along his spine, a condition he seemed to experience every time Nicolette was near. Another inch or two closer and they'd be touching…

He moved back a step so he could breathe. "No problem. I really need you to let me do it my way." He made his voice hard. "If you're not going to do that, I'm out of here."

She didn't have to know it was an idle threat. No way could he leave her, not until he had to. Until he knew she was safe.

"You're right. I overreacted. I promise, from now on I'll stay out of your way and let you do your job." She smiled. "Unless, that is, I catch you roughing up old ladies and infants. That's where I'll have to draw the line."

He gave her the grin again. "Hey, at least I know my boundaries."

She laughed. "Want something to drink?"

"Maybe some water."

She went into the kitchen and returned with a bottled water for each of them.

Heath gulped down a few swallows, then said, "Seriously, though. You do realize, just because Jerome is your maintenance man, and just because his reason for climbing to your window was legit, we can't rule him out as your blackmailer, right?"

She shrugged. "Yeah. But then we can't really rule anyone out, can we?

He nodded approvingly. "Now you're starting to think like a cop."

"Yeah? Then maybe I don't need you after all."

Heath stopped in the act of bringing the bottle back to his lips. "I certainly hope you do."

He'd meant to sound flip, but even to him, it sounded like a declaration.

She held his gaze for a brief moment, then said, "Did you eat?"

"I grabbed some lunch earlier."

"Before I go to the apartment, I have to go by Louisa's and make dinner for her. Want to come? We can eat with her."

"Sure."

"I'll drive. We'll take my Jeep. It gets around a lot better than the Buick in this kind of weather."

They walked outside and from down the street came the sounds of "Silent Night." When Heath glanced toward the source, he found a group of carolers standing on the sidewalk in front of a house three doors down.

"I didn't know people still did that," Heath said.

Nicolette unlocked her Jeep, and they climbed in. "Around here they do. Beautiful isn't it? I love Christmas." She pursed her lips, and an expression of longing came over her face. "I haven't been able to enjoy it this year like I normally do."

"It's no wonder. With Rudy gone, and then the crap with the blackmailer. Kind of casts a pall over the holidays."

She nodded, then reached out and squeezed his hand. "You being here makes it better."

The warmth of her hand in his made everything better. He squeezed back. "I'm glad."

She looked at him, her expression chagrined. "I just realized how selfish I've been. I'm sorry. This is your first Christmas without Rudy and your father. How's your mother doing?"

"She's doing pretty well. You know Mom."

"Yes. Tough lady. Wish I could be more like her."

"Hey. You're pretty damned tough yourself. You lost your husband. You're being harassed by a blackmailer, suspected of a murder, and you're running the duplexes and the charity. Doing everything you can to protect Rudy's memory, to keep his dream alive. I'd say that's pretty tough."

She smiled. "Not bad, I guess."

"Not bad at all," he agreed.

After she'd backed the Jeep out of the driveway and they were on their way, Heath said, "How about your father? Have you ever heard from him?"

In the dim lights shining in from outside, he saw sadness cross her face, and he wanted to kick himself in the ass for putting it there. He knew she'd gone years without talking to her father, but he hoped by now, they were back in touch.

"No. I haven't spoken to him since college."

"You haven't tried to get in touch with him?"

She shrugged. "I wanted to a few times. I mentioned it to Rudy, but he said it would be best to leave things as they were. He reminded me that if my father wanted to hear from me, he could get in touch with me. He pointed out that I was a reminder of a past he most likely wanted to forget."

Heath thought that was a little harsh. Even if it were true, it's not something Nicolette should hear. He knew a little about Nic's past. Her father had been accused of killing a neighborhood girl. Although no charges were ever filed, and the killer was caught and convicted, the suspicion that followed him ruined her family's life.

Her mother killed herself a few years later. Nic had gone off to college and she and her father drifted apart. Did her dad want it that way, or was he just respecting his daughter's wishes? Heath remembered while they were at MU, her dad tried to contact her. Maybe after years of being rebuffed, he'd given up. Rudy certainly hadn't helped matters by discouraging Nicolette from finding her father. Perfect or not, he was her father. And, perfect or not, Heath would give anything to see his own father one more time. He didn't want Nicolette to regret something once it was too late.

"I doubt that he wants to forget you. You know, he tried to reach you several times while we were in college."

"Yeah, but that was years ago. He hasn't found me since."

"Maybe he finally took the hint that you didn't want anything to do with him."

She glanced at him, then turned her attention back to the road. "So, you don't agree with Rudy that it was best to leave it in the past? To never see my father again?"

"No. No, I don't."

She seemed to consider his words for a moment, then she shrugged. "I think Rudy was right. If my father wanted to find me, he'd find me. He probably didn't want any part of his past. Doesn't matter anyway. We can't undo what's been done. It's better to leave things as they are. We're strangers now, after all."

Her words rang hollow to Heath. Underneath the bravado, he was sure he detected the pain of a lonely little girl.

Chapter Eleven

Louisa lived in an older section of Kansas City where neighbors still looked out for one another and kept their lawns in pristinely landscaped condition. Her house was a two-story that was too large now that her family was gone. Its coating of bright white paint gleamed in the winter sun.

Nicolette watched Heath as they pulled into Louisa's driveway. A multitude of emotions passed over his face. The corners of his mouth tilted upward in a melancholy smile, and a hint of pain touched his eyes.

"It looks the same," he said. "Except it's white now. Used to be yellow." A hint of moisture showed in his eyes, and he wiped it away with his thumb and forefinger. "Rudy's bike was always in the yard. His dad stayed pissed at him."

Nic offered a small smile, and they climbed out of the car.

As she unlocked the front door and pushed it open, Louisa's voice called, "Nicolette, dear. Hope that's you."

The sound of her wheels came, then she was in the hallway. Her face lit with joy when she saw Heath. "Oh my word, it can't be! Heath King, come here and give me a hug."

Heath laughed and bent down to obey her command. Nicolette could tell he purposely held her loosely, as if afraid he'd crush her brittle bones.

"Louisa," he said as he straightened. "As pretty as ever."

"Oh, Heath. You're such a charmer. Come in, please."

They followed her chair into the living room. Her house smelled of pine from the cleaning her provider must have given it that morning.

Louisa motioned Nicolette and Heath to sit on the sofa. As they eased into the cushions, she asked, "Are you in town for the holidays, Heath? I'm sorry about your father. He was a good man."

"Yes. Thank you. We all miss him terribly." Heath's face became inscrutable and he seemed in deep thought for a moment before his expression cleared. "I'm sorry I haven't been over to see you during my last few visits."

"Oh, don't worry about that." Louisa waved away his apology. "I know you're busy. I also know how difficult it must be for you. Being here. With Rudy gone. You two were like Mike and Ike growing up."

Heath laughed. "I'm sure you went a little nuts with us underfoot all the time."

Louisa's smile was wistful. "I did. And it was wonderful."

Nicolette cleared her throat, pushing back the poignancy that rose. "How are you feeling today?" She peered closely at Louisa's face, looking for signs of pain. Her eyes were clear, her smile relaxed. She must have had a good day.

"I feel fine, dear. Don't worry about me." She turned to Heath. "Nicolette is an angel, I swear. My Rudy was blessed to have her, as am I. Did you know she takes time out of her busy schedule to come and see me almost every day? Cooks for me, visits, runs errands. I don't know what I would do without this girl, I tell you. Nancy, my provider, comes in seven days a week to clean and do things for me I can no longer do, but still, my Nicolette here pitches in."

"That's very nice of her." Heath flashed Nicolette

a smile, and her heart sped up. "You don't have to tell me how terrific she is."

"I'm sure I don't. Everyone who knows her loves her."

Right. Other than the blackmailer, my husband's killer...and Heath.

"You don't need to make dinner for me, if that's why you're here," Louisa said. "Nancy left chicken salad in the fridge. I'll just have that, and the two of you can go have a nice evening, relax."

Nicolette shook her head. "No way. I made a meatloaf and left it in your freezer. Thought I'd heat that up and throw together a few side dishes for our dinner. Does that sound okay?"

"You two are staying to eat with me?"

"Absolutely." Nicolette stood and smiled down at her. "I'll get started."

Louisa clapped her hands together. "How lovely!" The TV was playing a game show and Louisa picked up the remote and shut it off. "Heath, let's catch up while we're waiting for dinner." She looked up at Nicolette. "Unless you need help?"

"I have it under control. You two chat. Dinner will be ready in half an hour."

In the kitchen, Nicolette took the meatloaf from the freezer, then slid it into the oven. While it heated, she opened canned green beans and wrapped baked potatoes in wet paper towels and plastic wrap to cook them in the microwave.

Louisa and Heath's conversation filtered to her ears. At first, they reminisced about the boys' childhood, then Heath asked, "Did you see much of Rudy in the days leading up to his accident?"

"Yes. Sure. I saw him every few days. He was just like Nicolette. Very attentive to me."

"Did he seem...different in any way those last few times? Like anything was troubling him?"

Great. Heath was interrogating Rudy's mother.

Nicolette took a deep breath and let it out slowly. She knew Heath would never hurt Louisa. He'd be gentle and was only trying to gather information to stop a blackmailer. She had to let him do his job.

"No. He seemed normal." There was a pause, then, "Are you trying to find out who killed him? Do you really believe it wasn't an accident?"

Heath also paused before saying, "I don't know, Louisa. That's what I'm trying to figure out."

Of course he wouldn't say he was also trying to stop a blackmailer. One very small plus to the suspicions surrounding Rudy's death was that it made a good cover for asking questions, without revealing the information about the blackmailer.

Heath and Louisa spoke for a little while longer. Heath didn't probe much, and Louisa seemed to be enjoying their conversation.

During dinner, they kept the conversation light. Louisa and Heath complimented Nicolette's cooking, but joked about the hours she must have toiled microwaving 'baked' potatoes.

"How would you two like to look at some old pictures?" Louisa asked while Heath helped her back into the wheelchair.

"Sure," Nicolette said. "I'll get them down from the closet."

"I'll help you," Heath offered.

Louisa pushed into the living room while Heath followed Nicolette to the back of the house.

"They're in here." She led him to the guestroom, glad they weren't kept in Rudy's old room. She still hadn't been able to go in there.

Heath cut his eyes toward Rudy's closed door as they passed and once again, that drawn look of pain appeared briefly on his face.

In the guestroom, Nicolette stood on her tiptoes in the closet, reaching for the albums on the top shelf. She managed to touch one with the tip of her fingers, but couldn't pull it all the way down.

"Here, let me."

Heath didn't give her a chance to move out of the way; he stretched up and over her from behind. His clothing brushed against hers. She felt the heat from his body along her backside. She held her breath, waiting for him to move as he fished the album down.

He held it out to her, and she took it, meeting his eyes over her shoulder. "Thanks." Tremors ran through her, along her skin and into her voice.

His eyes dropped to her mouth. He gave a short nod. "If you'll move, I can get the rest of them."

No. I want to stay right here, near you.

"Right." She stepped around him, and he snatched the remaining photo albums from the shelf.

They returned to the living room in silence. Louisa had maneuvered onto the couch, and they sat on either side of her as she thumbed through the albums.

Many of the photos included Heath, and Nicolette once more became aware of how close he and Rudy were, of how wrong it seemed to want Heath now.

Louisa pointed at a photo of the two boys in swimming trunks, holding Popsicles that melted and dripped over their thin chests. Nicolette laughed, but it died in her throat as she caught Heath's gaze over Louisa's head. His smile was maybe an eight on the Richter scale, but his laugh...the flash of white teeth, crinkles at the corners of those spectacular eyes...the rich sound that rumbled from his chest. *That* was totally off the scale and it made her job of resisting Heath King even tougher.

She forced her gaze away from him and back to the albums. After several more minutes and several more photos, they'd finally reached the end.

Louisa closed the last album and looked at

Heath, then sighed. "I miss my son, but somehow knowing you're around, Heath, taking care of my Nicolette, makes me miss him not quite as much."

****

They said goodbye to Louisa, after she extracted a promise from them to visit again soon.

In addition to his disturbing attraction to Nicolette, a sense of sadness and nostalgia stayed with Heath as they drove away. He and Rudy had shared a lot of good times at that house, in this neighborhood, and down at the corner lot where they'd endlessly played baseball or football, depending on the weather. Sometimes they gathered neighborhood kids and made a game out of it. Other times, it was just the two of them, passing a football back and forth, or Heath pitching a baseball while Rudy squatted in a catcher's pose. Heath would burn it in as hard as he could, and Rudy never complained, but he exacted revenge when it was time to toss the pigskin. Back then, to a younger and much smaller Heath, it seemed Rudy had an arm like Joe Montana.

The times weren't all good ones. He and Rudy had their share of fights. Sometimes over whether one or the other had cheated at whatever sport they were involved in at the time. As they got older, the arguments often centered around girls.

Heath snuck a glance at Nicolette. What if he'd put up a fight for her in college? He chuckled inwardly. That's a fight he'd surely have lost. The prize had wanted Rudy to be the victor, so it wouldn't have done any good for Heath to throw his hat into the ring.

"I'm sorry," Nicolette said, jerking him back from the past. "I have to go look at those apartments now. I'll drop you off at home. It wouldn't be fair for me to drag you all over town."

"No. I'll go with you. The only thing I have to do

is take care of you, so why not?"

And visit family, he amended silently, which he hadn't done enough of since he'd been here. He'd called his mom a few times to check in, and in one of those calls, his mom had insisted he come to the house and meet his sister. He hated thinking of that stranger as his sister. For God's sake, he'd never even laid eyes on her, and he didn't particularly want to.

That was a major reason he'd avoided going to his mother's house these past few days. He felt like a piece of shit because of it, but really, it was his mother's fault. She was the one who had welcomed Keeley Jacobs into her home, knowing how Heath felt. If she wanted him around, she should consider his feelings.

Of course, if he looked at it from the perspective of a loving son, he'd acquiesce to his mother's wishes. She'd been a terrific mom and deserved his respect, deserved to make demands, even if they were against everything Heath wanted. But for now, he couldn't bring himself to give in. If that made him a rotten son, so be it. He shifted in his seat, ignoring the voice that told him he was wrong.

Heath peered through the windshield at the rapidly deteriorating weather. Nicolette's knuckles were white on the steering wheel.

"You want me to drive?" he offered.

Her head made a quick, nervous shake. "No, thanks. I'm fine. It's not much further."

Heath didn't want to distract Nicolette with conversation, and the remainder of the ride was quiet.

Nic pulled into the parking lot of a haggard-looking apartment complex. Although darkness had fallen, Heath could make out peeling paint and cracked siding. The entire place seemed to droop as if giving in to the ravages of time.

He followed Nic through a dirty glass door and into a grimy hallway. The paint inside didn't look any better. Carpeting with red and black swirly designs showed multiple stains. Several long strands poked out where the fibers had started to unravel.

They took an elevator up to the third floor and stepped out into a similar hallway.

Loud music filtered through the closed door of one of the apartments. They made their way down the corridor. Nicolette jumped when a door opened and a large, tattooed man staggered out. He stopped and gave Nic a squinty-eyed appraisal, then looked back at Heath and turned away, heading past them down the hallway. Heath was glad he hadn't let her come alone.

"Here it is." Nic stopped in front of a door with 3A stenciled in faded lettering. She felt under the doormat and came out with a key. Heath followed her inside, nearly bumping into her when she halted abruptly.

"Jesus," she whispered in disgust.

The apartment was filthy. A rank odor hung in the air, like the combination of rotting garbage and body odor. Trash was scattered on the floor. A dilapidated brown couch missing its cushions sat beneath a grimy window.

Nic stalked through the apartment, swearing as she entered each room. From the kitchen where dishes still sat in the sink and garbage spilled out of an unlined trashcan, to a bathroom that looked like it hadn't been cleaned since before the millennium, everything spoke of neglect.

"She's out of her freakin' mind if she thinks Toddrick is going to live here. She thinks she can take advantage of him because he's got a drug problem. The hell she can." Nicolette kept up the litany of muttered complaints, sprinkled with cuss words as she headed out the door, slammin behind her and not bothering to lock it.

He followed her back to the elevator where she punched the button, then waited with her arms crossed, her foot tapping angrily on the nasty carpet. She punched the button a few more times before the elevator got the message and opened.

They stepped inside, and Nic did some more of the muttering and foot tapping while they slowly descended.

She marched off the elevator and down the hall, stopping to hammer her fist against the door that read Office. A thin woman with mean-looking eyes and long, stringy hair that could use a shampooing opened the door. Behind her, Heath saw a television playing some reality show. The sound blasted out at them as the woman scowled and demanded, "Can I help you?" not sounding like she really wanted to.

"I'm Nicolette Morgan from Renewed Hope, are you Benita Rogers?"

"Yep." The scowl deepened, making her even less friendly. "Didn't I say you could look at it, but if it's between seven and nine, not to bother me?"

"You did. And I used that key and I went into that hell-hole you call an apartment. I can't believe you'd expect a human to stay in there."

"Don't get your panties in a wad, girlie. Just needs a little spit shine." She peered back over her shoulder at the television screen as she spoke. "I'll knock a few bucks off the deposit."

"It needs more than a little cleaning, and you'll ᵈo more than knock a few bucks off the deposit. ʳe are all kinds of repairs that need to be done. ᵘilet doesn't flush, the kitchen tile is coming ᵉ back door doesn't lock. If you don't have it ᵃnd repaired, up to code, I'll have the city ᶜrawling up your ass. Got it?"

Rogers pulled her gaze away from the ᵈd stared at Nicolette as if she now had her full attention. "Okay, okay. You got it. I'll take care of all that before he moves in. I promise."

"I'll be back in a week to make sure."

"Look, it might take me more than a week to—"

"He needs a place to live. The apartment was advertised as ready to move in."

"Hey, I tell you what. It's gonna take me a while to get the apartment fixed up, but I have another one that's empty. It's nicer than that one anyway. Bigger, and it has a bath and a half. How about I take you up and we have a look at it? If you like it, Mr. West can move in right away."

"Is the key under the mat?"

"Yeah. I can take you up if you want." She cast another longing glance over her shoulder.

"I'll look at it on my own, thank you."

Benita seemed relieved that she wouldn't miss any more of her program. "It's apartment 4C. You'll like it. I promise. You call me or stop by, tell me what you think."

She shut the door, and Nic huffed out a breath. "Ugh. Didn't want to spend another second with that woman. Come on. Let's take a look. You mind?"

"After the reaming you gave her, I'm afraid to say no. Consider me your shadow. You lead, I'll follow."

She grinned. "Was I that awful?"

"You were pretty scary, but you're sexy when you're scary. I'm not complaining."

She laughed and they went back to the elevator.

While they waited, he said, "Do you often get into confrontations like that?"

"What do you mean?"

"I'm sure that lady was pretty pissed. Just wondering if that happens often with you. Did it happen with Rudy?"

"Not often, but yeah, from time to time. Why?"

"I just wondered if maybe the blackmail was

about revenge. Hatred even."

"Huh." She seemed to roll the idea around in her mind. "I just figured it was about money."

Heath shrugged. "No reason it can't be about both."

"Ah, ever the optimist."

"Yeah. That's part of my charm."

Her mood was less tense as they rode up to the fourth floor. As promised, this apartment was better. Bigger, cleaner, and seemingly everything worked.

"It could still use a cleaning, but it's a penthouse compared to that other hovel."

They left, and she placed the key back under the mat.

"So, this is what you do? What your charity does?" he asked as they walked back to the elevator. "Find housing for people? Help them get back on their feet."

"Yeah. We help them find jobs, housing, whatever they need to get their life back on track."

"What's to say you won't be just helping them into a life that will once again involve drugs?"

She shrugged. The elevator opened and they stepped inside. "We don't know that, but part of the program is that they have to come in once a week for drug testing. If they do okay, we monitor them for a year, then they're on their own. If they fail a test, they're out of the program, on their own. They can't come back until they've been off the drugs for ninety days. We don't want people in and out, using the charity as a way to get a roof over their head and a hot meal in between fixes."

Heath was starting to understand more about the importance of what she did. What Rudy had started. What the hell made him go back to the drugs? Maybe he'd never really kicked them.

"What would you say your success rate is? What percentage is still clean after that year?"

The lumbering elevator began its descent.

"Unfortunately, less than I'd like. I'd say maybe seventy-five percent. I wish—"

A grinding, clanging noise pierced the air, cutting off her words. The elevator jerked. The lights went out, and they were no longer moving.

Chapter Twelve

Nicolette let out a small scream. "Heath—what's happening?"

"There must be a power outage. Probably because of the weather."

"Shouldn't there be some kind of generator? Some kind of back up emergency plan to keep this sort of thing from happening?"

He couldn't see her in the dark, but he could hear the fear in her voice. He tried to infuse his with confidence. "Most of them probably do, but with this being an old building, maybe they don't. It's okay, though. I'm sure the power will come back on soon."

He felt around until he located the box that held the emergency phone. He picked it up and stuck it to his ear. Dead silence.

Shit. He took out his cell and said, "What's the number to the apartment office?"

"Shouldn't we call 911?"

"They probably won't be too concerned about a stalled elevator, especially in this kind of weather."

"Just call them. Please."

Heath sighed. "Okay. Just take it easy. I'll call."

He dialed 911 and the operator promised they'd send someone out, but couldn't promise how long it would take.

Heath relayed the news to Nicolette. "So, want to give me the office number?"

She quoted the number, and he dialed. Benita Rogers' irritated voice came on the line. When he explained the situation, he would have sworn he heard delight as she answered, "Yeah, that happens from time to time. Sit tight. We'll get it going as soon as we can."

When he hung up, he told Nic what she'd said, leaving out the glee in her tone at their plight. "They'll have it working soon," he promised.

"You think? Sometimes power outages last for days. Weeks!"

Her voice rose on the last word, and he moved in her direction, reaching out until his hands made contact with her body—her shoulder, he presumed. "Hey, now. Don't worry. We'll be fine."

She moved, and her hand gripped his. "Okay. Sorry to be a baby, but I'm slightly claustrophobic. And a little afraid of the dark."

"I never knew that."

"Well, you've never been stuck in a small dark box with me."

He laughed. "True."

Her cold hand trembled against his palm.

"Come over here." He tugged, and she let him lead her toward the back of the elevator. "Let's sit on the floor and talk. It'll make the time pass faster while we wait."

****

Nicolette felt better now. Heath eased her fears just by holding her hand. She would have told him that, but if he thought she was no longer frightened, he might let go.

She settled next to him, her back to the wall, so close she could feel the heat from his shoulder next to hers. "So, talk to me," she said. "Tell me about your family. What's going on with your brothers?"

"Well, Clint is in town with a horse, an actual horse, not an unattractive woman." Nicolette laughed softly, and Heath continued, "Alex is engaged to be married, but he recently received some surprising news."

"Oh, good or bad?"

"Very good, although it adds a bit of a complication to his life. He found out he fathered triplets, all little girls, five years ago."

"What! Triplets? With whom?"

"You remember Zoe Hillman?"

She frowned, trying to recall. "Wasn't she that assistant of his—the one he married during a drunken night in Vegas?"

Heath chuckled. "That's the one."

She liked the sound of his husky voice coming to her in the dark. What would it be like to hear him whisper in her ear while they made love? A shudder ran through her at the thought, but since she knew she'd never actually find out, she made herself stop wondering.

"Have you seen them? Do they live around here?"

"Yes and yes. They're adorable. Look just like Alex."

"What does his fiancée think about that?"

"She doesn't seem very happy about it. But then, Sydney doesn't really seem very happy about anything."

"Poor Alex. How's his relationship with Zoe? Too bad he can't be with the mother of his children."

"Well, yeah, but things really don't work that way, you know? Sometimes someone seems perfect for you, but for one reason or another you can't be with them."

He sounded dejected and she wondered if maybe he was referring to her. No. Not likely. He'd never indicated he felt that way. She was putting emotion in his words that weren't there. Instinct told her that what happened between them nearly a year ago, probably meant there was *something* there. But a physical attraction and reaching out to another person for comfort didn't equate with love or even a desire to pursue a relationship.

Heath was silent for a while. She could tell he wanted to say more. Her eyes adjusted to the dark where she was able to make out his silhouette. His head was bowed, and he looked down to where their hands were still linked, lying on the floor between them.

"What are you thinking about?" she asked.

He was silent a while longer, then said, "I have a sister."

"Pardon me? You have a sister?"

"Yeah. Seems Alex wasn't the only one to father a child he didn't know about."

"Your dad had a love child?" Nicolette knew how Heath felt about his father. How Heath felt about loyalty. That must have been rough on him to learn his dad had cheated. "How long ago?"

"Years ago. While he was in 'Nam. The daughter's a year older than Clint."

"Dear God, when did your mother find out? Have you met her? Where's the 'other woman' now?" Nicolette flushed. "Sorry. Didn't mean to fire so many questions at you. I'm just shocked, I mean, your dad? Who would have thought it?"

"Tell me about it."

She listened as he told the story of how he'd learned he had a sister, how he hadn't met her yet and didn't want to.

When he was done, she said, "It's not her fault, you know. She's a victim, too."

He snorted a humorless laugh. "You sound just like my mother." He lifted their hands and studied them in the near-darkness. "I just can't stand the thought of what my father did. Seeing the woman, the result of his infidelity, would make it so...I don't know. So real."

His thumb rubbed over the skin on the back of her hand, sending tingles along her spine.

"I know," Nicolette whispered. "I'm sure it's hard on you."

"It's hard on all of us, but I seem to be the one acting like the biggest jackass over it."

She squeezed his hand. "You're as far from a jackass as anyone I know."

Heath's eyes found hers in the gloom, and he placed a kiss on the back of her hand. "Truth is, you know another reason it bothers me? Another reason I don't want to meet my sister?"

"Why's that?" Nicolette asked, trying to ignore the warm spot where his lips had touched her skin.

"Because, it makes me wonder...makes me realize that I could be just like him."

"Like your father?"

She barely saw the nod.

"Disloyal. To Rudy."

"In what way?" she asked, but she thought she knew, and her heart seemed to beat loud enough for him to hear in the silence of the elevator. She waited breathlessly for his answer.

He sighed heavily. "In the way I want you. In the way I wanted you even while you were married to my best friend."

In spite of the guilt she heard in his voice, there was also longing. She turned her head just slightly. She wasn't sure exactly how it happened, but in the next moment, his lips found hers. He tangled his hand in her hair and pressed her more closely to him as his mouth moved urgently over hers. She moaned in the back of her throat, and he answered it with a growl.

Dear God. She was kissing Heath King. Those were *his* lips on hers. They felt as good as she'd always dreamed they would. Firm and skilled, his tongue warm and seeking. Her heart lurched, and for a moment, all the angst of the past year flew away. This was it. This was what it felt like to be kissed by Heath King.

They parted long enough for him to run his lips over her neck and down to the V above her top button. She ached to feel him loosen those buttons, for his lips to travel downward. Her nipples tingled with the need, and she almost reached up and undid the buttons herself.

Before she could consider the advisability of doing just that, a low roar sounded and lights blared on, as if spotlighting their shame. They froze, still touching, but then pulled guiltily apart. Heath stood and reached a hand down to her, helping her to her feet. He was breathing heavily, just as she was. He shoved a hand through his hair and looked dazedly around the elevator as it slowly began to descend.

"God. I'm sorry," he whispered, his voice hoarse.

She blinked as if waking from a deep sleep. "It wasn't your fault."

"Yes, it was." He reached out and took her hand again. "I don't know what I was thinking, but the last thing you need is for me to add to your emotional turmoil. For that, I'm truly sorry."

It was all she could do not to curse in frustration. Despite her earlier hysteria, she now wished they could stay stranded forever. Just the two of them, locked away in their dark cocoon, away from the real world of blackmailers and suspicious detectives and drug addicts needing her help and people who would shun her for loving Heath.

She sucked in a deep breath. Dear God. It was true. She loved him. Maybe she always had. The sad, hard truth was that it didn't matter. She could love him all she wanted, but she could never have him. It was that thought, that daunting realization that made her pull away from Heath's touch and say, "It was both our faults, but it was nothing to worry about. Let's just forget it ever happened," in the coldest tone she could manage.

****

In spite of the words she'd tossed at Heath, there was no way Nicolette could forget what happened. No way she could forget how it felt to finally lose herself in Heath's arms. That kiss. Wow. She'd never felt anything like it in her life. And, God help her, she wanted more.

She paced back and forth, going into the bathroom to brush her teeth. There was no way there could be anything between her and Heath. They were friends. People would think they were screwing around on Rudy the whole time. Sure, some day she wanted to find another man to love, although she couldn't imagine having what she had with Rudy, but the man couldn't be Heath. No one would ever believe she and Heath had been true to Rudy until nearly a year after his death.

But, really, had they? What about when they'd almost kissed while Rudy had been in a coma? She sighed as she thought back over it, something that had turned out not to be a big deal, but had stuck with her all these months.

They hadn't *actually* kissed. But the emotions were there; the urge was there. And if he hadn't pulled away, she wasn't sure she could have.

Then, she'd have known what it felt like to have Heath's lips on hers, to have passion explode between them. Would she have gone further? Would she actually have made love to her husband's best friend while he lay dying in the next room?

She'd like to think that she wouldn't, but if the way her body felt now was any indication, she couldn't be absolutely positive. But, Rudy wasn't dying in the next room now. He was gone. Forever. She was alone and had been for nearly a year. Heath King was the only other man she'd ever wanted like she wanted Rudy. Actually, she could finally admit, maybe she'd wanted him more than Rudy. In the past, Heath had only ever shown her friendship. But tonight had been different. He'd shown that he desired her, maybe as much as she desired him. Rudy was gone. Heath was steps away, nothing but sheet rock separating them.

It was true, they couldn't have a future together, not with the way people would shun them. Maybe Heath wouldn't even want a relationship, but they could have one night. They could find comfort in one another's arms, ease the sexual need. She jumped in the shower and quickly shaved her legs. She'd been alone for a very long time and in the winter seldom wore dresses, so shaving wasn't a task she performed daily. But, if she planned to seduce Heath, she definitely didn't want to be stubbly.

She rinsed the shaving cream and squeezed a dollop of scented body cream onto a sponge and liberally soaped her body. Shutting off the water, she grabbed a large, fluffy towel and dried her skin, the words to "We've Got Tonight" by Rod Stewart playing in her head. Tonight may be all she and Heath had, but if it were up to her, it would be a night to remember.

****

Heath shifted restlessly on the sheets, cursing, wondering how their softness against his skin could feel so irritating. Might have something to do with the boner that had come and gone, returning each time he thought about that kiss with Nicolette.

Finally, finally, after all these years of dreaming about it, he'd felt her soft lips yielding beneath his. Oh God, it had felt better than he could have imagined. He'd wanted to take her, right there on the nasty floor of the elevator. Strip her down and plunge into her softness, take from her what he'd been wanting since he laid eyes on her fifteen years ago. If the lights hadn't come on right then, he might have done just that.

What would she have done?

She'd certainly seemed into the kiss. The little noises she made in her throat didn't indicate she was feeling discomfort. Nope, she may have been all for fulfilling his little fantasy, the two of them stripped naked, tongues and hands roaming and tangling, flesh slapping flesh as he drove—

Shit.

Those images were not helping. He rethought his habit of sleeping in the nude. Certainly wasn't conducive to *not* thinking about Nicolette, to not needing relief for his recurring hard-on. Maybe he should just take care of it himself.

Yeah? And what about the next one, and the next, and the multitude of unfulfilled hard-ons to come? Because, truth was, no matter that Nicolette had been caught up in the moment. No matter that, even though they were supposed to only be friends, she seemed to desire him, too...he could never have her. Never ever. *So, bucko, just fucking get over it already.*

"Fuck," he growled into the pillow, punching it with his fist as he once more shifted and tried to get comfortable.

He closed his eyes, but his body was wound tight. He doubted he'd sleep at all.

He flung the sheet off and climbed out of bed. Maybe warm milk or some other bullshit might help. A little voice told him nothing would, other than relief from this hot burning need for Nicolette that had simmered for fifteen years and was now a raging inferno.

He was at the bedroom door when he heard a soft knock on the door adjoining Nic's duplex. He halted. Surely he was imagining things, but it came again. A little firmer this time.

He moved quickly to the door, but didn't open it. "Nicolette? Is something wrong?"

"No. I need to talk to you. Can I come in?"

"Hold on."

He grabbed a pair of boxer briefs off the chair and pulled them on. Looking down, he decided that was not nearly enough clothing and grabbed the jeans he'd worn that day and slipped them on, too.

Opening the door, he gasped when he saw Nicolette. Her hair was damp and tangled around her shoulders. She wore a short, white button down sleep shirt that gaped open just enough for him to see the tops of her breasts. She moved past him into the room, giving him a shot of her clean, citrusy sent. He nearly groaned aloud. Jesus. This was not going to help his boner one bit.

When she was inside his bedroom, he shut the door.

She looked at him, her eyes raking over his bare chest, and he suddenly wished he'd also grabbed a shirt. She brushed a hank of hair back from her face. "I can't sleep. I can't stop thinking about what happened in the elevator."

You and me both. Heath sighed and shook his head. "I know. I'm sorry. I was caught up in the moment. I shouldn't have kissed you."

He reached for the shirt that had lain with the jeans and started to shrug it on. Nicolette moved a few steps toward him, and took it from his hands, then tossed it back on the chair. He stared down at her, frowning.

She reached up and put two fingers against his lips. "I'm not sorry we kissed. I'm sorry we stopped."

Chapter Thirteen

Heath's heart rate shot up. As close as Nicolette was, surely she could hear it beating. He stared down into her eyes. They looked like deep green emeralds in the near dark of his bedroom.

"What? Do you know what you're saying?" His voice was hoarse, and he tried to clear it, but he could barely breathe.

"I know what I want. I know what I need. It's been so long. I've been so lonely. You make me feel safe, make me feel warm. I can't love you, but please..." Her voice broke, and a tiny sob escaped. "Please make love to me."

As if a dam burst inside him, feeling surged through his veins. Fifteen years, and he had never dreamed she'd say those words to him. Even if she couldn't love him, he could no more begin to tell her no than he could cut off his own hands. He'd waited too long. Dreamed too often.

He groaned and took her by the shoulders, yanking her against his body. As he stared down at her soft features, he memorized the mesmerizing play of light in her eyes. Light that filled him up, and made him feel like a drowned man begging for air. Drawn to the call of her parted mouth, he dipped his head and claimed her soft, full lips. Mint and citrus met the stroke of his tongue, and he drank deeply. God above, she tasted like heaven. Warm. Sweet. Intoxicating.

Her quiet moan vibrated against his mouth. Her fingers demanded more as they delved into his hair and scraped against his scalp. Drawing his body away, he reached between them, shaking fingers fumbling at the top button of her nightshirt. Good grief, this was insane. He could hardly function. He felt like a damn school kid all over again, fumbling in the dark with all the fineness of an elephant.

He sucked in a short breath and ordered his body to be patient. His fingers got the message, stilling enough that he could twist the remaining buttons free. The white cotton fell loose, and his knuckles brushed against satiny skin. He'd known her skin would be soft, but in all his fantasies, he'd never imagined one touch could set his gut to quivering.

Her nipples tightened, silently begging for his touch. He obliged. Cupping her breast, he rolled one hard bud beneath the pad of his thumb. Weighty fullness filled his palm perfectly, as it had a hundred times or more in his mind. His. She was finally his.

Dear God. This was real.

"Heath," she whispered against his mouth. Breaking the kiss, she held his gaze as her hands went to the button of his jeans. Unable to move, he stood still, his breath catching as he watched her work him loose. She slid the zipper down. Slender fingers slipped past denim to stroke his swollen erection beneath the cotton of his briefs. The warmth of her touch taunted. The confident squeeze tormented. His hips jerked forward in search of more.

On a hiss, he ground his teeth together, closed his eyes, and threw back his head, begging his body for control. He concentrated on touching her, teasing her nipple, massaging her breast. Yet when she slipped her hand inside, and those damning fingers closed around him, sensation rocketed through him. He went utterly still and gulped down air.

"If you don't stop," he whispered, "I'll be finished

way too soon."

She giggled and stroked her hand along the length of him once more before releasing her hold.

Freed from her delightful touch and the urgency it brought, he bent forward and ran a tongue over the top of her breasts. Her breaths came faster as she clasped the back of his head and maneuvered his mouth down to her nipple. He flicked out his tongue, wetting the nipple, then blew a breath on it. She let out a sound somewhere between a gasp and a scream and pressed against his head until he opened his mouth and took her nipple inside, working his tongue along the hardened bud, around, laving it over and over.

"Oh, please, oh, God, Heath, yes, please," she muttered as he brought his free hand up to give her opposite nipple a gentle twist.

It took all his will power to step back and away. But he wanted to look at her. Wanted to see the vision that made his dreams seem pitiful and colorless. He shoved the nightshirt off her shoulders. His gaze tracked its tumble to her feet, where it gathered in a pool of ivory. One crimson toe darted out to kick the shirt aside.

Long, lithe legs led to a flat belly and a waist narrow enough he could span his hands around it. He nearly cried out when he saw the tiny wisp of black panties that contrasted against her honeyed skin. He reached out, traced the minuscule strap of elastic, and slipped a solitary finger beneath the scrap of silk. One touch, and moisture met his fingertip. Heat soaked into his hand.

Her hips ground into his palm, and Heath choked back a groan. At this rate, he'd never get the chance to savor her. The jagged catch of her breath, the demanding press of her body, said she was racing right along with him. If he waited much longer, he'd beat her to that cataclysmic finish. And by all that was holy, he didn't intend to turn tonight into an embarrassment he'd never forget.

Withdrawing his hand, he cupped her cheek and sought her mouth once more. But Nicolette evaded his kiss. Scattering feather-light kisses across his chest, she worked his jeans down his thighs. The wash of cool air as she did the same with his briefs sent a shiver rolling down his spine. His erection bobbed against his abdomen, and then warmth flooded into his veins as her fingers closed around him.

"Baby," he gasped. "You've got to—" His words caught as she slid a cool palm down the length of his erection.

"Got to?" she teased, the hint of a smile playing at her lips. She lifted to tiptoe, mindless of the havoc she was working on his senses, and her teeth grazed the side of his neck. "What—stop?" Trailing the tip of her tongue to the lobe of his ear, she whispered, "I don't intend to stop. I want to feel you deep inside me. I've wanted this for too long."

Christ! How was a man supposed to say no to that? Or hell, hesitate for that matter? On a hoarse groan, he scooped her up and carried her the few steps to the bed. He tumbled into the covers with her, blanketing her with his body. A shudder ran through him at the enormity of this moment. At what was about to happen. For several heavy heartbeats, he held her gaze, questioning her in silence. Was this right? Would the friendship they'd built over the years fall into ruin? Was tonight what she really wanted?

When she slid her hand to the back of his neck, and drew him into a hungry kiss, he found all the answers he needed.

****

Nicolette's entire body trembled. Blood hummed through her veins like a live current. She wanted to scream at him, "Hurry, please, please hurry." But the heady sensation of his skin against hers made her want to hold on and treasure this fleeting moment for a lifetime.

His large, warm hands roamed over her body, now covered by only her panties. His confident touch, his inquisitive fingers, stoked her desire to intolerable limits. Her skin felt aflame, like at any minute she might combust. He dipped his head down and latched onto a nipple once more, his tongue doing those delicious things he'd done moments before. She arched off the bed, biting her teeth into her lower lip to silence a cry. Swear to God, just that velvety brush was nearly enough to make her orgasm.

His hand moved between them, skated down her stomach, and her entire body tensed with anticipation. *Please.* The thought ricocheted through her head.

His fingers brushed over her panties, then moved to the thin band at one leg. She shimmied her hips, helping him as he pushed the garment down her legs. When it caught on her ankle, she kicked it onto the floor with a shake of her leg. Cool air puffed over her skin, and then heat infused her. He cupped her feminine flesh and slipped a finger inside. Slow caresses stirred her growing need. Parting her legs to give him more room, she closed her eyes and murmured, "Yes."

What she thought was heaven, turned into unimaginable bliss as the moist heat of his mouth replaced the warmth of his hand. She arched off the bed, her fingers digging into his shoulders as sparks of light lit behind her eyes. His tongue teased and taunted, taking her up higher, lifting her to a plateau she'd never known before. Feeling intensified, built until it exploded and robbed her of all thought.

"Oh God," she cried as release rocked through her. Her nails bit into his skin, and she held on as something deep inside fractured into pieces. She was afraid if she let go, she might splinter right along with it.

As sensation ebbed, and she spiraled down from the heights of sensation, she opened her eyes to look at Heath. The strong lines of his face hardened with his effort at control. His breath came in hard gasps that matched hers. But the intensity that gleamed in his golden eyes stirred a feeling so unique she shuddered. Even Rudy, in all the times they'd been together, had never looked at her with such blatant appreciation. Heath made her feel womanly. Protected. *Cherished.*

"Nicolette..."

He closed his eyes on a deep breath. When he opened them again, he'd tempered some of that feral gleam, but it lingered just beneath the surface. Appeared in the rigidness of his shoulders. She let him go and tumbled back into the bed, watching all those fantastic muscles bunch and pull as he shucked his boxers, then positioned himself over her.

Bracing his hands on both sides of her shoulders, his gaze searched her face. In slow motion, he lowered his head. Touched his lips to hers. As his body melded against hers, he deepened the kiss, exposing her to the full onslaught of his fierce emotions. Hungry and possessive, his mouth demanded her full response, and Nicolette gave without hesitation.

His erection pressed against her, and she shifted to better accommodate him. In one breath-stealing thrust, he slid in deep. Nicolette cried out, but Heath swallowed the sound, his own cry vibrating between them. His hips retreated for a brief moment, then he plunged in deep. And then they moved as one. In sync, as if they'd done this their whole lives. No fumbling. No struggle over who would give pleasure and who would receive. The perfect dance of their bodies, the instinctual rhythm, defied the bliss of any practiced act. Wholly natural. As if their very thoughts blended in the same spectacular fashion.

Heath tore his lips away from hers. "I'm going to come," he growled.

"Yes. Please."

"I want you to," he gasped between words, holding back.

"No, please, I need to feel it, please." And she did. Before she could fully succumb to the vulnerability Heath exposed, she needed him to give her courage. To tell her without words he'd be there to catch her.

"Come with me," he murmured against her mouth.

That was all the encouragement Nicolette needed. She shoved her hips upward, grinding her pelvis against him as Heath thrust in deep and hard. His arms came around her, lifting her close as his body tensed. An orgasm raced through her body, blending with the trembling of his. In time with his ragged gasp, she called out his name.

****

Surely Heath had died and gone to heaven. Burying deep into Nicolette's soft warmth was the single best feeling he'd ever had. He pumped once, then twice, and the blood from his body rushed to his groin as he exploded inside her. She gripped his hips with her knees, taking all of him in as he poured into her like he'd never stop. Finally, the last of the spasms shook him and he collapsed, using his elbows to keep most of his weight off her.

He shifted to lie beside her, holding her soft, warm body close. "I can't believe I just scored with Nicolette Brandon," he murmured.

She laughed softly. "What do you mean by that?"

"All the guys in college wanted to. We were all jealous of Rudy. Now, I finally got to."

"So," she lifted up on an elbow to look down at him, "how was it?"

"Better than I ever dreamed."

She smiled and bent to give him a long, sensuous kiss. "Right answer."

He laughed. They lay for a moment, talking in the dark and Heath was close to drifting off when he felt her move.

He opened his eyes as she climbed out of bed, searching the floor for her clothing.

"What are you doing?"

"I'm going back home."

"You're not staying?"

She paused and turned to him, holding the sleep shirt one of them had tossed to the floor. "I can't stay over here with you, all night."

"Why not?"

Shrugging, she turned away and pulled the nightshirt on. "People will talk. Word might get back to the authorities."

"Who the hell's gonna talk? We're the only ones here."

"I don't know." She stood and looked at him beseechingly, begging him with her eyes to understand. "I'm just not sure what might happen. I can't take the chance."

He nodded, although he wasn't completely certain he understood. Without another word, she slipped back through the door. He threw an arm across his forehead and stared unseeing at the ceiling. His heart felt heavy, and he already missed her warmth. A frustrated groan issued from his lips.

What kind of man did it make him that, even after incredible sex, what he really wanted was to hold her while she fell asleep?

****

Heath slowly opened his eyes and squinted against the shaft of sunlight coming from the bottom of the window where the shades weren't completely pulled down. He looked beside him, at the empty spot where Nicolette had briefly lain. Her scent was still there and he just barely stopped himself from burying his nose into her pillow. His groin stirred just thinking about her, and he growled in frustration. Fool. Loser. Love-sick asshole.

Luckiest man alive.

He had, after all, made love to Nicolette last night. Even though it had meant more to him than it had to her, even though he was the one who'd spent fifteen years dreaming of doing that very thing, he wouldn't let it mar his happiness. No matter what happened from this day forward, he now knew what it felt like to kiss those lips, to share that intimate, timeless dance. To physically possess the woman he'd only had in his fantasies up to now.

For Christ's sake. He did sound pathetic. He shook his head and threw back the covers, heading to the shower, not able to erase the goofy smile he knew must be plastered on his face.

He was drying off when a knock sounded at the adjoining door. His groin tightened and heated. The last time she'd knocked...

Get hold of yourself, man. He threw a towel around his waist and went to the door. He wanted to jerk it open and pull her into his arms for a repeat of last night, but he had no idea how she felt about what had transpired between them, and he wasn't going to rush things. Wasn't going to blow it with Nicolette. Whatever *it* was.

"Heath?" Nicolette said through the closed door. "You up? I made breakfast and coffee. Come on over if you'd like."

He grinned. "I'd like. Let me throw some clothes on, I'll be right there."

There was a pause before she responded, her voice light and sounding almost as goofy as he felt. "Sure. Great. I'll see you in a minute."

He had a feeling she'd considered telling him not to bother with the clothes, but maybe he was reading too much into her hesitation and upbeat tone.

When he'd dressed, he went through the door and found Nicolette in the kitchen.

She turned and gave him a shy smile, and her eyes told him things were still cool between them. Impulsively, he walked over and planted a quick kiss on her lips. She smiled and handed him a cup of coffee.

This felt good. Felt right. Like an old married couple sharing their morning.

Except, they hadn't shared a bed. He had to remember that. Just because they'd made love and she was making him breakfast, didn't mean they could suddenly step into a life of happily ever after. Nope. Lots of obstacles still stood in their way. The main one being, judging from her flight last night, Nicolette apparently didn't want any more than sexual satisfaction.

He took a sip of the coffee and watched over the rim as she scooped pancakes onto a plate. She was already dressed, and her faded jeans hugged her bottom like an old glove. It made him think of the night before, when his hands had cupped that same delectable bottom.

Yep. Sexual satisfaction wasn't exactly a bad thing.

She joined him at the table, placing a stack of pancakes in front of each of them. He noticed her stack was as high as his, and he hid a smile. Apparently, she'd worked up an appetite last night.

She reached for a jar of peanut butter. He frowned as she knifed out a dollop and spread some on each of the pancakes, lifting them one at a time with her fingers.

"You eat peanut butter on your pancakes?" he asked.

"Sure. Don't you?"

"No. I've never thought about that. I use syrup."

She grinned and picked up the bottle of maple syrup, tilting it until the cakes swam in the brownish liquid. "Me, too."

He laughed. "Okay. I'm game."

He spread peanut butter on his pancakes and added the syrup as she had. The combination was surprisingly delicious. They ate in silence, washing their breakfast down with ice cold milk, until his plate was empty and hers nearly was.

She dropped her fork and pushed back from the table. "Stuffed," she groaned.

"Me, too. That was a great breakfast. Thanks."

"No problem. Just pancakes from an add-water mix. I'm not exactly Julia Child."

"Still. They really hit the spot." He stood and refilled his coffee cup, then took a gulp of the hot, strong brew. "And the coffee's great. Strong, just like I like it."

"Strong coffee and now peanut butter on pancakes. Guess we have something in common."

She rose from her chair, and he put the mug down. He took her hand and tugged her to him. "After last night, I feel like we have tons in common."

She smiled and relaxed against him. Reaching up, she cupped his face in her hands. "That, my friend, was the best of all."

He grinned, trying not to let the emphasis she put on 'friend' stab him too hard. "You mean the sex was better than strong coffee and peanut butter pancakes? Geez. I'm touched."

Still holding his face, she planted another kiss on his lips. "You should be. Up to now, very few things topped those." Her eyes lost their mischievous glint, and her mouth turned down in a frown. "Are we okay? I mean, after last night…"

"I don't know about you, but I'm more than okay. Last night was the most amazing night of my life."

Her lips tilted in pleasure. "Yeah?"

"Oh, yeah. Want me to show you how much I mean that?"

She laughed breathlessly and pulled back. "Although I think I would like that very much, I have to get going. I have to go into work and finish up a few things, then the charity is closed for the holidays. I don't have to go back until the Monday after Christmas. Maybe you could show me later?"

He thought his heart would burst with the joy of knowing it hadn't been a one-time thing for her. Their friendship was not ruined, and now they had this new and extremely pleasurable level added to it.

Today was arguably the best day of his life.

He swatted her lightly on the butt. "Then, I guess you'd better get to it. I'm not sure how long I can stand here so close to you without stripping your clothes off and showing you now."

She danced away with a laugh. "Later, stud. For now, I have work to do, and you have a blackmailer to stop."

The mood sobered at that, and he stepped closer, placing a hand on the side of her face. "I will stop him. I promise you, Nicolette. I'll find whoever is doing this, and I won't let him hurt you. You believe me?"

Her eyes moistened as she nodded. "Yes. Yes, Heath, I do."

****

Heath ducked his head in his coat and jogged out to the Tahoe, his steps light, his mood better than it had been in, well…ever. All he could think about was Nicolette. Everything bad that had happened to him in the past year; Rudy's death, his father's death, learning of his father's infidelity, learning he had an unwanted sibling, had fled, as if his soul was so overflowing with happiness, it had no room for anything negative.

The snow was increasing, the wind picking up and blowing it in sharp, freezing gusts across his face. He experienced a moment of concern for Nicolette. If the conditions worsened, she shouldn't be out driving. Her Jeep could handle hazardous roads well, and she was a cautious driver. Still, he didn't like the thought of her being out on these roads with bad weather coming in. If the snow continued to fall this heavily, he'd call her, offer to pick her up wherever she was.

Before then, though, he needed to follow up on a few things. His focus was identifying and stopping the blackmailer, but now he was beginning to wonder about his friend's death. It sounded more and more like it hadn't been an accident. But who would have wanted to hurt Rudy? Let alone kill him? Certainly not Nicolette. He didn't see any motive for Marla or Donovan to harm him. Of course, he didn't see any motive for anyone to harm him. That brought him back to the drugs. If Rudy's death was suspicious, most likely it had to do with his secret drug use. The blackmail and the murder—alleged murder—were probably related.

From what Heath gathered, the barbershop was linked to Rudy's drug use. Not the owner, Ted. Heath didn't get that feeling from him at all. He did, however, get that feeling from Noah Forsythe. He was certain the guy had used drugs with Rudy, if not sold or bought them. He'd just acted too squirrelly, too fidgety, not to be hiding something. The only other thing Heath could think of he'd want to hide would be if there was some other kind of relationship between him and Rudy, like maybe sexual.

But that was ludicrous. Forsythe claimed to be straight, although the jury was still out on that. However, Heath would bet his life that Rudy was straight as a board. Never in all the years he'd known him had there been even a hint that Rudy was anything but a female-loving heterosexual. Good God, any man married to Nicolette couldn't possibly be interested in anyone other than her, male or female.

He thought again of their night together, and a pleasant warmth filled his chest. This time, it had nothing to do with his dick. He really, truly, genuinely loved being with Nicolette, even on a platonic level. But now that he knew what it was like to know her on a level other than platonic, he didn't think he could ever get enough of her. Of course, most likely he'd have to.

Even though she hadn't indicated this was just a one night fling, it was doubtful and way too early to even entertain the idea of a future for them. First, he had to find the blackmailer, then make sure Nicolette wasn't charged with Rudy's murder. Then there would be the question of how Nicolette herself felt. Did she want a future with him, or was she too concerned about what people would think? Was she too worried they'd look down on her for besmirching the memory of her saintly husband?

Of course, there was also the very real possibility that she didn't feel the way he did. She cared about him, no doubt about that. She was attracted to him physically, something he hadn't really known for sure until last night. Boy, had he learned how true that was last night.

Even if Nicolette felt the way he did, even if she wanted a future with him, Heath had to get past the guilt. He couldn't shake the notion that he was betraying his best friend by wanting a future with that friend's wife. Mostly, he had to get past the question of whether that made him as disloyal as his father.

Shake it off, stop thinking about that shit. Stop thinking about Nicolette for right now. You have other things to worry about.

He headed to the barbershop, peering out the windshield at the ever-increasing snowstorm. Hell. Visibility was almost zero. Ice pellets pinged the windshield. The Tahoe's tires grabbed the road and held, but others weren't having as much luck. Several cars were abandoned on the side of the road, and Heath studied each of them, trying to see if it looked like people were still inside. If so, he'd stop and offer help, but all the ones he'd passed so far were truly abandoned.

He finally made it to the barbershop but he wouldn't get any more questions answered today. Just as he'd suspected it might be, the shop was closed. They'd left early because of the weather.

He tromped back through the deepening snow and climbed into the Tahoe. Digging out his cell, he dialed Nicolette.

****

Nicolette had never been so glad to be home in her life. The drive had been treacherous, the road worsening by the second. Nothing had ever felt better than being inside her cozy duplex, warming herself in front of the fire. Nothing, that is, until her phone rang, and she recognized Heath's number on the caller ID.

"I'm heading home," he told her in his husky, sexy tone. They were three simple words, but there seemed to be a wealth of meaning behind them.

"I can't wait until you get here."

"You and me both."

"So...tell me what's going to happen then." She was being purposely flirtatious. She wanted to make

166

sure Heath was as anxious to be with her again as she was with him.

"How about I *show* you what's going to happen?"

"Can you give me a hint?"

He laughed. "Let's just say clothing won't be involved."

A warm glow spread through her, happiness nearly making her head burst from her neck. Whoever would have guessed she'd finally have sex with Heath King? That it would be beyond her wildest expectations, that they'd settle into this easy, flirtatious, expectant rhythm and actually be planning to do it again?

"Promise?" she asked, lowering her voice to a husky, seductive purr.

"Oh, I promise all right. You just wait."

"What if I can't wait?"

His low growl carried over the phone. "God, woman. I'm driving in a snowstorm to get to you. Don't distract me like that or I'll never make—" he abruptly stopped, as if his remark made him think of what happened to Rudy.

Some of her eager anticipation dwindled, but the warm glow didn't completely go away.

"Drive safe," she whispered into the phone. "I'll be waiting."

"You got it." The relief in his voice was evident, as if he'd been worried that the mood was ruined. "I'll be home in ten minutes, fifteen tops, depending on how bad the roads are between here and there."

****

Steady snow covered the windshield quicker than the wipers could clear it off. Heath cursed the conditions that kept him crawling along the roads when all he wanted to do was rush home to Nicolette. He still couldn't wrap his mind around the thought that she was waiting, that the end of his journey would take him straight to her. He knew it was a temporary dream come true, but he would enjoy it as long and as fully as he could.

He flipped on the radio. Maybe music would make the drive seem less endless. Christmas music flowed from the speakers, and Heath grinned, thinking of how much sweeter it sounded now than it had just a few days ago when he'd been on his way to Kansas City. He didn't even cringe when the Chipmunks squeaked out their rendition of "Silver Bells."

Few vehicles were out on the roads, even though snowplows were busy clearing the streets the best they could under the circumstances. Through the dense white curtain, taillights shone like beady red eyes. The car was small, maybe a Cobalt or Focus. Heath was amazed it was actually moving on the icy, hazardous roads.

As if his thoughts had jinxed the car's odds, the taillights swung to the right, and a flash of headlights appeared for a few seconds before the car went into a slide. Heath watched helplessly as the vehicle slammed into a tree, looking like a hot wheels car tossed by an angry child.

Chapter Fourteen

The car shuddered to a stop, the driver's side door crunched by the massive oak.

"Shit!" Heath slowed and pulled to the side of the road. Grabbing his cell phone, he dialed 911 as he flung open his door. Icy wind fought his efforts, but he managed to climb out of the Tahoe. "There's been a car accident," he shouted into the phone when the operator answered. "They ran off the road, crashed into a tree."

"Where did this happen, sir?"

He gave the operator the location, making his way in the deep snow, hoping whoever was in the car was okay.

"Were you in the accident? Is anyone hurt?"

"It wasn't me. I was behind them. I don't know if they're hurt or not. I'm going to check now."

"Emergency vehicles are on their way, sir. Don't move the victim, okay?"

"I won't. Hold on."

He reached the car, but there was no way he could get to the driver. He stumbled around to the passenger side and yanked the door open. "Oh, shit," he muttered.

Jerome sat slumped behind the wheel. The deflated air bag lay on his chest like a fallen parachute.

Heath quickly looked through the car, but Jerome was the only passenger.

"Hey! Jerome?" He slid into the passenger seat and shut the door. He pressed his fingers into

Jerome's neck.

"Sir?" The 911 operator said into his ear. "Are you with the victim?"

"Yeah. I'm inside the car with him. Turns out I know him."

"What's his name, sir?"

"Jerome Badgett."

"Okay. We're going to take care of your friend. Is Jerome breathing?"

"He has a pulse. He's alive."

"Okay, sir. Does he appear to be in distress?"

"No. He's unconscious but he's breathing."

"Is he bleeding?"

A stream of blood poured from Jerome's forehead and dripped down onto his left shoulder.

"His head is bleeding."

"Okay. Just stay calm, sir. Help is on the way for your friend."

Heath didn't bother to point out that he wasn't *un*calm, or that Jerome wasn't his friend.

Jerome moaned, and his eyes fluttered open.

"Jerome?" Heath said.

Jerome's head moved until he looked at Heath. "What happened?" He blinked rapidly then squeezed his eyes shut.

"You were in an accident. Where does it hurt?"

"Ah, hell, man. Everywhere. My head." A low wail came from him. "My legs. Oh, God. Hurts."

"You're gonna be okay. Help is on the way."

"Sir, is he awake?" the operator said.

"Yes," Heath told her.

"Don't move him. An ambulance will be there soon."

"How long?" Heath asked.

"It may take a little while."

It was difficult to hear the operator with Jerome's whimpering punctuating their conversation.

170

"What are you doing here?" Jerome asked. He was breathing fast, his face scrunched in agony. "How did you find me?"

"I was behind you. I saw your car go off the road." Heath shifted his feet, noticing for the first time that the floorboard was littered with wadded up fast food wrappers.

"Thanks, man." Jerome reached out a hand. Heath hesitated a second before taking it. Jerome's hand closed over Heath's, then his grip tightened, and he stiffened. "Oh, God. Hurts so bad. Please. Help me."

"Calm down. You're going to be fine." Heath made an effort to keep his voice low, soothing.

"Get me out of here!" Jerome cried.

"I can't move you. Just stay still and try to be calm. Help is on the way."

Jerome's entire body shook, tears and blood mingling as they poured down his face.

"Take it easy," Heath soothed. "You'll be fine."

Jerome's terrified gaze darted around the car. "When will they be here? I have to get out."

"They're on their way."

"Am I going to die?"

"No," Heath said, although he realized that he couldn't be sure. "You'll be fine. Just breathe and try to relax."

Jerome nodded. "I shouldn't have been out in this. I knew I shouldn't."

"Where were you going?" Heath wasn't particularly interested, but he wanted to keep Jerome's mind off his pain.

"I had a date," Jerome bit out, then laughed. "Met her on the internet. Stupid to risk your life over a woman, huh? Especially one you don't even know."

Yes, that was stupid, all right, but it wasn't stupid to risk your life for the woman you loved. He thought of Nicolette waiting for him. Would they

171

make love again tonight? The thought sent a warm tingle through him, and he immediately felt guilty. Now wasn't the time to be thinking of his own pleasure.

"Is there someone I can call for you?" Heath asked.

Jerome shook his head. "No one."

"No family or friends who'd want to be there?"

For a brief moment, Jerome looked sad instead of just in pain. "No. My sister might be there. She's a nurse."

If his sister wasn't there, how could Heath leave Jerome alone and injured in a hospital? But, Nicolette was waiting for him...

Damn.

A siren's wail rose, followed by flashing lights.

"They're here," Heath said.

"Thanks for staying, man," Jerome choked out.

Heath nodded and climbed out of the car.

Two EMT's rushed over, and Heath moved back to let them work. His phone rang, and he looked at the display. Nicolette.

"Heath?" she said when he answered. "What's going on—are you okay?" Her voice rose hysterically.

"Yeah. I'm fine. Is everything all right there?"

"Where are you? It's been nearly an hour since I talked to you. I've been trying to call. What happened?"

He puffed out a sigh. "I'm sorry. I didn't mean to worry you. A car ran off the road, and I was on the phone with 911."

"Was anyone hurt?"

"It was Jerome. He's injured. They're taking him to the hospital."

"You stayed with him?"

"Yeah. I didn't want to leave him alone. I couldn't call you because I was on the phone with 911 the entire time."

Silence, then an exasperated sigh. "Oh, Heath. You're something, aren't you?"

He smiled. "I don't know. I guess I am."

She laughed. "I was so scared. I thought about the night I didn't hear from Rudy." She sucked in a breath. "And he died."

Heath's heart seized. "Aw, sweetie. I'm sorry." He looked up. The attendants had extricated Jerome and were wheeling him to the ambulance door. "Listen. I'm going to see if he's okay. I may go to the hospital with him. I'll let you know."

"Okay." She'd calmed now. "However long it takes, I'll be waiting for you."

"See you soon."

He closed the phone and slipped it in his pocket. He grinned. He hated upsetting Nicolette, but he liked that she cared enough to worry.

"Is he going to be okay?" Heath asked one of the attendants, a young guy with a goatee flecked with white snow.

"He's stable," the guy said as he slammed the door shut. "We'll know more when we get him to the hospital. Were you in the accident with him?"

"No. I was behind him. I saw the accident and stopped to help."

The EMT nodded his approval. "I'm sure you saved his life. We'll take care of him."

Heath thought of Nicolette at home and the injured Jerome, then reluctantly said, "Should I go with him?"

The attendant made his way to the driver's door of the ambulance, and Heath followed.

"I gave him morphine. He's kind of out of it," he told Heath as he climbed into the driver's side. "Will he have someone at the hospital?"

"His sister is a nurse there, but I guess he didn't have anyone to call."

"Your choice, buddy."

The door closed and Heath stepped back. He trudged through the snow, then climbed into the Tahoe and dialed Nicolette.

When he explained that they'd taken Jerome to the hospital, she said, "Are you going up there?"

"I hadn't planned to. I'm pretty sure his sister will be there."

"I'd like to know how he's doing, but I don't want you to drive on these roads any more than you have to. Why don't you come on home?"

"I will," he promised.

He smiled as he drove back onto the snow-covered streets toward the house where Nicolette waited for him.

****

Heath stomped snow off his feet on Nicolette's porch and reached out to knock. Before he could, the door swung open.

"Heath? Oh, God." She went into his arms while he was still outside. "Are you okay?"

He held her tight against him. "Yeah. I'm fine."

"How's Jerome?" she asked, still clinging to him.

"He'll be okay. We'll call and check on him in a little while, once they've had time to get him to the hospital and look him over."

She nodded against his shoulder. "Thank you."

He pushed her gently from him. "Let's go inside, how about it?"

She laughed and wiped at her cheeks. "Oh, yeah."

Heath took off his coat and hung it on the rack, then Nicolette took his hand and led him to the fireplace.

"You need to warm up," she said.

He held his hands in front of the blaze. Nicolette wore jeans and a soft pink sweater. Her hair was loose and her hazel eyes glinted in the light of the fire.

"Ah, much better." Heath grinned down at her.

"Thank you for helping Jerome. I know you don't even like him."

"He's not my favorite person," Heath admitted.

"I mean, just last night you were about to kick his ass. Today, you saved his life."

"Chalk it up to the Christmas spirit, I guess."

"Right. Or, the fact that you're just a really, really good guy."

Heath grinned down at her. "Yeah, there is that."

She smiled and Heath thought of their lovemaking. Was Nicolette thinking about it too? What had happened to the easy, flirtation between them earlier?

Nicolette rubbed her hands up and down her arms and looked at her feet.

"You think we should talk about it?" Heath asked.

Her head rose, and she looked at him. She pursed her lips and smiled. "About what?"

"About what happened between us."

She stared at him steadily for a moment then slowly moved toward him. He held his breath, watching her approach. She reached up and took his face between her hands. Her thumbs gently stroked his bottom lip. "I'd rather do this."

She lifted her face and touched her lips to his. He groaned and swept his arms around her, pulling her close. Her hands moved to the back of his head. He pushed her sweater up and slid his fingers over the silky skin of her back.

He wanted to strip her bare, take her to bed and slowly explore her body...take his time like he hadn't last night. He'd been too excited. As her tongue moved over his, the pressure against his zipper increased. Damn. If he wasn't careful, the same thing would happen now.

His cell phone rang, and he swallowed back a curse.

Nicolette pulled away and looked up at him, her eyes glazed with passion. "Guess you'd better get that," she whispered.

"Do I have to?" He grinned and dug his cell out of his pocket. Alex's number showed on the display. His baby brother had lousy timing. "Hey, bro," Heath said into the phone. "What's up?"

"It's the girls." Alex's voice was filled with uncharacteristic panic. "They're missing."

"Missing? The triplets?"

"Yeah. They were in their room, and now they're gone. Shit, Heath. I'm scared."

Heath's body tensed. He pictured the tiny girls out in this snowstorm, lost, cold, afraid. Or worse. He wouldn't think that. Wouldn't entertain the thought that some maniac had taken them. "Where are you?"

"I'm near Zoe's shop. We're out looking for them, but I could use your help."

"You got it. I'll call my buddy at the force. Have him get searchers out. We'll meet you."

Nicolette looked at him worriedly, her teeth gnawing at the pad of her thumb. When Heath hung up, she said, "What is it? What's wrong?"

"Alex's daughters are missing."

"Oh, God. How?"

"I don't know. They disappeared from their bedroom."

He dialed his friend, Peter McFarland. While he waited for him to answer, he told Nicolette, "I'm going over there. I'll be back as soon as I can."

Nicolette grabbed her coat. "I'm going with you."

"No, you don't—" Peter answered the phone and Heath quickly explained.

"I'll get some guys together," Peter said after Heath finished. "Give me the address."

When Heath ended the call, he sighed and kissed Nic's cheek. "You don't need to go. It's nasty out there. Stay here where it's warm."

"No way." She shrugged into her coat. "I couldn't rest here. I'd be a nervous wreck. I'm going."

"Nic, please. I need to concentrate on finding the girls, and I couldn't do it with you there, having to worry about you."

She pressed her lips together in disapproval, but nodded.

Heath kissed her on the forehead and charged out into the biting wind, a fear like none he'd ever felt taking hold of his gut. Those tiny girls were out in this? Dear God, they were too small, too vulnerable. No matter what the reason for their disappearance, the longer it took to find them, the more likely it was that something bad had happened. *No.* He wouldn't think like that. He'd only just gotten to know his nieces. He'd be damned if he'd let anything happen to them.

****

Nicolette had to do something to keep her mind off the lost little girls and Heath out there in this storm looking for them. First, she called the hospital to check on Jerome. She managed to get his sister, who told her Jerome would be fine. Thanks to Heath. Warm affection filled her heart. Was there no end to Heath's goodness?

After ending the call, Nicolette let herself into Heath's side of the duplex to clean. For a guy, his side had remained surprisingly neat. But then again, he hadn't been there all that much. There were a few whiskers in the sink. She used cleaner to scrub that, the bathtub, and the toilet.

In the bedroom, she found his Pez dispenser on the nightstand. Heath apparently thought a lot of his friend's child, and he'd been frantic about his missing nieces. He'd had a look of pride in his eyes when he'd told her about them. Children he'd only seen a few times, and though they were his nieces, he hadn't known they existed until a few weeks ago.

She bet he'd make a wonderful father. She'd thought that about Rudy, too. They'd talked about having kids, but it never seemed like the right time. Then the next thing she knew, their 'time' for having kids was over. Rudy was dead. And here she was, close to her mid thirties without a child and without a prospective father in sight. Heath was great with kids, but did he want them? Did it really even matter since the two of them could never be together?

Although the bed was made, she pulled back the covers, held Heath's pillow to her nose, and inhaled. His scent filled her nostrils, and she smiled and hugged the pillow to her. *You are a pathetic, lovesick fool.* What the hell was she doing?

Replacing the pillow, she smoothed the spread over it, then quickly went back to her side of the duplex. She was about one boiled rabbit away from being a stalker.

Her side was fairly clean, but the drawers in her office were messy with accumulated junk. When she'd been digging out Rudy's papers, she'd noticed she'd let crap pile up. One drawer at a time, she went through the junk, throwing away what she didn't need and sorting and filing things she did.

In the bottom drawer, a black jewelry box caught her attention, and she sighed, pain welling in her chest as she withdrew it. Lifting the lid, she looked at the blue diamond ring, a gift from Rudy, although one he'd never had a chance to give her.

It had been found among the wreckage, wrapped in a beautiful box with the words, *To the love of my life*, scrawled on a white card taped to the package. Rudy wasn't normally given to sentiment like that, but their tenth anniversary was coming up; he must have been feeling particularly romantic. Maybe he'd begun to think of how lucky they were to find each other and to have made it that many years in a day and age when over half of marriages ended in divorce.

Whatever the reason, when the police returned it to her, she'd been at once thrilled and devastated. One short week away, and Rudy would have given it to her himself. She hadn't been able to bring herself to wear it. Not only was it a little flashier than the jewelry she normally wore, it was just too painful to look at every day.

She took it from the box and slipped it on the third finger of her right hand. It fit perfectly now, but she'd lost weight in the past year. At the time Rudy bought the ring, it would have been too small. She smiled. Rudy most likely had no idea what ring size she wore and knew that once he'd given it to her, it would be her responsibility to have it sized.

She slid the empty box into the drawer. The pain of loss had dulled enough that now she could enjoy the ring's beauty. Now, every time she looked at her finger, she'd think of Rudy with a fond sadness rather than the gut-wrenching agony she'd endured the first several months after his death.

Her phone rang just as she finished going through the last drawer.

"Nicolette? It's Tonya."

Tonya was one of her tenants. She was a single mom with an eight-year-old son. Her voice sounded panicked.

"Yeah, everything okay?"

"It's taking me forever to get home from work, and Josh is there by himself. I wondered if you could maybe go sit with him until I get there. I hate to ask you to get out in this horrendous weather, but he's scared now that it's getting close to dark."

Eight years old was too young to stay alone,

even when it was light, but Nicolette didn't want to criticize Tonya's mothering skills. Sometimes, people didn't have much choice.

"Hey, no worries," Nicolette assured her. "I'll head down there now."

"Thank you. You're a saint."

Heath called as soon as she hung up to let her know the girls had been found, safe and sound.

Her legs went weak with relief. "Oh, Heath. I'm so glad. Thanks for letting me know."

"I'll be there in a little while."

How to tell him that although he'd told her not to come with him, she was going out in the blizzard anyway? "I may not be here, but I shouldn't be gone long."

"What do you mean? You're not going out, are you?"

"I have to."

She explained about Tonya and Josh.

"Nic, you don't need to be driving in this." His tone was harsh and authoritative.

"She only lives at the end of the block, I'll walk."

"The snow is a foot and a half deep and piling up."

Beneath his irritation, she heard worry, and she experienced a twinge of guilt. He'd dealt with enough of that for one day, but she couldn't leave a little boy by himself in this kind of weather.

"Heath, I have to help. He's all alone." As she spoke, she bundled up in her coat and gloves.

"I tell you what, I'll drive to her house and wait with you there."

"She'll probably be home by the time you get here." Nicolette opened the front door, and a cold blast of wind slapped her in the face. She couldn't stay on the phone and tromp through the snowstorm. "I gotta go. I'll see you at home in a bit."

Chapter Fifteen

Heath cursed as he closed his phone. Damn her and her stubbornness.

He headed to the duplex, his elation that his nieces had been found now tempered by concern over Nic. He had no idea which house the neighbor lived in, or he'd head over there now, even though she'd told him not to. She'd hung up without giving him the address, so he could either cruise her neighborhood hoping to spot the right place, or go home and wait like she'd asked him to.

Even if he drove through the neighborhood, Nicolette would be inside whichever house it was, so he still wouldn't know. He just had to trust that she'd be okay, although there were people stuck all over town, and he'd heard a report on the radio that an elderly man had frozen to death.

Damn. He didn't like Nic being out in this without him.

Sure enough, when he reached the duplex, she wasn't there. He paced as he waited, casting frequent glances at the clock. Had time ever moved this slowly? He started a fire to knock the chill off the room, and to give him something to occupy his mind, other than worry over Nicolette.

After a half hour of waiting, he tried her cell. No answer. The worry turned to abject fear. If she'd planned on being gone this long, she would have called him, or she'd damned sure answer her phone, knowing how worried he would be.

She would answer it, that is, if she were able.

181

Grabbing his coat from the rack by the door, he headed out into the blizzard for the second time that evening, praying someone he loved would be okay.

****

Nicolette made her way home in the freezing, blinding snow, barely able to walk against the rush of icy wind. She should have taken Tonya up on her offer of a ride home, but Tonya's little Kia had barely made it to the house. Nicolette hadn't wanted her to get back out. Besides, she hadn't known getting home would be this difficult. Walking *to* the house had been easier than walking back. She was against the wind now, plus, the weather had worsened.

She was only a few houses away. She could see her porch light, could see Heath's Tahoe in the driveway. Thank God. He was there, and just a few short seconds away. At almost the same time a figure rushed out of her house and headed down her porch steps, her foot caught on something, and she started to fall. She reached out to brace herself, but went down with a jarring crash, making it worse when her wrist bent back with the impact. Her knee slammed into the ground, and she cried out in pain. She only had a second to notice that she'd tripped over a fallen tree branch before she heard Heath shout, "Nicolette?"

"Over here," she called, trying to keep the tears out of her voice as she attempted to struggle to her feet. She put weight on her leg and cringed when shards of pain shot through her knee. She looked up to find Heath only a few feet away, his face clenched in worry.

"Nic? Are you okay?" he asked when he reached her, squatting to help her to her feet.

She sniffed and wiped a gloved hand across her frozen cheek. "I hurt my knee." She felt like a fool. Heath had asked her to stay behind to keep her safe and warm, and she'd ventured out into the mess anyway, only adding to his problems.

"Can you walk?"

She nodded, and he supported her elbow as he helped her limp her way home.

Inside the house, she nearly cried in relief. Heath had a fire going. She'd never felt anything so wonderful, so soothing. She stood in front of the fire, shivering, her hands stretched out to its blessed heat.

"Why didn't you answer my call?" Heath asked.

"I didn't know you called." Her teeth chattered as she spoke and she realized she wasn't going to warm up much as long as she kept her wet, now useless coat on. She started shrugging out of it and Heath moved over to help her. "I guess I didn't hear it ring. It was in my coat pocket."

"I was worried sick about you," he murmured as he slid the coat off her shoulders. "Let's get you into some warm clothes. Tell me where they are so you won't have to go upstairs."

"Just get my robe, please. It's hanging on the bathroom door."

Heath disappeared up the stairs. Nicolette eased onto the couch to wait for him. He was back in seconds, holding her fluffy pink robe. She stood and he tossed the robe onto the couch. Reaching down, she gripped the edges of her sweater. Heath's hand stopped her. She looked up at him and allowed him to pull the sweater over her head. Letting him undress her felt scary, yet right. He reached behind her and unclipped her bra. Warmth spread through her, and she swallowed nervously.

When her breasts were bare, Heath stared at them for a moment, then picked up the robe and slipped it over her shoulders. Strangely, modesty didn't swoop down on her. Standing naked in front of Heath felt like the most natural act on earth. Only, she craved far more than the appreciative touch of his hands. Her body keened for his touch.

But the resolve that glinted in his eyes told her she'd have to wait. Reluctantly, she put her arms in the sleeves. Heath unbuttoned her pants. Tingles wafted across her skin. She held her breath while he tugged them down over her hips. God if only…

She pushed the longing aside, wilting a little when Heath's hands didn't glide over her thighs. When her jeans rested at her feet, she stepped free, kicked them aside, then cried out as pain shot through her knee.

Heath frowned down at her. "You're hurt?"

"Just my knee. I'm sure it's not bad."

"Let me see."

Heath closed her robe, then squatted in front of her. His voice was hoarse when he spoke, "We need to get that tended to. Here, sit in front of the fire. We also need to get you warmed up."

She nodded, trying not to show her disappointment at his chosen method of warming her up. He led her to the chair in front of the fireplace, and she settled into it.

"First aid kit?"

"Bathroom cabinet."

He disappeared and returned after a few moments. Sitting on the ottoman in front of her, he moved her robe back far enough to expose her knee. Gently, he cleaned the wound with a peroxide-soaked cotton pad, dabbed on antibiotic ointment, then bandaged it.

"There you go," Heath said. "All better now?"

"Much. Thanks."

Before releasing her, he slid his hand gently up and down her calf. She held her breath, waiting to see what would happen next, wondering if she should *make* something happen. He let go and the moment was over.

"I'll make you something to drink," he said. "Tea

or coffee?"

She forced a smile. "Hot chocolate."

He grinned. "I'll be right back."

Nicolette stared into the fire while she waited. What was she doing? What were they doing? Would their sexual relationship continue for the brief time he was here? He hadn't tried to touch her when he'd helped her into the robe. She'd made it pretty obvious that he could have. Standing bare-breasted in front of a man was a pretty good indicator. Had he just been concerned for her comfort, or did he not want to make love to her again? The look in his eyes said otherwise, as had the kiss they'd shared earlier. If he hadn't gotten the call about the girls, she was pretty sure how that kiss would have ended. But maybe now he'd had time to think things through and knew, as she did, that it wouldn't be wise to engage in a sexual relationship with no future.

Maybe not wise, but whether it lasted no more than three days, she wanted Heath, however she could get him.

Heath came in with a mug in each hand. He held one out to her, and she took it. A sip of the warm chocolate made her feel instantly better. Heath lowered back onto the ottoman.

To fill the silence, she said, "I can't wait for the Christmas party we're giving the kids. I wish you could stay around for it. There's nothing like watching the joy on their faces."

"I bet." He took a drink of his chocolate. "Did you and Rudy ever want to have kids?"

"You know, we were married for nearly ten years, and we talked about it from time to time, but we just sort of let the conversation die. It never really went anywhere. I don't think he really wanted them."

"What about you? Do you want them?"

She noticed he said 'do' not 'did,' like maybe it

wasn't too late. She thought about having kids with Heath, and a warm glow moved through her.

"I think I'd like to have kids, but it's almost too late for me. I mean, I'm not even close to being in a relationship, or getting over Rudy enough so that I can be." He flinched, and she realized she'd hurt his feelings. Well, hell, they'd had sex one time and had never said anything about it turning into more. He certainly wasn't acting like he wanted more right now.

"You know, Jesse is adopting a kid," Heath said.

"Yeah? How wonderful."

"His name is Ethan and he's thirteen. I haven't met him yet, but when Jesse talks about him, she has this glow like I've never seen. He seems to have filled a void in her life."

She frowned in thought, then took a sip from her mug. "Are you saying I should adopt?"

Heath shrugged. "I don't know what you should do, Nicolette. But you seem lost. You seem like there's a void you need filled."

She did have a void, but she had no idea what she needed to fill it. Sadness opened up in her soul, but she shook her head. "You know, right now we have a blackmailer to catch and cops to get off my back. No time for void-filling."

Heath narrowed his eyes, studying her, and she shifted uncomfortably. Did her loneliness and despair, her bleak outlook for the future, show on her face?

****

Heath's heart ached at the lost look in Nicolette's eyes. She was right. First things first, and that was to make her safe. There was nothing he wanted more than to erase the pain and fear from her life. "We'll catch the guy," he vowed.

Nicolette smiled, but the haunted look remained. "You really think so?"

He wondered what had happened to their earlier sexual banter, the promise in her voice when they'd spoken on the phone before the triplets were lost, before she'd been injured, before they'd had time to let uncertainty and awkwardness settle between them. Had the passage of time given her a chance to rethink being involved with him, even temporarily?

Heath moved his hand back to her leg and squeezed, telling himself he should let go. If she'd changed her mind, he needed to remember not to touch that soft skin of hers. But he left his hand there. "Yes, I really think so."

Even as he said the words, he knew finding the blackmailer and getting the cops off her back wouldn't take that bereft look out of her eyes. She had no family; she'd lost her husband; she had few friends. There was Donovan, Marla, and of course, Louisa, but they were all inherited. She had no one around who was her blood. He thought of his own sometimes jacked up family, but he *had* family. They were there for one another no matter what.

He knew how to take that lost loneliness out of her soul. Or at least how to try. Tomorrow, he'd call Burke, have him do some checking around. Heath would do whatever he could to find Nicolette's father.

"So, should we go over the plan again for the money drop?" Nicolette asked.

Reluctantly, he nodded. The thought of her doing something so dangerous made his gut clench. "I suppose so. I'll be watching from a short distance away. You'll have a mic in your ear that's also a transmitter, so we can communicate. You must do exactly as I tell you."

"I carry the backpack into Dave and Buster's and put it beneath the Elvis machine, then leave."

"Right. I'll watch the escalators for anyone carrying a black backpack and follow him until I can catch him alone."

"Got it."

He held her gaze, his brow furrowing. "You know I don't want you there," he said.

"Yes, but you know I have to be. Each time I've done it, I've been terrified, but this time, you'll be with me."

He hoped her faith in him wasn't misplaced. If something went wrong and his presence caused her to be hurt...or worse...he couldn't live with himself.

She watched his hand on her leg for a moment, then lifted her eyes to his. "I'm scared."

"I'll be there. I'll take care of you. We'll find the guy, find out what happened to Rudy, whether or not the two things are related."

"I don't mean I'm scared about that."

"What then?"

She held his gaze. "I don't miss Rudy as much as I did."

"Time helps. That happens."

"No. It's not time. It's you."

His mouth went dry, and his heart thudded into his ribs as he searched her face. "Nicolette..."

The look in her eyes said she wasn't just referring to the physical. Was it possible she was falling in love with him? He was afraid to bring up the word, afraid it would sever the fragile bond they'd developed. If he couldn't yet show her by his words, he could show her by his actions.

He set his mug on the end table and scooted forward on the ottoman. Slowly, he eased away the edges of her robe and heard her sharp intake of breath. Moving his hands along her legs, the insides of her thighs, then further, he teased the soft curls and she moaned, laying her head back on the chair. He removed one hand to take the cup from her and placed it next to his.

Careful not to hurt her knee, he pulled her from

the chair and laid her down on the floor. In the warm glow of the fire and beneath the lights of the Christmas tree, he made slow, thorough love to her, delighting in the sounds of pleasure that came from deep in her throat.

Afterward, Heath moved away only long enough to tug the throw from the couch and spread it over their bodies. He was loathe to release her even briefly, not knowing how many more opportunities he'd have to touch her...to listen to the soft, contented sounds of her breathing.

"That was amazing," she whispered, wiggling her body even closer to his.

"Mmmhmm," was all he could manage. His limbs felt heavy, his mind and body sated and relaxed. The only blight on this perfect evening was the knowledge that tomorrow, Nicolette would be thrust into danger, and he couldn't absolutely guarantee that he could protect her.

Chapter Sixteen

Heath leaned against the wall next to the dinosaur restaurant and watched Nicolette ride the escalator up to the entrance of Dave and Buster's. She wore jeans and a snug blue sweater beneath a black leather coat. Her blonde hair glinted in the bright winter day. A black backpack containing ten grand in cash hung off her right shoulder.

"You okay?" he asked into the mic. She wore an earpiece and even though they'd already tested it, he wanted to be sure it was still working.

"I'm fine," she said with a smile in her voice.

"Remember the plan. You drop the backpack under the Elvis game and get the hell out of there."

"I remember. You know, I've done this a few times without you." Her voice was barely a murmur, and he knew she was speaking with as little lip movement as possible.

Yes. He remembered she'd done this without him, and it caused a tightening in his gut. He couldn't stand to think of the danger Nic had been in the past four months, or that she'd faced it alone.

"I'm right here," Heath said. "I got your back."

"Yes, you do. And last night you had my front."

Heath laughed and heat spread through him. He didn't know how long this thing with Nic would last, but words couldn't describe how good it felt to hear her making sexual innuendos, and know they were based on real sex, not just the fantasies he'd entertained for fifteen years.

"No more talking. You're getting close, and he

might be watching. Take care of yourself, sweetheart."

She didn't answer but he saw her head nod just before she disappeared into the restaurant.

Time seemed to drag on endlessly, but when he looked at his watch, he discovered only five minutes had passed. *Only* five minutes? Five minutes was a very long time to go without breathing.

Nicolette appeared, sans backpack, and stepped onto the escalator. They'd made a deal that she would head to her car. The two of them wouldn't meet up until they arrived home. Heath wasn't sure if the blackmailer would be watching her; he couldn't take the chance the guy would see them speaking to one another.

Nicolette slowly meandered along the sidewalk in front of the shops, and Heath glanced back and forth from her to the escalators. Several moments passed before a youngish guy carrying a black backpack wandered nonchalantly out the door and to the escalators.

"Nic," Heath whispered into the mic. "I think I see him. This guy is about 5'8 and young. Sort of thin with shaggy dark hair hanging over his eyes. I know you never got a good look at the blackmailer, but does that sound like it could be him?"

"Hold on. I'll head that way and take a look."

"No!" Heath's heart sped up in panic. "Don't go near him. If he spots you, no telling what he'll do. Just tell me if you think it sounds like him."

He watched as she paused indecisively. "I'll be careful."

"Jesus Christ, Nic. He's going to see you. I'm too far away to do anything if he hurts you. Hell, if nothing else, you'll tip him off, and he'll run. Just stay back!"

"Okay. You're right. I'm sorry."

She continued toward the lot where she'd

parked her Jeep. Heath let out a sigh of relief.

"Thanks," he said.

"Sure thing." She gave a little wave without looking in his direction. "Good luck."

The suspect was almost to the bottom of the escalator. Heath waited until he stepped off, then quickly moved toward him, keeping a discreet distance behind. The guy headed toward the parking garage. Good. That would be an out of the way place to have a little chat without being spotted.

Heath caught up to him on the second level. Not seeing anyone around, he grabbed the guy by one shoulder and clamped a hand on his mouth. The guy yelled out, but it was muted. Heath dragged him between two SUV's and slammed him up against one.

His eyes rounded. Behind Heath's hand, he mumbled, "What the fuck?"

"I'm going to let go, but if you scream or try to get away, I'll hurt you, got it?"

The guy nodded.

Heath released his mouth and jerked the backpack off his shoulder.

"What's this about, man?" he asked, his voice frightened, but as Heath instructed, he didn't yell. "What are you doing? I ain't got nothing in there worth taking, but you can have it."

Heath yanked open the zipper and his heart sank into his stomach. A couple of textbooks and some paper. A few cans of energy drink.

"School's out for Christmas break," Heath said stupidly. It was the only thing he could think of to say. Why was the kid carrying textbooks?

"No shit." His voice was reedy but defiant. "I carry them around. Study when I can. College is tough, man."

He had the wrong guy. Shit. "Sorry. Look. This was a mistake. I thought you were someone else." He pulled two twenties from his wallet. "I know this doesn't make up for it, but here you go."

The kid took the bills. Fear cleared from his face. "I guess I won't call the cops."

Heath nodded, and the kid scurried away.

At a run, Heath went back to Dave and Buster's. The lobby was crowded with people waiting for a table, but he skirted around them and went to the right, into the game room. Making a beeline for the Elvis game, he looked beneath it. No backpack. He searched the crowd and didn't find anyone holding one.

He went into the bathroom. Two stalls were occupied, but he checked each of the empty ones. He cursed when he looked into the second. An empty backpack lay on top of the toilet seat, unzipped and deflated.

Heath cursed and snatched it up. The blackmailer had obviously taken the cash and stashed it on his person, in a heavy coat or another bag. He probably made his escape while Heath was chasing the innocent college student.

Damn and double damn.

Heath took the pack with him, hoping but doubting he could get some kind of fingerprints or something to lead him to the actual blackmailer. He'd have to send it back home to Burke, and it would take a little while, if he ever got a good print, not to mention a match.

Dejected, he slid into his car and headed to Nicolette's.

****

The detectives were waiting for Nicolette when she arrived home. *Great.*

As if her nerves weren't strung tight enough from the money drop. Another ten thousand dollars gone. But this time, at least Heath had been there with her. He'd called her while she was on the way

193

home and told her he hadn't gotten the guy. That the suspect he spotted wasn't him. Even if it had been, then what? They still couldn't turn him over to the cops. But if nothing else, Heath would figure out a way to stop him, she was sure of it.

She stepped up onto her porch where Detectives Patella and Berry stood.

"You've been gone a while." Patella smiled and pulled a stick of gum from his pocket. He slid it into his mouth and chomped down, speaking around it, "We were beginning to think you'd skipped town."

His tone was light, but his eyes were serious.

"Sorry. I was checking on one of my units." She felt dirty and guilty as soon as the lie tumbled free. It was the first time she'd lied to the police, yet they still suspected she'd killed her husband. "What can I do for you gentleman? You were just here a few days ago."

"Can we come in?" Detective Berry asked.

No. "Yes. Sure."

Nicolette unlocked the door and led the detectives inside. She didn't offer them anything to drink or a seat. She didn't want them settling in for a lengthy visit, not only because they made her nervous, but Heath might arrive any moment. She hoped.

They helped themselves to a seat, each of them settling at one end of the couch.

Patella looked around. "You have a guest staying with you?"

Nicolette frowned. "No. Why would you say that?"

"Seems like Heath King has been spending a lot of time around here. Just thought he was staying with you."

Nicolette tensed as her suspicions about being watched were confirmed. "Are the police spying on me?"

"Not spying. Keeping an occasional eye out. All part of the investigation."

"Heath is not staying here with me."

"When we interviewed him, he said he *was* staying here." Patella seemed pleased at catching her in an untruth.

"Well, yes. He's staying at the empty duplex next door."

"Ah. Why is that?"

"He's in town for the holidays, and it's crowded at his mother's house. We're old friends. It gives him a place to stay and a chance for us to catch up." Sort of a lie. *Mostly* a lie.

"Catch up?" Detective Patella's forehead wrinkled in a frown. "Exactly what is the nature of your relationship with Heath King? Are you lovers?"

Her face flushed, and she told a third lie to the detectives. "No. We're not lovers. We're close friends. Nothing more."

She'd been fooling herself these past few days. No way could she and Heath continue their affair. They'd surely be caught. A deep, troubling sadness entered her chest. She knew what she had to do.

"Are you being honest with us, Mrs. Morgan?"

"I am being as honest as I know how. I wish you would just leave me alone and find the real killers."

"Ah, so now you *do* believe your husband was murdered."

"I'm not sure. If you believe it, then it's likely true. I just mean, if he was killed, I hope you find the killer. Soon."

"Yeah. We do too."

They stood. "We'll leave you alone for now, Mrs. Morgan, but you be sure to give us a call if you decide to tell us something that will help with the investigation. Pass that on to Mr. King, too."

****

Nicolette opened the door to Heath's knock and

stepped back to let him in.

Her mood seemed troubled, subdued. Had something else happened, or was it just the unending list of problems she was dealing with?

"Would you like something to drink?" she offered, going to the bar.

"I'll take a beer."

She handed him a Budweiser and poured a glass of Chablis for herself.

When they were seated, he gave her the details of his mistaken identity encounter and finding the empty backpack.

She rubbed her forehead and sighed. "I don't think we'll ever find him."

Heath reached out and squeezed her uninjured knee. "Don't give up yet. We'll find him."

"I know you'll do your best." She smiled and took a sip of her wine, then moved her knee away from his touch. As small as the rejection was, it still caused a shaft of pain to his heart. Something had changed between them. He wasn't sure if he really expected to continue sleeping with her, but he'd hoped.

"Has something happened?" he asked.

"What do you mean?"

"You seem like something's on your mind."

She barked a humorless laugh and stood, pacing to the fireplace. "Yeah. A lot of things."

He rose and joined her as she stared into the flames. "This is different, though. You seem like you want to say something."

She took another sip from the glass, not looking at him. "What's happened between us has been amazing."

"It has. I sense a but in there."

Now she looked at him, her eyes searching his. Pain and uncertainty showed in hers. "I never wanted to ruin our friendship."

He frowned. "Is that what we've done? Ruined our friendship?"

She moved away and stalked to the patio door to look outside at the still-falling snow. "You and Louisa are really all I have left. I mean, there's Marla and Donovan, but I haven't known them as long as I have you and Louisa."

Even though she was obviously trying to put distance between them, he couldn't help himself. He walked up behind her, but resisted the urge to touch. "You've still got me, you know. I don't want the sex to ruin that either. You'll always have me."

In the reflection of the glass, her mouth tilted in a wry smile. "Even if I told you I couldn't do it anymore? That the sex has to stop?"

Another stab of pain shot through him, this one deeper. It wasn't entirely because she said the sex was over, but because she thought he would no longer want to be her friend.

"You really think that?" When she didn't answer, he took her shoulders and turned her to face him. "Do you really think I'm that kind of man?"

She looked up at him, her eyes misty with unshed tears. "Of course not. I don't think that at all." She shook her head and wiped a hand over her face. "It's just all such a mess."

"Did something else happen?"

"The detectives were here today. They were asking questions about us. About our relationship. I had to lie to them for the first time, and it made me feel guilty. Almost as if I was responsible for Rudy's death."

"Oh, sweetie." He pulled her against him and hugged her, rubbing a hand up and down her back. He tried to ignore the surge of sexual desire that washed over him. He needed to prove to her that he was still her friend and not some man who just wanted in her pants. "You have nothing to feel guilty about. Rudy's been gone for almost a year. Maybe we shouldn't have slept together, but it doesn't make you a bad person. Doesn't make you responsible for his death."

She pulled back and smiled up at him. "Of course not. It sounds crazy when you put it that way. Damn. It's just that my emotions are so raw, so mixed up. I no longer know what's right and what's wrong."

He tilted her chin up and placed a quick, chaste kiss on her lips. "Let's just take this one day at a time. You don't have to figure everything out right now, okay?"

"Okay."

"Let's concentrate on finding out who's doing this to you and let the rest take care of itself."

"Sounds good, but how are we going to do that? We don't have a clue."

Heath released her. "Not yet, but it doesn't mean we won't figure it out. Did you give me all of Rudy's papers?"

"That's everything I have."

"What about at the office—are there any papers there?"

"Yes. I left his desk alone. But anything there is probably just business. Charity stuff. You want to go through it?"

Heath shrugged. "It's worth checking into."

"Okay. Let's go now. I'll let you in, and you can search his desk."

He glanced out the window with a frown. "The weather's getting worse. Why don't you give me a key and stay here where it's safe and warm."

"You sure?"

"Absolutely."

"Okay. I'll get you that key."

She returned in a few moments and handed him a key. "I hope you understand why we can't...you know. As much as everyone loved Rudy, if they knew about us, they'd hate me."

"I do understand. We're attracted to one another, but the friendship is more important." The words were hard to say, but he felt he had to say them to help assuage her guilt. "We can't do anything to jeopardize your freedom, or your safety."

She nodded. "I am attracted to you, and you remind me of Rudy." Taking in a deep breath, she said, "I think I was lonely, missing him. Maybe I was just trying to fill the emptiness he left by making love with you."

Heath felt like he'd been slammed in the gut with a baseball bat. *Fill the emptiness, my ass.* Maybe he should remind her of what she'd said earlier...*I don't miss Rudy as much now that you're here.*

No. He wouldn't do that. He didn't know if she was putting distance between them because she was afraid of what the police might learn, or if she truly felt that way. In either case, he wouldn't push her. They had too many things to deal with right now. Later, though, he'd force her to confront her feelings. Find out once and for all if there was hope for a future together.

He'd allow her to play it her way. Not letting the effect of her words show in his voice, he nodded. "You're probably right."

He slipped the key in his jeans pocket and turned away before she could see the hurt in his eyes. Grabbing his coat, he headed outside. The frigid cold felt oddly similar to the spot where his heart once beat inside his chest.

Chapter Seventeen

Heath shivered as he made his way through the dark chill to Rudy's office. Behind the closed door, he started with the filing cabinet but only found files on the charity.

Going to the desk, he sat in Rudy's chair and opened the top drawer. Nothing but pens and office supplies there. He opened the second drawer and found a small paper-clipped stack of papers at the back.

Taking them out, he removed the clip and began thumbing through them. Most of them were receipts; restaurants, gas, ATM withdrawal slips. All were dated in the months before Rudy died. One particular receipt caught Heath's eye. It was for a hotel in town and was dated a week before Rudy's death. Why would he need a hotel room in town? A hotel receipt for a married man spelled cheating. Unless he and Nicolette shared the room for a special night out? Heath didn't want to consider the thought of his best friend cheating on his wife—he'd had enough of that kind of disappointment when he'd learned of his dad's affair—but somehow the thought of Rudy sharing the room with Nicolette was just as painful.

That was ridiculous, though. Rudy and Nicolette were husband and wife. Of course they'd shared a bed. While logic told him they'd made love countless times during their ten year marriage, he still didn't want to think about them sharing a romantic interlude at a hotel. Crazy.

He tucked the receipt in his pocket and went through the remaining drawers, but didn't find anything else of interest.

Driving to the address on the receipt, he found himself at Stratford Arms. While not exactly a five star hotel, it wasn't a seedy, trashy place either.

The lobby was deserted, and a lone clerk stood behind the counter.

"Can I help you?" he asked Heath.

"I hope so." Heath pulled out the photo of Rudy and showed it to the clerk. "Do you recall seeing this man here?"

The clerk was young and dark-skinned and spoke with a faint middle-eastern accent. "I see a lot of people here, men and women. Why would I remember this one?"

"I don't know why. I'm just asking if you do."

He shrugged. "Maybe."

Heath slipped a twenty across the counter. "I'd appreciate anything you can tell me."

The man grinned, showing a row of even, white teeth. "Ah, big spender, are you?"

Heath flipped out two more twenties.

"Yes. I know this man," the clerk said. "He was in the papers often. For his charity work. Then when he died, his picture was in the paper again."

"Right." Heath tried to hold onto his patience. "But have you seen him here? Like nearly a year ago? Was he a guest?"

The man raised his eyebrows, looking at Heath's wallet expectantly. Heath pulled out another twenty. The clerk pocketed the bills and said, "Yeah. I seen him check in here a few times."

"Was he with anyone?"

A sly grin. "Now what do you think?"

"Why don't you tell me?"

Again, the expectant eyebrow raise.

Heath jerked a hundred out of his wallet and

slapped it on the counter. "Look, I'm running out of patience and cash. If you tell me everything I want to know, this is yours. If you can't tell me any more than any thug on the street can, you're not getting another dime. I don't have time for this, so spill what you got. If I like what I hear, it's yours, and I go."

He reached for the hundred, but Heath pulled it back.

"Nope. Talk first."

The clerk sighed and looked around the still empty lobby. "Yeah. Okay. He was a guest, pretty regular. Not alone, though."

Briefly, an image of Noah Forsythe flashed through Heath's mind, but he dismissed it. Rudy may have been a lot of things, drug user, liar, maybe cheater, but he was pretty certain he was a *heterosexual* cheater.

"A woman?"

"Bingo, Einsten."

Heath took out a picture of Nicolette. "This her?"

The clerk whistled through his teeth. "Nah, but I bet he wishes it was. Chick's a looker, not that the one he had here wasn't. I wouldn't say no to a tussle with either one of them, know what I mean?"

"So it was the same woman each time?"

"Yep. And they both wore rings, but didn't act like they were married to each other. They never spent the entire night. I ain't no Einstein like you, but I guessed they were fucking around on their spouses."

"Can you describe the woman?"

"Can you give me the Franklin?"

Heath handed him the money.

"I never got that good a look at her. She always wore dark glasses and a scarf around her head. Always sort of stood back. They seemed to be in a rush, like they couldn't wait to get upstairs and fuck each other's brains out."

Heath hurt for Nicolette, but also felt betrayed by Rudy in some strange way. Almost like he did with his father. Did all men eventually cheat? Hell, Rudy had Nicolette, and he fucking cheated? What was wrong with the guy? Who had the woman been?

Heath would keep looking until he found out, but unless she was the blackmailer or the killer, he didn't really give a damn who Rudy had cheated with. His only concern was the woman he'd cheated *on*.

Moments later Heath sat in his car without starting the engine, wondering how to handle this last bit of information. Could he tell Nicolette and shatter her even further? She'd been through enough She didn't need to know her husband had cheated, on top of everything else.

Then again, it was possible she knew, or at least suspected. Most of the time, when a spouse cheated, the other knew. With or without proof, deep down inside, they knew. Often, they stayed in the marriage. Take his mother for instance. She knew without a doubt and still stayed with her husband.

His cell phone rang and he recognized Nicolette's number on the display. A mixture of pity and joy washed over him as he answered.

"Heath?" Her voice sounded shaken. "He called."

"Shit. What did he say?"

"He said I'd done well today. That he appreciated the donation, and he'd call when he was ready for another."

"Bastard. I'm on my way. I'll listen to the call when I get there."

Heath drove to the duplex and went to his side first to retrieve the recording equipment. Then he took it to Nicolette's.

"Did a number show up on the caller ID?" Heath asked as he set up the equipment.

"Yeah. It wasn't blocked or anything, so I doubt

if he called from his cell or home. I didn't try to call the number back. I didn't want to do that until you got here."

Heath took the piece of paper she handed him and dialed the number. A beep like a fax machine sounded on the other end. If the call came from a business, it was likely that the number wasn't an incoming one.

He pressed Play and they listened to the recording together. The dialogue was pretty much what Nicolette relayed. Heath tried to listen for more than what was said, concentrating on background noise. He caught the faint sound of voices in the distance. Turning up the volume, he played it once more.

"Did you hear that?" he asked Nicolette.

"What?"

"Someone talking in the background. Listen."

He played it again.

She nodded. "I heard something. It sounded like people talking."

"Can you understand what they're saying?"

He pressed Play again and as they listened, Nicolette's brows scrunched in concentration. She shook her head, and he repeated the process.

On the fourth try, Heath was able to make out the words. He repeated them to Nic, "Be gone, you miserable little beggars. Take your infernal Christmas carols and get away from my door." He sighed in frustration. "But I have no idea what that means."

"I do."

"What?"

"It's a line from a *A Christmas Carol.*"

"Someone's watching the movie in the background?"

"Didn't sound like the movie. It sounded live."

"A play? Is it showing around here?"

"Let's look it up." He followed her into the office where she booted up the computer. She typed the name of the play into the Google search engine.

"It's showing at the Northland Playhouse," she said. "Their number has the same prefix of the number that showed on the caller ID." She took out a pen and jotted the address on a sticky note. "There's a production going on now, then it shows again tomorrow."

"I'll drive over there, ask around. See if I can find a link to anyone in Rudy's life and the theater. Then I'll check with a few more people."

He thought again of what he'd learned at the hotel. Now wasn't the time to bring it up to Nicolette, if there ever would be. He wasn't sure it was something he should share with her, but he didn't feel right about keeping it quiet. Until he sorted out the pros and cons and made a rational decision, he'd keep the knowledge to himself.

"What people are you going to check with?"

"I don't know. I'll talk to the cops, but I doubt if they'll tell me anything. I'll go to the barbershop, too. They should be open tomorrow. I'll check it out."

Nicolette nodded. When she stood, it brought their bodies close together and Heath's breathing slowed as he looked down into her beautiful face, at her tantalizing lips. Rudy had cheated, it wouldn't be wrong to...

Nic stepped back, crossing her arms over her breasts as she turned away. "I'm sorry," she said quietly.

Heath wondered if she'd change her mind if she knew Rudy had betrayed her. If he told her, would that mean he could once more hold her body next to his? Feel her soft warmth as he slipped inside her?

No. He couldn't hurt her just to satisfy his lustful cravings. Cravings that would apparently never cease.

****

The parking lot of Northland Playhouse was packed. It would be too crowded inside to learn anything. Heath would come back later tonight, maybe the cars would be thinned out some and he could look for a match to the vehicles he'd seen in Salarber's lot.

He drove to the police department and asked for Patella or Berry. The dispatcher made a call, then buzzed him through to the squad room.

Patella's brows rose when he saw Heath. "Hey, it is you. I didn't believe the dispatcher when she told me who my visitor was. Sit."

Heath took the chair next to Patella's desk. "Is Detective Berry here?" he asked.

"Not right now. You got something for us?"

"I was hoping you had something for me."

Patella used a finger to smooth his mustache as he studied Heath. "We checked you out. You used to be a cop. Some of the guys downtown know you, speak highly of you." He narrowed his eyes. "You're not sniffing around on your own, are you? Impeding the investigation into Mr. Morgan's death?"

Heath had to tread carefully. "I stumbled upon some information. Might mean something, might not. I just wanted to run it by you."

"I'm all a quiver."

The corner of Heath's mouth tilted in a grin. "You know anything about Northland Playhouse?"

"I know my wife must enjoy torturing me. She drags me to that bullshit at least once a month."

"I mean, in connection to Rudy's death."

"No," Patella said slowly, but his eyes lit with interest and he scribbled something on a notepad. "Is there anything you want to tell me about it?"

Apparently, Patella didn't already have information on the theater, but he would check it out. If the blackmailer had nothing to do with Rudy's murder, it was unlikely the cops would find him through the Northland link, and Heath would be able to keep the blackmail angle under wraps.

If the blackmailer had a connection to the theater, and he was involved in Rudy's death, the police would likely find him. In that case, at least the blackmail would stop and Rudy's killer would be apprehended. Leaked publicity was a small price to pay for killing two birds with one stone.

Heath's shrug was intentionally nonchalant. "I just heard it mentioned. I'm not sure it means anything."

"You find out it does mean something, I'm sure I'll be the first to know, right?"

"Right."

Patella snorted a laugh. "So, tell me, why'd you quit the force?"

Heath thought for a moment before speaking. "You ever feel like you're trying to push a wheelbarrow full of bricks across a sand dune?"

"Every day of my life, *amigo*."

"After ten years, it occurred to me I'd never get them to the other side."

Patella shrugged. "That's when you take them out and carry them one at a time."

Chapter Eighteen

Heath was heading back to Nicolette's when his mother called. "Heath, Keeley's here."

"Okay. And..."

His mother made a frustrated *harrumph*. "I want you to meet her. You're the only one in the family who hasn't, and it's ridiculous. She's your sister."

"I'm not the only one. Dad never met her."

A heavy silence followed. Damn. He'd hurt his mother again.

"Hey, I'm sorry, Mom. I've been a little tense lately. Would coming over to meet Keeley make it up to you?"

Her voice filled with delight. "Absolutely. Besides, Alex wants you to come for dinner. He has some news." Then she said firmly, "If you show up, I'll forgive you, but don't think you can continue to smart off to me, young man."

"Yes, Mother." He smiled, but the smile disappeared when he realized what he'd just agreed to.

Dammit to hell, he would have to meet Keeley Jacobs.

****

The entire family, except for Clint, gathered in his mother's family room. The triplets attacked him with enthusiastic kisses, and his mother gave him a tight hug.

"I've missed you," she said when she released him.

"I've missed you, too. Where's Clint?" Heath asked, not letting his eyes gaze on the strange woman in the room.

"He won't be joining us tonight. He's having a rough time."

"Is he okay?"

"He will be. He just needs some alone time right now." She peered at Heath's head. "You got your hair cut. I like it."

"Thanks."

"Now come over here and meet Keeley."

Heath couldn't bring himself to speak the first time he laid eyes on Keeley Jacobs. She was a few inches shorter than he, maybe 5'7 or so, and slender, graceful. She wore beige slacks and a red blouse. Her blonde hair was pulled back in a tortoise shell clip, revealing a detail that no longer allowed him to deny her. At the top of her left ear was a tiny indentation that had been passed down through generations of the King family. His father had that same birthmark...the King notch. Like it or not, when Heath stared into those vibrant green eyes, he knew he was looking at his sister.

Keeley Jacobs reached out a slender hand, and Heath took it in a reluctant shake. "I heard you would be the hardest sell of all the King brothers," she said.

Heath was taken aback by her bluntness, but decided to respond in kind. "I don't know you, don't trust you. If you are indeed my father's child, then you're proof he was unfaithful to my mother. I don't need those kinds of reminders."

"Heath!" His mother's horrified shout cut through the thick silence.

"It's okay," Keeley said. "I understand. But you have to understand something, too. I didn't choose this any more than you. I've gotten to know the rest of your family, and I've already come to love them. I don't expect you to warm up to me right away, but I hope someday, we can at least be friends." She inhaled. When she spoke again, tears clung to her voice. "I know you're hurt, so am I. At least you were able to grow up with your father. That's more than I can say."

Heath was silent as he contemplated her words. She was right. He'd been an ass. He gave a short nod, and she smiled. It was almost like seeing his father's smile, and it gave him a chill, making him feel sad, yet oddly comforted at the same time. "I tell you what," he finally said. "I'm willing to try if you are."

"Deal," she whispered.

He turned to Alex. "So, what's your news?"

His eyes went to Zoe and he had an idea what Alex would say before he spoke. There was no mistaking the glow of pleasure on Zoe's face, not to mention, Sydney was absent from the gathering

Alex slipped his arm around Zoe's shoulder. "Zoe and I are getting married."

Heath lifted his brows. "Does Sydney know?"

Zoe laughed and Heath held out his arms to her. She hugged him, then pulled back and looked up into his face. "I'd like to ask a favor."

A grin tugged at the corner of his mouth. "If it's marrying Sydney in Alex's place, forget it."

She laughed again. "Nothing that horrible. I wondered if you'd walk me down the aisle."

A surge of emotion rose in Heath's chest, and he cleared his throat. "Sure. I'd like that very much."

"Thank you."

Zoe released him, and Heath shook his brother's hand. He'd never seen Alex look so happy. "Congratulations, man. I think you're doing it right this time."

"Hey, practice makes perfect, right?"

"You ought to know."

Alex punched him lightly in the sternum. "Shut the hell up and let's eat."

"Daddy, you're not supposed to say bad words, and hell's a bad word," Macy admonished.

The room burst into laughter.

The dinner discussion centered on the last minute changes in the wedding plans. Alex explained how he and Zoe had fallen in love, and he'd realized that Sydney wasn't the kind of woman he wanted to spend the rest of his life with, or the kind of woman he wanted around his daughters. In Heath's mind, Alex had definitely made the right choice.

Although Heath wasn't completely sold on the idea of having a new sibling, he found himself warming up to Keeley as the evening wore on. Watching her interact with the triplets moved her way up in Heath's estimation. She was great with them and they seemed comfortable with her. Like the saying went, animals and children can sense the difference between good and evil. Maybe Keeley didn't have horns and a pitchfork after all.

When it was time to leave, Heath hugged the females, except for Keeley, who received a handshake like he'd given Alex. He still had a few reservations about her; he didn't want her to think she'd completely won him over until she proved she could be trusted. After all, her arrival into their lives was precipitated by a lawsuit against his mother. That still didn't set well with him.

As he drove away from the house, Heath thought about how his mom had loved his dad, even though he'd cheated. Rudy hadn't been loyal to Nic, but Heath knew *he* could be. He and Nic deserved that chance, right? He'd learned a lot in the past few days about forgiveness and second chances. Look at Alex and Zoe. He'd never seen a couple look at one another with so much love. Then there was Keeley.

She was the one who'd had a rough life, a single mom and not getting to grow up with a great father like he had. Yet he was the one who'd sat in judgment of her.

Life was too short for that kind of bullshit thinking. He'd loved Nic for years. Maybe she cared enough about him to give it a try. He wouldn't ask her to marry him, not right off. She had a lot to lose in the community. But he had to try to convince her to give love a shot.

He should wait until the investigation was over, until he decided how to tell her Rudy had cheated, until he figured out how he could hurt someone who'd had enough hurt in her lifetime.

Right now, he would concentrate on the case.

****

Heath drove back toward Northland Playhouse. The last performance was to end at around ten, so by now, the crowd should be thinned out a great deal. Maybe the blackmailer wasn't a theater-goer, maybe he was an employee. After all, if he was using their phone, it was likely he worked there. It would be unusual for a theater guest to make a call from the house phone since everyone these days had a cell.

Heath had no idea if checking out the theater would pay off, but right now, he had nothing. He'd called information and gotten Ted Wellington's phone number, but there had been no answer, so he couldn't ask if anyone at the shop worked part-time, or had any ties, to the Northland Playhouse.

As he'd predicted, the lot was nearly empty. A small group of cars were parked at the back of the theatre, in an area reserved for employees. Heath cruised back and forth along the rows, looking for a familiar vehicle, or a person he could speak with who might know something.

A white Altima caught his attention. He'd seen that car before. White Altimas weren't all that uncommon, but this one had a dent on the right side. Heath thought he remembered seeing a similar dent in one of the cars at the salon. He fished for his notepad and pulled out the list he'd made of vehicles in Salarber's parking lot. The Altima matched one on the list, license plate number and all.

Adrenaline surged through him. This was one thing he missed about being a cop. The thrill of the chase, but mostly, the elation when closing in on the prey.

He chose a space in a darkened corner and slid the Tahoe in, shutting off his lights and the engine. Now, he'd wait.

One of the drawbacks to waiting, besides being bored as hell, was that it gave him too much time to think. He thought about Keeley Jacobs and how he hadn't wanted to like her. Not that he *loved* her or anything, but he didn't hate her, and that sucked.

It forced him to rethink his plan of action, although admittedly it hadn't been the greatest, anyway. Holding out after everyone else in the family had accepted his father's love-child—a nice girl who was totally blameless—and pouting about a mistake his father made nearly forty years ago, wasn't exactly brilliant military strategy.

He smiled. Maybe it wouldn't be bad to have Keeley around during the holidays. Jesse could use a little female competition. She'd had all the King brothers' loyalty and devotion for long enough. Although, if he was reading the signs right, one particular King brother wanted to give Jesse something a little more intimate.

Before his thoughts could turn to how and when, or whether, Heath would tell Nicolette that her dead husband had not only kept his drug use from her, but had also been banging another woman, the back door to the theater opened. A small group of people exited, then headed to various vehicles. No one went

213

to the Altima.

Heath shifted in his seat. This could take all night. What if the Altima owner had left with someone else? Heath had searched the sea of faces as they exited the theater and none had looked familiar, not like anyone he might have seen at Salarber's, but then, his position didn't allow a close look.

It only took a few moments for the door to open again. This time, a lone man exited and headed straight to the Altima. Heath's adrenaline spiked higher when he recognized the guy. He couldn't place him exactly, but he'd seen him somewhere before.

Heath started the engine and followed the Altima out of the parking lot. He didn't want to confront the guy at the theater, not with the likelihood of someone interrupting. He'd see where the car went and hope it was somewhere he could have a nice, private chat with the driver.

Heath and the Altima drove for five miles or so before the car slowed and pulled into the lot of a strip club. Great. The asshole was going to dole out Nicolette's money to pole dancers, probably a few bucks at a time.

When they both parked and the guy stepped out of the car, Heath got out and approached him as he was thumbing a key fob to lock his door. He was short, maybe in his late twenties, with close-set eyes and a long, thin nose.

"Hey, pal," Heath called. When the guy looked up, Heath recognized him. He'd been sweeping floors at the barbershop.

"What? Who are you?" The guy seemed more puzzled than frightened, but when Heath grabbed him and shoved him into the open door of the Tahoe, he made a grunting sound, then yelled for help.

Heath shoved him over and climbed into the

driver's seat. Clamping his hand over the guy's mouth, Heath held his head down on the seat while he drove around to the back of the club. An alley stretched behind the strip club and the other businesses in the shopping center. Quiet. Deserted. Perfect.

When Heath released his hold, the guy sat up and started slapping at him like a sorority girl. "Let me go. What are you doing? Who the hell are you?"

"Knock it the fuck off." Heath opened his door and tugged the guy out by his collar, then slammed him against the side of the Tahoe, retaining his grip.

"Hey, what the fuck!" He looked around the darkened alley. "Help! Please, somebody help!"

Heath grabbed the back of his hair and jerked downward until the guy was staring directly up at the night sky. "Pipe down, or I'll snap it right off."

His Adam's apple protruded with the strain of holding his neck in that position. He managed an almost imperceptible nod.

"I'll let you go," Heath said, "but if you scream again, I'll put you back in the truck and take you on a trip you'll never come back from."

Heath released him, and the guy pressed his lips together tightly as if not trusting himself to keep quiet. He blinked back tears and rubbed his throat, then peered closely into Heath's face. "I've seen you before. At the shop."

"Yeah. You sweep the floors there. What's your name?"

His lips tightened again, and Heath said, "Look, I'm going to get your name one way or the other. Might as well make it less painful on both of us."

"Barney Frost," he bit out resentfully. "What do you want with me?" He was panting heavily, fear making his eyes large and round.

"Just want to have a little chat."

The eyes narrowed. "About what?"

"Do you know Nicolette Morgan?"

Something flickered in his eyes before he looked away. "Never heard of her."

"You don't lie very well. Blackmailers should be a little better at it."

His gaze rose back to Heath's face. "What? I don't know what you're talking about."

"The hell you don't. I have video of your car going into the parking garage where you accosted Nicolette. I have your voice recorded in several of the calls you made to her. I called the voicemail on your phone and did a voice print comparison. They match. You were caught on camera at Dave and Buster's." Most of that was a lie, but Barney Frost had the look of someone who could be easily bluffed. He was.

"Okay, man. You got me. You're a cop?"

"Not a cop. Just a friend." He pulled Barney with him and reached into the open Tahoe door. Digging through his brief case, he pulled out a tape recorder, then shoved Barney sideways into the driver's seat, while he remained standing outside, blocking the guy's escape. "Tell me everything, and if you can convince me you won't bother Nicolette anymore, and that you'll pay back the money you took from her, I'll consider not calling the police."

That was also a lie. Although Nic wanted to keep the blackmail out of the media, there was no way in hell Heath would let a criminal walk, especially not one who'd threatened her and made her life hell for all these months.

"You're going to record me, man? Why, if you're not going to turn me in?"

"Insurance. As long as I have this tape, I know you'll keep your word."

Barney frowned and crossed his arms mutinously. "I don't know."

"Offer expires in sixty seconds. After that, I'll let you deal with the authorities. I have enough on you that they'll make a case. Your choice."

"Fuck." Barney reached up on either side of his head and clenched his hair in his fists. "I'm fucked either way."

"Yeah. But you'll be literally fucked if you go to prison. Talk." Heath pushed the record button and lifted his brows expectantly.

"Fine." Barney released his hair and shook his head. "I'll tell you everything. You got a smoke?"

"No. I have Pez candies."

"What?" He frowned and shook his head again. "Never mind. Okay, here goes. I work in the shop right? Cleaning up. Half the time, the stylists don't even know I'm around. I see Rudy Morgan come in every six weeks or so, and he's this big shot, you know? Noah does his hair and everything's normal in the beginning. Except, after a while, they seem sort of chummy. I always figured Noah was gay, but he swears he's not. Don't know why he'd deny it. These days, there's no shame, no reason to hide it. Either way, though, I don't think for one second Morgan has a gay bone in his body. One day, I'm leaving the same time as Noah and I decide to follow him, keeping my distance, you know?"

When Heath nodded, the guy went on, his voice becoming more animated as if now that he was caught, he enjoyed telling the story.

"Noah drove to a park at the river. He got out and walked down the bank toward a guy standing near the water. I'm still behind him, but staying back. I'll be damned if it wasn't Rudy Morgan waiting on him. I didn't know if they were going to start some guy on guy sex or what, but Noah pulled out this pipe and the two of them start smoking crack. I couldn't fucking believe it."

Barney shook his head and gazed out the windshield of the Tahoe with a faraway look, as if picturing the scene in his mind.

"And?" Heath prompted.

"Anyway. Long story short, I knew the guy was rich. I don't make jack shit with both jobs combined. I followed them a few more times, took some pictures, and called Morgan. I didn't even feel bad. The asshole ran a charity to get people off drugs, and he was a crack head himself. So, that's when it started. Blackmailed him for ten G's a month."

"What'd you do with the money? You're still working those jobs that don't pay shit."

"Yeah. For now. I was going to wait until I had a hundred grand, then get the fuck out. Go to some Mexican island or somewhere in the tropics and disappear forever. Margaritaville and shit, know what I mean?"

"So why did you kill Rudy. He was paying, right?"

Barney's eyes got big and round. "Kill him? I didn't. No fucking way. Blackmailing just about made me piss my pants. No way could I kill someone."

"But you can attack helpless women in a parking garage." Heath bit back his fury at the thought of this asshole's hands on Nicolette.

"I didn't hurt her, man. Just wanted her to know I was serious. She seemed about to put a stop to it."

"You say Rudy deserved it, so you didn't feel bad. But what about Nicolette? She'd lost her husband. She kept the charity going, and she wasn't doing drugs. You sleep okay at night after what you've done to her?"

He shrugged. "Once I got going, I didn't want to stop until I had enough to get the fuck out of here for good."

"Yet you left clues all over the place. You practically drew me a road map right to you."

"So, what was it that tipped you off?"

"Last call you made, the play was going on in

the background. Tracked you here. Noticed your car was parked at Salarber's when I was there before. You didn't exactly cover your tracks that well. You made some really dumb ass moves."

"Hey, dude, if I was a fucking Mensa candidate, would I be sweeping hair off floors, or for that matter fucking talking to you? That's a clear sign I didn't exactly pull off the crime of the century."

"But you expect me to believe you didn't kill Rudy."

"No way I did that. I freaked when he died. For one, I didn't want to be blamed. For another, that meant no more cash. Then it occurred to me his widow would have cash, if nothing else, with the life insurance. I gave it some time to cool off and started in on her. I was about twenty thou away from the hundred grand, and I'd have been fucking history."

Heath shut off the recorder and grabbed Barney by the back of his head.

Barney jerked as if shot through with electricity. "What the fuck you doing, man?"

"I lied about the cops."

While Barney was trying to assimilate this piece of information, Heath slammed his head into the open door and knocked him unconscious. He pushed his limp body into the passenger seat and slid behind the wheel.

Heath considered forcing Barney to take him to his stash, so he could retrieve Nicolette's money. But if he did that, there would be no proof of Barney's crime, other than the tape. Heath wanted all the evidence against this weasel they could get. It was best to let the cops find the cash in Barney's possession. With that in mind, Heath drove his unconscious hostage to the police station.

Chapter Nineteen

Nicolette dug out the gigantic bag of toys for the Christmas party. She gathered wrapping paper, tape, scissors and bows and spread everything out on the floor. Marla was coming over in the morning to help her wrap gifts, but Nicolette would do part of them tonight. She needed something to keep her mind occupied while she waited to hear from Heath.

The phone call from the theater was their first good clue. Would it lead him to the blackmailer? If so, what would happen then? Most likely, the police, therefore the media, would be involved. Then everyone would know about Rudy's drug use and the charity would be in trouble. The alternative was letting a criminal go free. Talk about a rock and a hard place.

One thing she definitely hadn't counted on in all this mess was falling in love with Heath. Or maybe she'd always been in love with him but hadn't allowed herself to acknowledge it until now. Either way, it was both wonderful and terrible, scary and thrilling. Mostly, though, it was futile. In spite of the level they'd taken their relationship to, nothing had been said about love, about the future.

In two days, Heath would be gone, and Nicolette would have to start the grieving process all over again. For the first time, she truly knew what Elvis meant when he sang about a blue Christmas.

She would always have this last week, though, the memories of what it was like to make love with Heath, to see her through the long lonely nights.

Barring a miracle, that was all she'd have. She'd told Heath he was a replacement for Rudy, but that had been a lie. If anything, fifteen years ago, Rudy had been a replacement for him.

She'd wrapped over half the gifts and was putting the finishing touches to the package that held an X-Box 360 when a knock sounded at the door.

Through the peephole, she saw Heath standing on the porch. She jerked the door open and impulsively went into his arms. Releasing him, she stepped back to let him in.

"I found him," Heath said.

"You found him? The blackmailer?"

"Yeah."

"Who was it?"

"His name's Barney Frost. He worked at Salarber's." Heath sighed and scrubbed his hands over his face. "How it came about is a long story, and I'm drained. Give me a minute, and I'll explain it all."

"Did he kill Rudy?"

"I don't know yet. I don't believe he did, but the police are checking into it."

"The police?"

"I had to. If it comes out about Rudy's drug dealing, then so be it. I don't know how we could stop or punish the guy otherwise."

Nicolette closed her eyes tightly as fear clawed at her stomach. "I know. You're right. We'll just have to do as much damage control as possible and hope for the best. I just can't stand the thought of what will happen to all those people. I wanted to make the charity successful, and now I don't know if it will survive."

"No matter what happens, it's not your fault. You've done the best you could. You've paid your dues, protected Rudy's reputation as long as you could. Whatever debt you think you owed, it's been paid. You've suffered enough for it, and now it's in the hands of the authorities."

She sighed. "I suppose. Thanks, Heath. I can't tell you how much I appreciate what you've done. You saved me."

Heath smiled. "Hey, what are friends for?"

There was that word again. *Friends*. Hoping for anything more had been foolish.

Nicolette forced an answering smile on her face. "Why don't you come in and sit down. When you feel up to it, you can fill me in on the details of what went down tonight."

****

Heath spent nearly an hour telling Nicolette how he'd tracked Barney Frost and why he didn't think the guy had anything to do with Rudy's death. She listened attentively, asking questions and making comments from time to time.

Once he was done, an awkward silence settled between them. Nicolette seemed deep in thought, as though she had something on her mind, but couldn't bring herself to say it.

He couldn't stop thinking about what he'd learned about Rudy's affair. Who was the woman Rudy had been cheating on Nicolette with? What kind of woman could possibly tempt a man who had Nicolette in his bed? And, how could Heath bring himself to tell Nicolette and pile more hurt on after what she'd been through?

One thing he knew for sure. He wouldn't tell her tonight. They'd dealt with enough turmoil for one evening. They needed to assimilate all that had happened before introducing a new catastrophe. Not to mention, there was still the matter of Rudy's death. Accident or murder? If murder, who? Knowing the police could knock on Nic's door at any minute and haul her to jail was unthinkable for him.

It must be terrifying for her.

"I'm exhausted," Nic said. "I know you must be too. We should probably go to bed."

He caught her eyes, trying to detect if there was invitation in her statement. He saw none, and he wasn't going to be the one to make a move. It was as though they were stepping through a minefield, one wrong move and everything would blow to pieces. He couldn't tell her Rudy had cheated, yet he couldn't be with her again that way until he did.

"Goodnight." He stood. Nicolette stood with him.

She gave him a quick peck on the cheek and he retired to his side of the duplex. He brushed his teeth and stripped off his clothes. Dropping heavily into bed, he lay in the darkness with an arm over his forehead, staring at the ceiling.

He felt like things between he and Nicolette were unresolved, but for now, he had to leave it that way. Maybe after they put some distance between them and had a chance to clear their heads, they could talk about a future. He might even admit that he loved her, that he had from the first moment he laid eyes on her.

For now, though, he'd go back to Oklahoma as planned. He'd make the deal for his security firm and then he and Nicolette would see where they were.

He might be leaving her on Christmas, but there was no way he'd be leaving Nic alone. He took his cell phone from the nightstand where it was charging and dialed Burke.

"Hey, man," he said when Burke answered. "Did I wake you?"

"Nah. I never sleep. I just hang out with my phone in my hand, waiting for you to call."

Heath chuckled. "That's good, because I need to know if you found Robert Brandon, Nicolette's dad."

"I found his number, and left a message. Haven't

223

heard back."

"Check again tomorrow, okay? Let me know as soon as you hear anything."

"You got it."

They hung up and Heath went back to staring at the ceiling. It was a long, torturous time before he finally fell asleep.

****

Nicolette's mood was morose when she opened the door to Marla's knock. She hadn't seen Heath that morning. After the awkwardness between them and the climactic turn of events, he probably needed some down time.

"Ready to get those gifts wrapped?" Marla asked brightly.

"Sure. I wrapped a few last night, but I saved plenty for you."

"Great." Marla rolled her eyes, and Nicolette laughed.

Pulling out the remaining gifts and the wrapping tools, Nicolette carried them to the table, and the two of them got busy.

They chatted as they worked. Suddenly in the middle of a sentence, Marla stopped talking. Nicolette looked at her. She was staring at Nicolette's hand, her face pale, her mouth frozen in a stricken O.

"What's wrong?" Nicolette asked.

Marla reached out a trembling hand and took Nicolette's right hand in hers.

"Where did you get that?" Her voice was hoarse with some unidentifiable emotion.

"From Rudy."

"Rudy gave it to you?"

"Yes," Nicolette said, puzzled. "It was his last gift to me."

Marla's grip was tight. Nicolette tugged loose from her hold.

"He bought it for you?" Marla asked, not taking her gaze off Nicolette's finger.

"Yes. Well, he had it on him when he had the accident. He hadn't had a chance to give it to me yet."

Marla shook her head slowly from side to side. Tears filled her eyes and spilled down her cheeks. "Not for you."

"What? What's the matter with you?"

Marla stalked over to her purse and dug around. Turning, she thrust a jewelry box toward Nicolette. Frowning, Nicolette took it and lifted the lid. Inside was an expensive, gorgeous pair of earrings. Blue diamond earrings. An exact match for the ring.

Nicolette's frown deepened. "I don't understand."

Marla's eyes shimmered with tears. "He said they were the exact color of my eyes." She swiped a hand over her face. "God. I miss him."

"Marla..." Nicolette dropped the box onto the coffee table, not wanting to touch the object that was starting to represent something she didn't want to acknowledge.

Marla lifted her chin and met Nicolette's gaze. "The ring wasn't for you. It was for me."

Cold realization twisted through Nicolette's belly. She remembered the note that had been found with the ring. *To the love of my life...*

"Jesus Christ," Nicolette whispered. "You and Rudy were having an affair."

****

Heath stepped out of the shower and was toweling off when a loud knock sounded on the door connecting his unit to Nicolette's.

He tucked the towel around his waist and hurried to answer. Nicolette stood on the other side. Her face was streaked with tears, and she twisted her hands together. Her entire body visibly trembled.

"Nic? Sweetie, what's wrong?"

Her gaze lowered to the towel and stayed there a moment, then moved back to his face. She took a deep breath.

"Rudy..." She shook her head, wrapped her arms around her body.

"Hey, come here." Heath took her arm and led her into the room. "Tell me what's happened."

She swallowed and closed her eyes. When she opened them, the hazel depths were filled with pain. "Rudy and Marla were having an affair. He cheated on me, Heath. With Marla."

Shit. So, the other woman was Marla. Heath should have figured that out. Some detective he was. The 'who' didn't really matter, though. The fact was, Nicolette knew, and she was obviously shattered. How much more could she take?

He drew in a long breath. Time to come clean. He had to tell her that he knew. She might hate him, but she had a right to know.

"I'm so sorry." He pulled her against him and slipped his arms around her, trying to ignore how her body felt with the insubstantial barrier of the towel between them. He'd better hold her while he could. After his confession, it was unlikely he'd have another chance. "There's something I need to—"

"No." She drew back slightly, but stayed in his embrace. Her eyes locked on his, and she reached a hand up, running her fingers over his lips. "Don't talk. I don't want any more talking."

Her lips replaced her fingers and she kissed him, hard and fierce, thrusting her tongue between his lips and pressing her body more fully against his.

With every ounce of strength he possessed, he broke the kiss and took her shoulders, setting her away from him.

"Wait. I have to tell you something."

"No." She reached up and pulled his head down

to hers, once again locking onto his lips. Her hand moved to the towel and tugged it loose. It dropped to the floor, and his erection sprung free, pressing against her clothing, the friction making him harder than he'd ever been in his life. "Make love to me," she whispered against his lips. "I need to feel you inside me. Now."

With a groan, he undid the buttons on her blouse and his searching hand found her soft breasts. He tugged the bra away and kneaded her nipples with his fingers.

She moaned, and they stumbled to the bed, still locked together, hands groping, seeking, clothes peeled away until she was as naked as he was.

He fell with her onto the bed and kissed her deeply, filling himself with the sweetness of her hot, wet mouth. It was wrong. Oh, so wrong to make love to her before telling her he'd known about Rudy's affair, but God help him, there was no way he could stop.

When they came up for breath, she moved on top of him, guiding him into her. As she rocked against him, she gasped out, "For the first time, I'm able to make love to you without feeling guilty. I love you, Heath. I've loved you all along."

He closed his eyes. She'd said it. The words he'd longed to hear. A shudder moved through him and he gasped out, "Oh, God, Nicolette. I love you, too."

And then there was no more talking as Heath was swept away into the wonder that was Nicolette.

Chapter Twenty

Nicolette's soft warm body lay pressed against Heath's. Her slow even breathing was the only sound in the still aftermath of their lovemaking. Heath didn't want this moment to end. He could happily die right now. No moment would ever be as perfect as this. Especially not after he told Nic the truth.

"So, how long have you loved me?" she murmured. Placing a light kiss on his shoulder, she ran her fingers in lazy circles through the hair on his chest while he slowly stroked his fingers along the velvet skin of her arm.

He smiled against her hair. "Since the moment I saw you."

She leaned her head back to look into his face. "And you let Rudy have me?"

"Yeah. Dumb move on my part, huh?"

"Yeah, dumb move. But you've more than made up for it."

They fell silent again until he finally gathered the courage—or maybe it was the idiocy—to tell her. "There's something you should know."

"Oh?" Running a hand over his stomach, she felt her way down to his groin. "Like maybe that you're about ready to do it again?"

He sucked in a breath, already growing hard beneath her touch. Gritting his teeth, he reached down and gently removed her hand. "I'm always ready for you, sweetheart. But we should talk first."

Rising up to her elbows, she looked at him.

"Okay. We'll talk. This sounds serious."

He couldn't say it with her tantalizing, nude body so close to his. He rose and swung his legs over the side of the bed. Plucking his jeans off the floor, he stood and slipped into them. He turned and stared down at her, shoving a hand through his hair.

He took a deep breath. "Nicolette, about Rudy's affair…"

A shadow of pain crossed her face. "Yes?"

"I knew."

She frowned. "I don't understand."

"I knew about the affair before you told me."

Coming abruptly to a sitting position, she pulled the sheet up to her chin. "You knew Rudy cheated on me? This whole time you knew, and you didn't tell me?"

He shook his head. "I found out yesterday."

Tears sprang to her eyes, and she clamped her lips together, taking a deep shuddering breath before speaking. "How?"

"I found a hotel receipt in his papers. I went to check it out and…" He shrugged.

"Oh, God." She shook her head and leapt from the bed, dragging the sheet with her. "Oh my, God. You knew and you didn't tell me? How could you do that to me? How could you keep something like that from me?"

"I don't know. I'm sorry. I just couldn't bring myself to tell you. I tried but—"

"If you told me, then maybe I wouldn't have fucked you, right?" Her voice shook with rage and tears. She paced the floor, shaking her head, running one hand through her hair while the other kept the sheet over her body. "Dear God. Of all the people I thought I could trust." She whirled on him. "I can't believe I said I *loved* you. That I actually believed you loved me."

"Nicolette, I do love you. I just didn't want to

hurt you. You've been through so much, were already dealing with enough. I wanted to keep you from suffering any more than you were."

He went to her and reached out to take her in his arms, but she jerked away from him.

"No! Don't touch me. Don't you ever touch me again."

A sharp pain cut through his body, and he fought back tears of his own. "Please. You have to listen to me."

"Get out!" She pointed to the door. "I want you the fuck out of here, now."

"You don't mean that. I know you're hurting, but if you just calm down and think this through, you'll understand I was trying to protect you."

She attempted an incredulous laugh, but it came out as a sob. "I think I've had about enough of your kind of *protection*." Gathering the sheet around her hips, she turned and stalked to the door. Without turning to look at him, she said, "Get your shit, and get out. I don't want to see you again. I won't calm down, and I won't change my mind. You've gotten all you're getting from me, Heath. I mean it. I never want to see you again."

"Nicolette—"

But she jerked the door open and stormed out, slamming it behind her.

Deflated, he sank to the bed, despair making his limbs weak and his gut feel like it was filled with hot lead. He was a fool. The last thing Nic needed was for someone else to betray her, and that was exactly what he'd done. He rubbed a hand over his eyes, not even ashamed to feel the dampness of tears. He'd blown it. For a few brief moments his fantasy had been in his reach, now it was gone forever.

****

With all the enthusiasm of a condemned man preparing for the gas chamber, Heath dressed for his brother's wedding. He'd gone to his mother's house shortly after he'd broken Nicolette's heart and had done his best to respond appropriately to the joyous wedding talk. As pleased as he was for Alex and Zoe, seeing all the wedding decorations and hearing the buzz of preparations had only deepened the yawning hole of grief in his soul. He'd gone for a drive earlier that evening, needing some space, and had nearly been late getting back in time for the wedding.

Although they hadn't spoken of marriage, for a little while, he'd imagined he and Nicolette would someday be doing all the sappy shit the people downstairs were doing. *How's that working out for you, asshole?*

He shook his head and made an effort to push away his black mood. The family he loved was counting on him. He'd promised Zoe he'd walk her down the aisle. Parade her to her place at Alex's side while a handful of guests looked on with sickeningly sweet smiles.

As much as Heath wanted his brother to find happiness, putting on a fake smile and pretending his heart was in the celebration felt like climbing Mt. Everest. The whole ordeal only reminded him of the chasm between him and Nicolette. Drove home exactly what he couldn't have. There was nothing he wanted to do less than watch two people vow to love one another till death parted them. Come to think of it, death sounded pretty appealing right now.

He checked himself in the mirror and straightened his tie. His face was drawn in lines of tension. He tried on a smile but it looked like a death grimace. Turning away from the mirror, he dropped to the bed to put on his shoes.

What was Nicolette doing right now? It was Christmas Eve. She was all alone, sad, and no doubt feeling lost. This was her first Christmas without Rudy. It would have been hard enough without all

Alicia Dean

the other shit, but Heath had made sure to heap on a little more pain. At least he'd caught the blackmailer. Nic wouldn't have to worry about that. They still didn't know who'd killed Rudy, and although there was nothing to indicate the killer was a threat to Nicolette, Heath couldn't get rid of the worry that tugged at his gut.

She shouldn't be alone tonight. He would call Marla, but of course, other than him, Marla was the last person Nic wanted to be with. Nicolette didn't really have anyone else. Louisa wasn't able to go over there. Donovan? He seemed to care about Nic.

Nicolette had given Heath Donovan's number in the list of people he may need to talk to during the investigation. Picking up his cell, he dialed the number.

When Donovan answered, Heath said, "Hey, Donovan, this is Heath King."

"Heath? How you doing, man?"

"I'm good. I'm worried about Nicolette, though."

"Oh? What's wrong with her?" Heath detected concern in his voice. He did care about her.

"I'm not sure. We had a disagreement, and she's alone. I know it's Christmas Eve and all, but I wondered if you could do me a favor. You have plans tonight?"

"Nope. Nothing going on. We don't do much until Christmas day. What do you need?"

There was nothing to indicate he was distressed. Maybe Donovan was the only person in town who didn't know his wife had been screwing Rudy.

"I wondered if you would go see Nicolette, maybe spend the evening with her. She's alone, and this is a rough time of year for her."

"Yeah. I imagine so. Her first Christmas without Rudy. What'd you two fight about, if you don't mind my asking?"

He minded all right. No way was he going into

232

the whole sordid thing with Donovan. In order to do that, he'd have to shatter his world by telling him about his wife's affair. He'd done enough world shattering for one day.

"It was a stupid misunderstanding. No big deal, but I can't be with her. My brother's getting married tonight."

"Hey, that's great. Tell him congratulations. And, yeah, I'll be happy to go stay with Nicolette. Marla's not home, and I'm kind of at loose ends myself."

"Great. Thanks."

"No problem."

"One more thing," Heath added. "It might be best if you didn't tell her I asked you to go over there."

"Okay. Yeah. Got it."

Heath felt marginally better when he hung up the phone. If he couldn't be with Nicolette, at least he knew she wouldn't be alone.

He took in a deep breath and released it, then headed to the door. Time to perform his brotherly duty. He hoped he wouldn't make a mess of that, too.

****

Nicolette sat on the floor in front of the Christmas tree, staring at the twinkling lights, pretty much the same thing she'd been doing since she'd stormed away from Heath.

Throughout most of the day, the lights had blurred behind her veil of tears. The tears had stopped hours ago, and now she just felt hollow and drained, like a dried husk of corn. This was better than the pain, though. She could live with the numbness.

She'd gone over it all in her mind. Heath telling her he loved her. The way he'd stroked and held her, she'd believed he really meant it. But how could he love her and keep something like that from her? Let

233

her go on thinking Rudy's only sin had been his drug use? She'd had to find out from Marla, in the most devastating, humiliating way possible. All because Heath had chosen to deceive her.

She'd lost her parents, she'd lost Rudy, and she'd lost Marla's friendship, although she'd come to learn that Marla had never been a true friend.

The loss that cut the deepest, the one from which she would likely never recover, was losing Heath. She'd had his friendship, then his love, and now they were both gone.

Yeah, that's it. Feel sorry for yourself. How about a nice pity party for Christmas? Right. That was sure to make everything better. She barked a laugh, but it only made her throat hurt. She hadn't had anything to eat or drink all day. Probably not a good idea.

She was debating whether to try choking down some food, or at least a drink when a knock sounded on the door, causing her to jump.

Who could that be on Christmas Eve? Her heart started to pound, the most active it had been since it had cracked this morning.

Heath? Was he here to try one more time to convince her he was sorry? Too bad. She wouldn't let him in. To hell with him.

The knocking continued and a man called out, "Nicolette? Are you in there?"

Not Heath. Donovan. Poor, sweet, Donovan. Did he know about Rudy and Marla? Probably not. Not yet, anyway. Maybe she should tell him. Why should she be the only one suffering?

Because Donovan was a good man, and he didn't deserve to be hurt. No, she wouldn't tell him. She'd do the same thing Heath had done for her. *Protect* him. It was Marla's place to tell him, anyway.

Donovan banged again, louder this time, and she forced herself to her feet.

On legs that were shaky from despair and lack of activity, she made her way to the door.

Cold wind rushed in as she opened it, and Donovan stared down at her in concern. "Are you okay? You didn't answer my knock. I was worried about you."

"I-I'm fine. I was just..." She motioned behind her with her hand, but dropped it when she realized she wasn't sure what she was going to say. "Come in."

He entered, and she closed the door behind him, then led him to the living room.

"Marla's out doing some last minute shopping," he said. "I thought I'd come hang out with you. You busy?"

"No." She forced a smile. "Not busy at all. Have a seat."

He took off his coat and laid it over the back of the couch. They sat, and he peered at her with a frown. "Is everything okay?"

"Yeah. Sure."

"You seem upset. Did something happen between you and Marla?"

Her eyes flew to his face. Did he know? "Why would you ask that?"

"She seemed upset when she came home after seeing you. She wouldn't talk to me about it. Now you seem bothered about something. Just wondered."

"No. Nothing happened."

Now she was doing the same thing Heath had done, deceiving someone she cared about. Only this was different. Heath owed it to her to tell her. He would have been saving her pain. If she told Donovan, she would ruin his marriage. She was tired of pretending and wanted the whole thing out in the open, but she wouldn't be the one to tell him. That was on Marla.

"Hey, you hungry?" Donovan asked. "How about we go grab a bite to eat?"

Nicolette shoved a hand through her hair and looked down at the sweats she wore. She must look a mess. She'd showered after her roll in the sack with Heath, but hadn't bothered to even run a comb through her hair. "I look like hell. I can't be seen in public."

"You look great." Donovan smiled. "Not that many restaurants are open on Christmas Eve, anyway, so we can just go to a fast food place. You don't have to get out of the car. I'll run in and grab our food. At least you'll be getting out of the house. The fresh air will do you good. Plus, I'm guessing you haven't eaten much today."

She shook her head. She hadn't eaten anything. "I'm not hungry."

"Maybe not, but I am. You wouldn't let a friend starve, would you?" He stood and offered his hand. "Come on, let's get you a blast of that nice frigid air."

She forced a smile and let him pull her to her feet.

They both donned coats and Donovan held the door open for her while she braved the winter outside. Donovan tried to engage her in conversation as he drove, but all she could manage was a brief nod from time to time. The tears she'd emptied from her body wanted to surface again. She just *thought* she had no more left. Somehow, being out of the house, even being with Donovan, made her loneliness increase. The soft Christmas music playing on Donovan's radio, the Christmas lights outside the window twinkling amidst the lightly falling snow, the few people who were out, no doubt finishing up last minute holiday errands so they could settle in with their families, only magnified what she didn't have.

"Is LC Burgers okay?" Donovan asked.

She hadn't even been aware they stopped, but they sat in the parking lot of her favorite burger joint.

"Sure, yeah. That's fine. Just get me whatever you get."

Not like she'd be able to choke it down, anyway, whatever it was. The lump in her throat was growing. Heath was at a wedding right now, surrounded by loving family and friends. Their friendship, and whatever else had been developing between them, was truly over. Forever. Tomorrow he'd go back to Oklahoma City and she'd never see him again.

Wasn't that what she wanted? No, not what she wanted, but after what he'd done, it had to be.

The tears surfaced and she searched her purse for a tissue. When she didn't find one, she opened the glove compartment, shuffling through the items inside. She tugged out a napkin to wipe her eyes, knocking a cell phone out in the process. Her hand reached out to catch it, but it tumbled to the floorboard.

"Shit."

Barely able to see in the dim lighting of the car, she dabbed at her eyes and felt around until her fingers touched the phone.

She was about to shove it back into the glove compartment when its familiarity caught her attention. This wasn't the phone she'd seen Donovan use, but she'd definitely seen one like it before. It was identical to the one Rudy had. Of course, it couldn't be Rudy's. Maybe this was one of Donovan's old phones she'd never seen before.

The words made sense, but something told her they weren't true. A sickening dread filtered through her heart, compelling her to find out. She flipped the phone open, but the power was off. Pressing down on the 'End' button, she waited as the lights and noise announced the phone was powering up.

When the cell phone was fully on, she stared down at it, her body beginning to tremble with the awful realization. The phone laying in her palm most definitely wasn't Donovan's. It belonged to Rudy. The one missing since the accident.

Chapter Twenty-One

Nicolette stared at the phone. Rudy's wallpaper—a movie poster for the tear-jerker movie *The Notebook*—stared back at her. She'd always teased him about having such a girlie photo on his phone. She grinned at the memory as tears rose to the back of her throat.

Then, fear, confusion and betrayal overtook nostalgia. There was only one reason Donovan would have Rudy's phone. Donovan had been with Rudy the night of his accident. If Donovan had been with Rudy that night...if he'd lied all this time...if he'd kept Rudy's cell phone...

Dear God.

Donovan had killed him.

Her hands trembled as her mind tried to work out her best course of action. Had Donovan known about the affair all along? Was that why Rudy had died, because he couldn't keep his dick in his pants?

She should call Heath. Or should she? The last conversation they'd had, she'd screamed at him that she never wanted to see him again. Now she was going to call him begging for his help? No. She should call 911.

Before she could decide, she saw Donovan come out of the restaurant, heading for the car.

She looked at the phone. Rudy had Heath in his speed dial on number two. Her finger pressed the 'two' and sure enough, Heath's name popped onto the screen.

"I hope you like grilled onions on your

cheeseburger," Donovan was saying as he climbed into the driver's seat. "I also got you fries."

If she called 911, she'd have to speak to them and Donovan would hear her and get to her before help arrived. She put her thumb on the Send button and whipped the hand holding the phone behind her back.

"Thanks." She attempted a nonchalant smile but wasn't sure she pulled it off. "That sounds great."

Over and over, her thumb pushed the Send button. She wouldn't be able to speak to Heath, but if he saw multiple consecutive calls from Rudy's phone...hell, when he saw *one* call from Rudy's phone, he'd realize something was wrong and, hopefully, he'd come to her rescue.

A twinge of guilt shot through her. Heath was probably smack dab in the middle of a wedding right now.

The ride home was silent and when they arrived at Nicolette's, Donovan carried the food inside. Nicolette continued to hold the phone behind her back, managing to shrug out of her coat while keeping the phone tucked out of sight.

Donovan placed the bags on the coffee table, then frowned as he peered closely at Nicolette. "Nicolette? Is something the matter?"

Her terror must have shown in her expression, because realization dawned on his face. In place of his puzzlement, she saw a cruelty she'd never known him capable of.

"Ah," he said with a slow nod. "You know."

The guilt went away, and her thumb began to frantically press the Send button. *Please, Heath, please figure it out, and please don't be so mad at me you won't bother to respond.*

****

Amelia had managed to decorate the family room in a Christmasy, weddingish way that seemed to work well, like Santa and Mrs. Claus had used Martha Stewart for their wedding planner.

The triplets looked cute in their frilly dresses. Zoe was gorgeous. She wore his mother's wedding gown and stared adoringly up at Alex as Judge Parker performed the ceremony, his balding head reflecting the shine from the lights above. On the other side of Zoe, Jesse was radiant in a blue beaded gown, though Heath couldn't help notice that her blue eyes didn't shine with the same joy they normally did. Had Clint hurt her, in spite of Heath's warnings? If so, his eldest brother would have him to answer to.

Heath returned his focus to the ceremony and tried to keep his mouth spread in a smile, but the glow on the faces of the bride and groom only magnified the hollow ache in the pit of his stomach.

The judge read passages from the Bible, then Zoe and Alex spoke their vows. Heath nearly grinned at the incongruous sound of his suave little brother speaking the flowery words. On his cue, Heath handed Alex the ring.

Heath's cell phone vibrated with a low buzzing sound, but he reached in his pocket to silence it, watching as Jesse handed Alex's ring to Zoe.

After Zoe slipped the ring on his finger, Alex turned to where the girls stood, each of them in different states of restlessness, shifting and tugging at the edges of their dresses.

"Michaela, come here, please," Alex said.

When she moved toward him, Alex went down to one knee.

Placing a hand on her father's shoulder, Michaela said, "Can we be done yet?" The too-loud whisper carried in the still room and laughter erupted.

Alex chuckled and placed a chain holding a locket around her neck. "Just about, sweetie."

As his baby brother performed the same ritual with his other two daughters, Heath tried hard to blink back tears. He gritted his teeth and blew a breath out between his lips. Since his arrival in Kansas City, he'd become a blubbering fool. Time to haul his ass back to Oklahoma. In less than twenty-four hours, he'd do just that.

His phone continued to buzz and he frowned. What the hell? He was in the middle of his brother's wedding, for God's sake.

Finally, he discreetly pulled the cell from his pocket and looked at the display.

A chill coursed through him, and he found it hard to draw breath. Rudy's phone number appeared, over and over.

Fuck. Nicolette?

Mumbling a quiet apology, Heath slipped away from the wedding and rushed out the door, not looking back to see the reaction of the wedding guests, or the bride and groom.

He punched in Nicolette's number, his heart pounding as he waited for her to answer.

When the call went to voice mail, his worry increased. Was she ignoring him because she was angry with him or was she in trouble? He tried to call Donovan, but didn't get an answer.

Shit.

****

Donovan shook his head as he moved slowly toward Nicolette.

"I can't believe you killed him," she said tearfully. "You were his friend."

"Right. He was *my* friend, and he screwed my wife."

"So you murdered him?"

"I was with him that night. I knocked him unconscious, choked him until I thought he was dead, then rolled his car down the hill. Little did I know that he wasn't quite dead. I never figured on him slipping into a coma. Lucky for me he never recovered." He shook his head, still moving toward her as she backed away. "I didn't want you to end up getting hurt. You and I are innocent. It's Rudy and Marla who should pay."

"Why did you kill Rudy and not Marla?"

He smiled as if she'd asked the most obvious question in the universe. "I love her." He shook his head again, his voice filled with regret. "I can't let you go free. It will ruin my life."

"I won't say anything, I promise."

He laughed. "Yeah, like I believe that. You do see why I couldn't let Rudy live, right? I mean, he was a liar, a phony. Running a charity for drug addicts while he was one himself. Preposterous. And then, what he did to me. With my wife..."

Nicolette didn't remind him his wife had done it to him, too. He knew that. Besides, if she did, he might say, "Oh yeah, that's right. Let's go back and get her, and I'll off you both at the same time." Even though Marla had broken her trust and screwed her husband, Nicolette didn't want to watch her die. Not much anyway.

Nicolette searched her mind for something to say that would stall him, but her brain was frozen in disbelief and terror.

Donovan sighed as he continued, "Marla knew I had something to do with Rudy's death. I lied to her about where I was that night. She knew I knew she was fucking Rudy. She put two and two together and accused me of causing the accident. She threatened to leave me right after he died, but I told her I had proof of what had happened between them. I told her I had the phone with all her text messages back and forth, the sick, twisted things they said to one another. That I would ruin her chances for a political career. Destroy her family."

Alicia Dean

Nicolette finally found her voice. "Wow. The ingredients of a happy marriage. Fear, threats and intimidation."

He shrugged. "Whatever works to get what you want, right? Very soon, all this will be over for you, but first I need you to write a note letting everyone know how despondent you are over your husband's death and the subsequent humiliation of his drug use. You cheated with his best friend, and now you've lost him too. You have nothing more to live for."

"No one would believe that."

"Come on. It's all true. I mean, you don't have any family. You and Heath are done, even though the two of you probably rutted like pigs in heat for a while. The charity will most certainly fold." He moved closer, the look in his eyes sending a terrifying chill through her soul. "Really, Nicolette. What the fuck do you have to live for?"

He'd backed her against the cocktail table. She had nowhere else to go. Her cell phone rang, and hope rose in her chest.

Heath? It had to be Heath.

"I need to get that," she said. "If I don't answer, whoever is calling will become suspicious."

He laughed. "Right. Because no one ever misses a fucking phone call." He reached out and clamped a hand around her neck. "Now, be a good girl and come with me. We have to do this all exactly right to make it look convincing. And, we have to make sure there are no disturbances, so I need you to come peacefully."

"No." She shook her head. "I won't come quietly. I'll fight you like a crazy woman, and you can explain why I wrecked my house before I killed myself."

A hard look came into his eyes. "I'll make you a deal. You're going to die no matter what. If you cooperate, I'll make it quick, painless and no one else will be hurt. If you make me fight you, after I leave here, I'll go over to Louisa's. Her Christmas gift this year will be a great deal of pain. Is that what you want?"

She looked into his face and knew he was serious. He would do it. Her shoulders slumped, and she reached back to grip the edge of the table behind her.

Heath, please call. Please come. You're my only hope.

Hope rose when she heard a loud knock on the door, then Heath's voice shouting, "Nicolette? Are you in there? Let me in."

Shit. She must have locked the door after letting Donovan in, an unconscious habit she'd developed since living alone. "Heath!" she screamed as loud as she could. "I'm in here. Donovan is—"

"Shut up!" Donovan hissed. Confusion, then anger crossed his face. He looked toward the front door.

Nicolette's fingers touched the Santa's workshop figurine. She brought it around just as Donovan turned his attention back to her. She slammed it into the side of his head. He dropped to his knees, a dazed look in his eyes. Blood trickled from beneath his hair, and Nicolette let the figurine fall from her shaking fingers to the floor.

She paused, momentarily paralyzed before her brain kicked into gear. *Run, get the hell out of there.* Turning, she started toward the door.

Before she'd gone two steps, Donovan's hand shot out and grabbed her ankle. He still seemed dazed, but his grip was like steel.

"Heath!" she called out. "I'm here. Donovan's trying to kill me."

She tried to kick out at Donovan's hand, but he held tight. No more sounds came from the front door.

Had Heath not heard her and left? Maybe he was calling the police. Maybe—

A loud crash of breaking glass sounded at the patio door. *Heath.*

Glass shards clung to his hair and his clothing. His golden eyes searched frantically until they fell on Nicolette. He grinned with relief and started toward her.

Donovan released her ankle and moaned, then pushed his hands against the floor, trying to rise. Heath was on him so fast, Nicolette was barely aware he'd changed directions.

Jerking Donovan up by the shirtfront, Heath slammed his fist into his face, over and over. Nicolette clamped her hands over her mouth, frozen to the spot. She shivered as she watched in disbelief. She'd never seen Heath violent. Never seen him harm a soul.

"Heath!" She rushed over and grabbed at his arm. "Stop. You're going to kill him."

Heath paused at her touch, his fist drawn back. Donovan, his face bloody and battered, was no longer conscious. Heath released him, and his limp body dropped to the floor with a dull thud.

Heath came to his feet, his chest rising and falling with deep breaths. He looked down at Nicolette, and she reached up to pick broken glass from his hair. He captured her wrist in his hand and brought her fingers to his lips.

"Heath," she breathed his name on a sigh, then fell into his arms, sobbing and covering his face with kisses.

"Be careful." Heath laughed, his voice hoarse from exertion. "I'm covered in broken glass."

"I don't care," she murmured, still clinging to him.

"Are you okay?" he asked roughly.

"I'm fine. I was so scared. I was afraid you

wouldn't come. You saved me again."

She felt his smile against her hair.

"It's what I do," he said. "I'll always save you."

She pulled away and looked into his face. "Here I thought you were a King. Turns out you're a knight."

He brushed the hair back from her eyes. "Are you sure you're all right? He didn't hurt you?"

"No. I'm fine."

Heath shook his head, and a dark expression took over his face. "Good God. It's my fault you almost died."

"What are you talking about? Like I said, you saved me."

"You were only in danger in the first place because of me." He drew in a deep breath. "I sent that son of a bitch over here to *protect* you."

Nicolette shook her head. "You had no idea. None of us did. If not tonight, then some other time, I'd have been alone with Donovan. We thought he was a friend. Thought he was harmless." She lifted a hand and stroked Heath's cheek. "I'm not going to let you take the blame for this, hear me?"

He jerked a short nod. "If you say so."

"I do. Besides, truth is, this is my fault. It never would have happened if I hadn't sent you away. I'm so sorry for the way I treated you this morning. I've been so mean to you. I think my emotions just exploded, and I wasn't thinking straight. All you were doing is exactly what you said, protecting me, just like I tried to protect Louisa, out of love. And even how I protected Rudy, although he was gone and as it turned out, didn't necessarily deserve my protection, my loyalty."

"It's okay. That's all behind us now."

He removed one arm and dialed his cell phone. He spoke to Detective Patella, explaining what happened. He hung up the phone. "They're on the way."

She laid her head on his chest and wrapped her arms around his waist. "I don't care," she whispered. "All I need is you."

Chapter Twenty-Two

"The wife had already called us." Patella scowled at Donovan as a patrol cop hauled him, handcuffed, out the front door. "Been looking for this joker a couple hours."

"Marla called you?" Nicolette asked. The last time she'd spoken with Marla, nothing had been said about her suspicion that Donovan killed Rudy. Of course, once Nicolette learned of the affair, she hadn't wanted to hear anything else from Marla, not the explanations, not the apologies.

"Yeah. She told us everything she knew about her husband's involvement with Mr. Morgan's death."

"She damned sure took her time about it." Heath's eyes blazed, and a muscle ticked in his jaw. "She almost got Nicolette killed. Not to mention arrested for murder."

Nicolette reached out and squeezed his hand in a comforting gesture.

"Yeah." Berry nodded as he gazed at Nicolette. "No hard feelings, right? Just doing our job."

"I know." Nicolette didn't care anymore. All that mattered was that she was no longer under suspicion, and that the blackmailer *and* Rudy's killer had been caught. Then, of course, there was Heath. She pushed back the smile working its way to her mouth. Now was not the time to let her joy burst forth.

"Course, there's a good possibility we'll file charges against Mrs. Sussman for not coming

249

forward," Patella said. "She knew her husband had the cell phone all along. That alone might have been enough to file murder charges against him."

"He kept the phone in his car all this time?" Heath asked. "Kept it charged and ready?"

Patella shook his head. "Apparently he'd kept it hidden at the house, but this morning when Mrs. Sussman came home from her visit with Mrs. Morgan, her behavior made him nervous. He was afraid she was going to spill the beans, so he took the phone with him. I guess he's kept it off all this time. Phone still had enough charge for Mrs. Morgan here to do what she did." He grinned and a glint of admiration entered his eyes. "Smart move, by the way."

Nicolette grinned back. "Thanks."

****

It took nearly two hours for the police to finish the questioning and for the techs to go over the crime scene. Yellow police tape surrounded the area where Nicolette had nearly taken Donovan's head off. The police had seized the chipped Santa workshop figurine as evidence.

After the police left, Heath took Nicolette by the shoulders and looked down into her face. "Did you mean it when you said you loved me, or was that just a way to get me to sex you up?"

She laughed. "Oh, I meant it. Maybe I wasn't convincing enough, but I can show you again."

He smiled. "Is that a threat or a promise?"

"Both."

"Okay, but one favor after I allow you to ravish me."

"What's that?"

"I'd like for you to go with me and stay at Mom's tonight. Not only is this place a mess and a lot of bad shit went down here tonight, but I'd like to wake up there on Christmas morning. I mean, we've had so many additions to the family that it would be kind of cool to be with them all on our first Christmas as a family."

"Are you including Keeley Jacobs?"

"I am."

"See, Heath King, I knew you couldn't be an asshole for long."

He laughed. "That may have earned you a spanking."

She gazed at him from beneath her lashes. "Is that another promise?"

He placed a lingering kiss on her lips. When he came up for air, he said, "There's something you should know. I'm not going to let you use me and not make an honest man out of me. I want to marry you, Nicolette."

"Any time, any place."

"Yeah? You're easy. There is one problem, though. Mom has her heart set on her sons following hers and Dad's tradition of getting married on Christmas Eve."

"I thought you resented your dad so much you wouldn't care about something like that."

"I've been an unreasonable dick head. People make mistakes. Besides, something pretty special came out of it."

"What's that?"

"My sister."

"You have matured in the past few days. But there's only one problem about that tradition. Christmas Eve is almost over, and I don't want to wait a whole year to be your wife."

Heath moved his hands, tightening them around her waist. "I have a solution. We'll get married right away, maybe New Year's Eve, then next Christmas Eve, we'll renew our vows at Mom's house."

"Wow, you're Mr. Problem Solver, aren't you? What are we going to do about where we live?"

"Damn, woman. One problem at a time. I don't care where we live as long as I can look into your beautiful face every morning. Now, enough talking. Let's get to Mom's house. I have a fiancée to ravage."

****

On Christmas morning, Amelia's living room looked like an army of giant rats had invaded it...rats with a taste for wrapping paper.

Discarded bows and paper littered the floor and three very happy little girls flitted from one gift to the other, seeming to be bothered only by the fact that they couldn't play with all of them at the same time.

Stockings were strewn among the other debris. In the past week, four had been added. One for Keeley, who had the advantage in that she'd been the only one who was an adult at the time the stocking was created, and therefore, compared to the others hers looked like it had been done by a professional artist. Each of the triplets had also made their own glitter-name stocking, but to be honest, Heath couldn't tell whose was whose. The lettering all looked the same. Uncle Heath had added a Pez dispenser to each stocking—one Santa, one snowman, one Rudolph—with extra candy refills for each of them, earning a mock disapproving frown from Zoe.

He supposed that now there would be one for Ethan, Jesse's son who Heath had only met that morning. Then, sometime in the future, his and Nic's children would make their stockings. A fissure of contented delight moved through his body.

The family had just finished a late Christmas breakfast that Amelia had decided to make instead of an early Christmas lunch, and were lounging around the living room.

Heath stood. "Sorry to end the party, but we have to run."

"Where are you going?" Amelia asked. "I thought you canceled your appointment with that client, and you didn't have to go back today."

"I'm not going back to Oklahoma. We'll be back here later this evening. We told Louisa we'd have a late meal with her."

"You should have asked her to join us," Amelia said.

"We did, but she didn't feel like getting out."

"Heath?" Nic said. "We're not supposed to be at Louisa's for a couple more hours."

"I know, but we have to make a stop on the way."

"What stop?"

"You'll find out soon enough."

"Yeah, what stop?" Zoe and Keeley asked at once.

Alex chimed in, "Spill it, bro. What's up?"

"You people are nosy as hell." Heath took Nic by the hand and led her to the door, calling over his shoulder, "We'll be back later."

Nicolette frowned as she followed Heath to the Tahoe. "Stores are closed, so it's too late to buy me a gift. By the way, don't think I've forgotten you owe me one."

"Greedy, aren't you?"

He closed her door once she was seated, then climbed in on the driver's side and headed out of his mom's driveway.

****

Heath drove in silence and Nic cast confused glances his way the entire time. What was he up to?

When he took the exit for the airport, she scowled. "If we're going on a surprise trip, that's really sweet, but unlike you see in the movies, I'm not crazy about the idea of an impromptu vacation where I don't even have a chance to pack. I need clothes, my makeup, my nighties, my own pillow,

253

toiletries—"

He pulled into short-term parking and reached over to plant a kiss on her mouth.

"Good grief, woman, do you ever shut up?"

"Hey!" she shouted, but her protest was cut short as he climbed from the Tahoe and came over to open her door.

She clamped her lips together to stop the flow of questions. It was obvious Heath wasn't going to let her know what the hell was going on.

MCI was nearly dead. On Christmas morning, people would have already come in and wouldn't be leaving until later tonight or tomorrow. Heath strode down the terminal and she hurried to keep up.

He stopped by a row of plastic chairs against the wall outside an American Airlines gate.

"Have a seat," he said as he settled into one of the chairs.

She huffed and fell into the seat beside him. In moments, through the glass door, passengers disembarked.

Among the sea of people, one man seemed vaguely familiar. Nicolette stood and craned her neck. He intermittently disappeared as other passengers moved in front of him. Her heart started to pound as the man came closer. People continued to exit, each filing away until the familiar stranger was the next one out the door.

She squinted, then feeling as though she were in a dream, she slowly moved toward him. He saw her and dropped his bag, his eyes moving over her.

"Daddy?" she whispered, then she was in his arms, laughing and crying and hugging.

"My baby girl." His voice was muffled against her hair. "God, I can't believe it's really you. I'm sorry. I'm so sorry."

She finally pulled away and turned to see Heath watching them, a smile bigger than a 747 plastered on his face.

"You did this?" Nic asked

"I figured you'd need someone to walk you down the aisle."

Tears flowing, she went into his arms. "Thank you," she whispered, but the words seemed so inadequate.

Pulling away, she looked into his face. "Not only did Rudy cheat on me," she said quietly. "He didn't love me enough to make this happen. No one has ever done the things for me that you have."

"You're special. You deserve this and more. I want to spend the rest of my life putting that beautiful smile on your face. Maybe without the tears, though."

She laughed. "I guess fifteen years ago, I didn't make the right choice. We've lost so much time."

"Maybe we had to go through all that to get where we are. If that's true, it's fine by me. Because I really, really like where we are."

"Yeah? Me too."

"Hey, remember me?"

She turned at her father's voice. His smile was as broad as Heath's had been. He looked the same as she remembered, tall and handsome, although the full head of blond hair had started to thin and was now gray.

"Let's get your father's luggage," Heath said, clapping her dad on the shoulder.

Nicolette linked her arm in her father's as they headed toward baggage claim.

She placed her free hand in Heath's and squeezed tightly. Looking up into his sexy, golden eyes she winked at her knight in shining armor, who'd given her by far the best Christmas of her life.

A word about the author...

Author Alicia Dean has had a love for reading since she was a small child. That love morphed into a desire to write, and she was thrilled when she finally realized her dream of publication.

There is nothing she enjoys more than creating stories to share with others. Her favorite genres are suspense, paranormal, horror and contemporary romance. She has been inspired by such authors as Dennis Lehane, Michael Connelly, Lisa Gardner, Jordan Dane, Tess Gerritsen, Sharon Sala, Merline Lovelace, Mel Odom, and Stephen King, to name a few.

She resides in Oklahoma City and has three beautiful grown children and a multitude of amazingly wonderful and supportive friends and family.

Turn the page

for an exciting preview

of Alex King's story

in the first *Three Kings* novel

from author Dyann Love Barr

A Perfect Bride for Christmas

The Three Kings, Book I

Available now from The Wild Rose Press

Chapter One

December 2005, Kansas City

Scrooge had it right. Bah, humbug! Christmas sucked long and hard.

Lights twinkled on the tree, reflecting off the windows of the darkened office. The smell of holiday spices wafted from the potpourri dish on Zoe Hillman's desk, filling the room with false cheer. It was Christmas Eve, and not even the large, make that huge, bonus check lifted her spirits.

"Bah, humbug." She sniffed, wiped her tears for the umpteenth time before she checked her resignation letter to Cox, Zuckerman, Howe and Stanford. No matter that her heart was shattered, her life over, it wouldn't do for her last act as Alex King's personal assistant to be sloppy and unprofessional.

She reached into the candy dish on her desk, absentmindedly unwrapped one of the truffles, and popped it into her mouth. The chocolate melted in a creamy, dark lushness designed to put a Band-Aid on her broken heart, but tonight her drug of choice didn't work. Candy wrappers littered the floor, along with half a box of used tissues. The clock on her computer read seven p.m. Alex would be married and on his way to Las Vegas by now. Bianca Freemont would be his bride. Zoe's brain whipped up an X-rated vision of the wedding night, and she grabbed another tissue to wipe her red nose and puffy eyes.

Her breath hitched, and she hit the SEND key before she could change her mind.

God, she was so stupid.

She'd been in love with Alex from the first day he walked through the door of the law firm. He winked at her as he passed her desk. How could she not fall for all that dark hair, startlingly blue eyes, and a smile designed to charm the panties off any woman under the age seventy?

Not that Alex ever tried with her.

Another wrapper and tissue hit the floor.

Alex relied on her. She organized his office, his life—hell, she even organized his house when he complained he never could find his socks. Zoe became his best friend, his confidant. She sent flowers to his women, found a housekeeper to keep him from living in bachelor squalor. She did everything a wife did for a man, except share his bed.

The hours they spent working together, alone at night in the office, were the gems in her pathetic life. He'd drop by her apartment after his Sunday jogs with Lamar's donuts. They'd discuss various cases, the news and sometimes watch a DVD. She had him to herself for those few brief hours. But nothing she did could get him to see her as a woman, a woman who'd walk over hot coals if it meant he would say he loved her.

Instead, he told everyone she was his right hand, and sometimes his left. His pal. Zoe blinked tears out of her eyes and turned off her computer.

Over the last three years, he'd risen in the firm from a new hire to partner. Everyone loved him. The man could do no wrong.

Except marry the right woman.

Bianca Freemont was cold, calculating, and just plain mean. Alex's life didn't have room for both Bianca and Zoe. He couldn't see the two were like two cats in a bag. Hissing and snarling at each other. But Alex saw Bianca as the perfect wife for an attorney going places. So did the partners.

Zoe sniffed and reached for another truffle. She suffered in silence, despising herself for being the stereotypical   secretary-falling-in-love-with-her-boss like the plots of many of the romance novels she devoured, along with six thousand calories a day. So, here she sat with a hundred and fifty extra pounds of unrequited love.

How lame. All she got for her efforts for years of devotion was a stuffy head, runny nose, and puffy eyes to go with a broken heart.

A surge of anger replaced the hurt.

Let Alex find out who really watched over him, cared for him, loved him. He wouldn't be able to function without her. Bianca wouldn't know where his socks were, but then again, there'd be no need for socks on the honeymoon.

She had to strike out on her own, find a new life that didn't center on a man she could never have.

She opened the drawer of her desk where she stashed her purse, grabbed up another tissue to stem the tears washing over her cheeks. The clutter on the floor by her chair made her stop. Her bulk made it impossible to bend down and pick up the evidence of her emotional tsunami. Zoe let out a sigh and got on her hands and knees. Voices on the other side of the door stopped her cold. Zoe's hand smothered her squeak of surprise. Everyone had left for the Christmas holiday. She'd thought she was alone in the office, maybe even the building.

The cleaners had already come and gone. Her heart stammered in her chest, her breath came in short pants. Part of her breathing problem came from the effort of getting to the floor in the first place, but she didn't want to be caught alone by some burglar...or worse. She couldn't get to her feet and run, not with bad knees and ankles. She scooted under the cubby of her large antique desk, hoping the small enclosure would provide an adequate hiding space. Zoe held her breath.

The door of Alex's office burst open, and she heard Tommy Dunn's voice slur, "Why the hell do you want the tickets to Vegas if the bitch dumped you at the altar?"

Relief washed over her. No rapist, just an asshole. What had he said? Dumped at the altar? Alex hadn't married Bianca?

"Because, my friend, I'm getting married tonight." Alex sounded as drunk as his best man.

"You're full of crap, and booze. Who are you going to get to marry you?" He paused. "At seven in the evening?"

"I'll marry the first single woman I see," Alex snorted. "I'll bet you a thousand dollars, no make that five thousand, I can get someone to do it."

"I still say you're full of crap, but it's a bet."

"Just watch me. Bianca isn't the only one who can make a point. I'm getting married on Christmas Eve, so screw her. Family tradition and all that. Got to get married on Christmas Eve. Mom and Dad got married on Christmas Eve, and they have a perfect marriage." Anger wove through his voice. "Bianca overreacted. A pretty girl smiles at me, I smile back. I wasn't flirting with her bridesmaid. Damn it, I'm not going to walk on eggshells just because I smile at a woman. I like women, I can't help it. It's my nature."

"I noticed."

"S'not my fault she backed me up against the wall and tried to kiss me."

"Not your fault at all."

"S'truth."

"Right." Tommy Dunn's voice held a touch of disbelief.

"Honestagod," Alex slurred his words together.

Zoe leaned back against her desk, hoping they would go into Alex's office so she could make a hasty and quiet escape. No such luck.

"Where are the tickets?"

"Zoe's desk."

Oh, dear God, don't let them come over here. She stuffed her hand into her mouth. The tickets were in Alex's desk. She'd put them there this morning and specifically told him they were in the upper left drawer. How could he have forgotten? *Oh yeah, she was talking about Alex.* If it didn't involve jurisprudence, Alex was an organizational disaster waiting to happen.

She heard one of them come closer.

"Know s'it's here somewhere." Alex shuffled things around on her desk.

"S'not here. Wait, wait, s'it's in my office."

She held her breath until little spirals of color and black dots danced in front of her eyes. Zoe squeezed her eyes shut, but it didn't stop her internal light show.

"Zoe?"

Busted. She let out the breath with a whoosh. "Yes?"

Alex came around the desk and perched his fine butt on the edge. Tommy couldn't resist following Alex.

"Whatcha doing, Zoe Pie?" Tommy smirked.

Zoe ground her teeth. She disliked Tommy as much as she loved Alex. How could he have such a stupid and offensive friend? Being rich shouldn't give him a license to be an asshole. In his mind, however, it did.

Tommy came up with the vile nickname. Alex told her he liked it but hadn't known the real reason behind it. The nasty barb resulted when Tommy once found her face-first in a large piece of French

5

Silk pie. Sending flowers to Alex's flavor of the month always took its toll.

"Leaving." She threw the trash into the waste can and picked up her purse. Her position made it hard to look dignified, but she managed to stand. Her hands brushed down over her loose brown slacks. "For good."

Alex jumped to his feet and wobbled. "Whoa, head rush." He steadied himself by using Zoe's shoulder. His hand sent little shivers of delight through Zoe's body, the tingling sensation landing square between her legs. She closed her eyes, trying to resist the pull Alex had on her. Maybe she should seek professional help. That's it. She planned to thumb through the Yellow Pages as soon as she got home.

"Wait, wait, what do you mean?" Alex frowned. "You can't leave me."

"Check your interoffice memo. Not only am I leaving the firm, you, and your charming associates..." She gave Tommy the stink-eye. "I'm moving to St. Louis. I've got a job there starting in the middle of January and a new apartment."

"No, no, no." Alex waved his hand around as if trying to wipe away her words. "I won't allow it." An edge of panic crept into his voice. His eyes went a bit wild. "Who's going to take care of me? You're my friend, why didn't you tell me any of this?"

Zoe heaved a sigh. "It's already done, Alex. Your new bride will take care of the house. A new PA as well. Her name is Virginia Hamilton. She's very sweet, very efficient. Be nice to her."

Tommy sniggered. "Wait, why don't you marry Zoe, win the bet, and that way, she can't leave."

It took a millisecond for Tommy's suggestion to hit Alex's alcohol-soaked brain. "S'it's perfect. You'll be my perfect bride for Christmas."

"You're crazy and drunk." Zoe tried to go around

Alex.

"No, Bianca dumped me, and we're pals, Zoe. Come on, let's do it. The three of us," he nodded toward Tommy, "can go to Vegas. We'll get married and have a great time. What do you say? Hmmm?"

The temptation to say yes beckoned to her. She couldn't say yes, could she? Could she? Maybe this was her chance. It might be so wrong, on so many levels... Screw it. She'd grab for the golden ring while she could. She could change Alex. It might take more than a few prayers in the process, but given enough love, he'd come around.

Alex needed someone to guide him. That someone was her.

"All right." She hitched her purse high on her shoulder. "Let's go to Vegas."

Turn the page

for an exciting preview of

Clint King's Christmas homecoming

in the third *Three Kings* novel

from author Claire Ashgrove

A Christmas to Believe In
The Three Kings, Book III

Available from The Wild Rose Press

Chapter One

Snow crunched beneath the Chevy pickup's tires as Clint King navigated around a turn. In the silent dark, his blinker clicked a steady beat that tempered his nerves. In the rear-view mirror, he checked that the two-horse trailer on his bumper didn't slip in the light sheen of ice. The last thing he needed was a wreck.

As if today wasn't bad enough.

He mumbled as he glanced down at the gas gauge. A few more miles and the warning light would come on. Thank God Mom's house lurked just around the next bend. He could finally get off the snow-covered highways between Brandenburg, Kentucky and the Kansas City Northlands. Eight hours of treacherous roads was enough strain to turn a saint into a sinner.

Then again, if his mother hadn't dosed out a heavy round of guilt, he'd be happily tucked into his couch, watching the latest DVD release. Even a saint couldn't stand up to Mom's masterful manipulation. He could still hear her heavy sigh. The carefully chosen words echoed in his head. *But Clint, you missed your father's last Christmas.*

He had. Certainly not intentionally, but he'd missed it all the same. None of them had foreseen their father would die the following summer. This last summer. When Clint had been too busy prepping for the track to come home for the Fourth of July.

Guilt rose up to curdle his stomach and

compressed his chest. He tightened his hands on the wheel. Damn, he didn't want to do this. Coming back here stirred up all kinds of memories. Each mile he crossed brought pictures of the past. Dad taking him and his brothers sledding. Dad holding the camera as they all opened gifts. Even the last Christmas Clint had spent with his family his father had maintained the specific role of photographer. Who would take the pictures this year—Alex?

Clint shook his head. No, *he* was the eldest. That should be his responsibility. Alex had other things on his mind. More important things like a long-lost sister none of them had known about until a few weeks ago. Alex also had new triplet daughters to worry about. News Clint would have loved to see Alex's high and mighty fiancée hear. That ought to be quite the twist to Alex's Christmas Eve wedding.

Heath would be too caught up in the festivities. Hell, for that matter, Heath probably hadn't even thought to bring a camera. Even if Dad's sat in the closet, Heath would be goofing off. He'd always gotten away with it too. As the peacemaker of the family, he'd never been on the receiving ends of Mom's down-the-nose looks, or Dad's stern, "I expected more from you" frowns. No, Heath fixed everything with an innocent expression and humor.

Letting out a heavy sigh, Clint steered around a slow left hand curve. Up the hillside, pale blue lights dangled from high gables. White strands wound around the porch beams. Even from this distance, the deep red glow of his mother's Christmas wreath shone from the front door.

Home. Five years later, and he was home.

Further off in the distance, he observed the festive red and green bulbs that always decorated Jesse Saurs' folks' barn. Some things never changed. Odd though, Mom had mentioned something about the Saurs moving. Did that mean Jesse still lived in that old house on the hill?

His spirits brightened at the thought. If Jesse were around, things would be like old times. Too bad they were all too old for car-hood sledding—she'd been the best driver out of the whole gang. They weren't, however, too old for a good, old-fashioned snowball fight. And if his memory served, he still owed her for an ice-ball in the nose.

A grin quirked the corner of his mouth. That girl knew how to throw. His nose had bled for almost an hour.

Man, if he had to have a sister, why couldn't it have been her? Instead, he had to deal with some stranger. Keeley Jacobs might be his father's daughter, but Clint was pretty damn certain she didn't know how to cheat at arm wrestling like Jesse did. He was also pretty certain neither of his brothers would put up with a strategically placed toe in the ribs from her either.

Guess he'd find out. As much as he didn't care to meet his new half-sibling, Mom made it clear she intended to welcome the woman with open arms. Which meant this family get-together would come with strangers.

He shifted into second to climb the steep driveway. The trailer skidded, threatening to pull him back onto the road. Scowling, Clint dropped the truck into four-wheel drive, and gave it a bit more gas. The rig jumped as the trailer bounced forward. Slowly, he inched up the gravel drive.

At the top, he pulled straight into the yard. He still had to find stabling for his horse, and turning around up here wouldn't be easy. Mom could deal with the tread marks. She'd wanted him to come. Insisted on it. She could deal with the fact his prize mare was due to foal any day. If he were lucky, the trailer ride hadn't stressed her, and she wouldn't choose tonight.

He opened the door to her sharp whinny. Jumping down into the snow, he tromped to the rear of the trailer and threw open the top half of the loading doors. She twisted her elegant neck around to give him an expectant look.

"Not yet, Angel."

Clint closed the door and made his way around to the escape door. The hinges creaked as he pulled it open. He stepped inside, kicked his way through the loose bedding, and moved up to her head to give her an affectionate pat. She rode free, not tied to anything, in the event sudden labor set in. Not familiar with her foaling habits, he didn't dare take the risk she might try to lie down, despite the unlikelihood.

"Eat your hay while I run inside. We'll get you settled in soon." He scratched her behind the ears, ran his hand down her mane, and patted her shoulder. "No foals, Angel. You gotta cook that one until January."

She answered his order with a lazy blink.

Satisfied they were in agreement, Clint climbed out of the trailer and secured the door. He crossed behind his bumper, stepped over the hitch. His gaze fell on the house. Bright lights flooded the snow-covered porch with a warm yellow glow. The Christmas tree twinkled behind the front window. Through the frosty panes, he glimpsed Alex seated on the couch. Alex laughed at something, and though the sound didn't filter outside, Clint could hear the rumble of his voice.

Maybe coming home wouldn't turn out so bad after all. He hadn't seen his brothers in years.

He made his way to the porch, stopped in front of the door to stomp the snow off his boots. Bells jangled as he opened the door.

A chorus of laughter greeted his ears. Alex looked up with a broad grin. But what caught Clint's immediate attention was the flash of movement near the hearth. He glanced over in time to see a woman punch Heath in the arm. She tumbled back into her chair, giggling, then turned bright blue eyes on him.

Jesse.

"Clint!" Her excited greeting blended with his brothers' hellos.

Her smile, however, made his breath catch. Something deep in his gut tripped as he took another step inside and Jesse eased to her feet. Long black hair tumbled to her waist, just as she'd always worn it. He'd seen those raven locks a thousand times, but they'd never shone quite like they did as she crossed the room.

To his shame, his gaze skipped down to her toes, taking in curves he'd never noticed, and a waist so tiny he could span his hands around it. She wore jeans that hugged thighs he knew were muscular. Only, five years ago, they'd just been Jesse's legs. Now, they belonged to a...

He caught the sweet scent of lilacs as she slipped her arms around his neck and hugged him tight. Soft curves melted against his chest.

A woman.

When in the hell had Jesse grown up? She'd been thirty when they'd last spent any time together. Even as an adult, he'd still seen the tomboy she'd always been. His little sister. But damn... She felt good. All feminine.

He collected himself enough to return her hug. "I'll be damned, Jesse. I didn't expect to see you here."

"Is that Clint?" his mother called from the kitchen.

"Yeah, Mom. I'm here."

Jesse pulled out of his embrace, leaving his skin tingling where they'd touched. Good grief, what was the matter with him? He'd *wrestled* with her, for

God's sake, and hadn't ever been affected by touching her. For that matter, they'd all skinny dipped in Longview Lake one summer. And those breasts hadn't been anywhere near as compelling as they were beneath her light blue sweater right now.

Shoot, he hadn't even known she'd had breasts back then.

Well, he'd *known*, but there was a distinct difference.

"Clinton, come give your mother a kiss." His mother's call jarred him back to sense.

Thankfully, it also offered a means of escape. He glanced about the room, offered a short nod and said, "Be right back." Avoiding eye contact with those disturbingly unsettling blue eyes, he followed the aroma of apples and cinnamon into the kitchen.

****

Stunned, Jesse curled into her chair with her feet tucked beneath her and trained a smile to her face. Though she pretended interest in Heath and Alex's conversation, her gaze followed Clint's retreat. Loose blue jeans pulled around firm buttocks, tapered down thick thighs to bunch at the neck of his tan hiking boots. He ducked his head as he stepped under the doorframe, and thick dark waves touched the neck of his beige sweater. Wide shoulders hunched to shorten his long frame.

She could not be staring at the same Clint who she'd grown up with. *That* Clint's one-dimple grin made her want to poke her finger in his cheek. *This* Clint's lazy grin had temporarily stopped her heart.

Where had this one come from?

"Dontcha think, Jesse?" Alex gestured her way, his look expectant.

She blinked. Not knowing what to say, she stammered, "Oh. Ah, yeah."

"See, little brother?" Alex tossed a rolled up paper at Heath. "No way can Arizona beat K-State.

6

Don't you know Jesse's never wrong about football?"

Once upon a time, maybe. But until right now, she hadn't even known her Alma Mater had made it to the bowl. Or which one for that matter. However, now wasn't the time to clue the King brothers in on the fact she'd given up her tomboy ways years ago. That would require conversation. Until her heart stopped this ridiculous hammering, she didn't dare brave her voice.

Clint's deep laughter rumbled from the kitchen. Her gaze pulled back to the open doorway. A strange tingling sensation tripped down her spine. Somehow, he'd changed his laugh too. It no longer made her want to join in. Instead, the urge to giggle set in. *Giggle*, for heaven's sake.

How come that hadn't happened when he came back earlier this year for his father's funeral?

Because he wasn't laughing, dummy.

Well that logically explained the prickling of her skin. Yet, it didn't reason why she hadn't noticed the *man* in July. He'd worn a suit and tie, but even all dressed up, she hadn't really seen him. What did jeans and a cable-knit sweater have over formal wear?

Why in the world did she care? This was Clint. Clint, who lived in Kentucky. Clint, who liked horses, and she didn't know the first thing about them. Clint who knew the embarrassing secret that at sixteen, she'd let Mark Hammond, the school nerd, put his hands up her shirt in exchange for the right to copy off his Algebra quizzes.

Of course, she hadn't told Clint. He'd found out when Mark asked if Clint could barter up a better payment for answers. Still. Clint knew things about her no man should.

His heavy heel squeaked the board just inside the kitchen doorway. He stepped through carrying four small plates of homemade apple pie. His gaze flicked to her, and to Jesse's shame, her stomach clamped into an anxious ball.

Lord, he was handsome.

Amelia King hobbled to her chair beside the twinkling Christmas tree, her recently broken ankle slowing her usually quick pace. She bent over to set her plate and a coffee cup down on the end table and paused. With a tip of her head, she peeked out the front window. "Sweetheart, is that a horse trailer in my front yard?"

His arm half-extended to offer Jesse her plate, Clint froze. His amber eyes locked with hers. A touch of color flushed his cheeks as he answered, "Ah, yeah."

Amelia sat down and frowned at her oldest son. "Why?"

"Well..." Clint handed Jesse the plate. Their fingers brushed, sending a jolt of pleasant energy rippling up Jesse's arm. Clint's gaze flashed with something she couldn't define. He pulled his hand away so fast he nearly dropped the pie in her lap. She caught it at the last moment, then dropped her gaze to stare at the sugar-dusted crust.

He eased himself into the couch cushion closest to her and fixed his stare on his mother. "I was going to ask you if old man Jameson still ran that boarding stable on the north end of town. I had to bring my mare along. She's due to foal any day."

Jesse let her gaze stray sideways to his knee. It rested close enough that if she unwound her legs they'd touch. Solid, sturdy—she could almost feel the way his leg would lean into hers in a silent expression of affection.

She gave herself a mental shake. What was she thinking? Clint would never do something like that. At least not with her. She had no business even letting the thought register. He might be handsome, but he was still Clint, and she was still his little sister. The way he'd jerked his hand away said more about his thoughts on touching her than anything.

Blinking, she pushed aside the thoughts that clouded her mind and focused on the conversation. All three raptly discussed who might have a boarding stable, who might be willing to take on a pregnant mare on short notice, and how far Clint would have to drive to tend to his horse.

"Clint," she began with a slight frown. His gaze pulled to hers so quickly she stumbled over her immediate thoughts. Swallowing, she willed her voice not to shake. "Why don't you use Mom and Dad's old barn? I put a new roof on it last year, so it should be watertight. I use half for storage but there's a stall we could fix up. You'd be close to your mother and your horse."

"Hey good idea. I can help you fix it up tomorrow, Clint," Alex offered.

Clint's gaze held Jesse's, spreading unfamiliar warmth through her veins. The urge to move, to somehow extract herself from that rich, amber intensity, gripped fierce. A woman could get lost in those expressive eyes. Dangerously lost.

Thank you for purchasing
this Wild Rose Press publication.
For other wonderful stories of romance,
please visit our on-line bookstore at
www.thewildrosepress.com

For questions or more information,
contact us at
info@thewildrosepress.com

The Wild Rose Press
www.TheWildRosePress.com

9 781601 548559